Lou 1019

a novel

RICHARD G. TUTTLE

Cat's Paw Publishing, Inc.
P.O. Box 385
Spring House, PA 19477

Cat's Paw Publishing will be happy to assist you in bringing the author of this work to your live event. Please contact us at our email address set forth above.

Print ISBN: 978-1-66786-349-8
eBook ISBN: 978-1-66786-350-4

Printed in the United States of America on SFI Certified paper.

First Edition

For Patrick, Catherine, John and Juliette. You know, family.

PART I

CHAPTER 1

Lou Incaviglia was sitting on his front stoop smoking his second cigar of the day. "Hey, Lou," said his neighbor Gloria, who was passing Lou's stoop on her way to the 7-Eleven. It was early Friday afternoon.

"Hi Doll," said Lou, with a tip of his cigar. Lou was not big on long conversations while he was smoking, but his neighborhood presented a million opportunities for short ones. He loved those.

"How you doin', Loretta?" Loretta was passing his stoop going the other way.

"Good Lou, how 'bout you?"

"Good, real good. Nice dress, Doll. Is that new?"

"You like it?"

"Yeah, it's nice."

Lou's next-door neighbor came out his front door carrying a trashcan. "Yo, Juan, don't forget trash day is a day later this week, 'cause a the holiday."

"Oh, yeah, thanks Lou."

Juan carried his can back through the house to his back porch. The trash trucks couldn't get down the alley in back, and it was a long way to the corner from Juan's house. So once a week he had to carry his cans – trash and recycling — through his living room to the curb out front. Not ideal. So Lou's tip was important. No point dragging your cans to the curb early and having them blown around by the wind for an extra day, or knocked over by dogs or kids.

A few minutes later, Lou's other next-door neighbor, Ada, stepped out on her stoop, on her way somewhere. She spotted Lou. "D'ja hear Noreen's daughter is gettin' married?"

"A course I heard that. I hear everything. Are you goin' to the wedding?"

"Probably," Ada replied. "Have to see who she invites."

"Where you headed now?"

"Just to the bank. It's payday. Be good, Lou."

"You too, Doll."

Overall, Lou probably liked the company of men better than women – you don't ever have to think of nothin' to say with men – but he loved talking to the women in his neighborhood.

Lou's house sat on Walnut Street in Norristown, Pennsylvania. It was a rowhouse, in the middle of a block. Lou stayed in his house out of inertia, sure, but also because he believed that a rowhouse was the ultimate in no-apologies living. You paid your mortgage if you still had one, you kept the grass cut in your back yard, and you lived the way you wanted. The trade-off, of course, was that everybody on the block knew everybody else's business. For example, Lou knew that when Gloria passed his front stoop on a Friday, she was on her way to buy lottery tickets at the 7-Eleven. She bought a lot of tickets for the games with the big jackpots. Lou thought Gloria was out of her mind to spend so much for one-in-a-gazillion bets. When Lou gambled, he preferred to win.

CHAPTER 2

Lou grew up on Walnut Street, five doors down and across the street from the house he moved into later. His dad, Roberto, was a tailor from South Philadelphia. His mother, Gina, stayed home to raise Lou, his younger brother Mario, and his younger sister Rita.

Lou's dad smiled often, loved people, and played the saxophone. When he was younger, he played his horn in a swing band, and as he got older he would jam with friends. Sometimes he would play for an hour on Sunday afternoon, while kids were running around and dinner was cooking.

Roberto Incaviglia – Bobby to his friends – moved the family to Norristown when he opened his own tailor shop. Lou was three. There was nobody in Norristown who didn't know Bobby Incaviglia, nobody who didn't take clothes to him for resizing or repair. He wasn't one of these guys who would scowl at you when an alteration needed further adjustment, or find something about you lacking because you didn't like a bump in a seam. Bobby, on the contrary, was always happy to see you come into his shop. He wasn't satisfied with a seam or the placement of a button until you were happy with it. He loved people and sought out human contact relentlessly. Lou figured he was 80% like his dad on that score – the other 20% of the time he wanted to be alone with his cigar. And he hated when the phone rang.

Lou's mom was different. She lived for her three kids, and family was everything. Although she was kind to strangers, Lou never saw her really trust anyone she wasn't related to.

As different as they were, Lou's parents were happy together. If it pained Bobby that he couldn't coax Gina into spending more time with their friends, he never showed it. If Gina struggled to interact with the people Bobby brought into their lives, she at least made the effort. She always showed up for life. And she fought like a tiger for her children.

Lou agreed with his mother. Family was everything. And he agreed with his father — people were all that mattered. He didn't see anything inconsistent about those two absolutes.

When the Incaviglias moved to Walnut Street, the neighborhood was all Italian. Twenty years later there were Puerto Ricans, Vietnamese, African Americans, Arabs, Indians, Pakistanis, Filipinos and Thais. And a bunch of others. And that was just in a four-block radius from the Incaviglia home. Norristown had turned into the U.N., but on less expensive real estate. Bobby Incaviglia didn't care. He figured you could either accept change, or you could be miserable all the time. He knew plenty of people who were miserable all the time, and he didn't see the point. Lou felt the same way.

Bobby and Gina died within a year of each other, Bobby from too much veal parm and too little aerobic exercise, and Gina from breast cancer. Lou was in his mid-thirties at the time. Lou's brother Mario took care of the estate, and sold the tailor shop to a rude guy who lived in Lansdale and commuted to Norristown. Such was the power of Bobby's personality that his customers continued for years to take their clothes to the shop, notwithstanding.

Mario owned a burger and soft ice cream place in Delaware County. Mario's wife, Paulette, worked for a car dealership, and they had a couple of grown kids. Lou's sister Rita was a buyer for Macy's and lived with her partner, Karen, in Doylestown. The three siblings – Lou, Mario and Rita – got together often, and they all knew each other's kids and in-laws and cousins and stuff. They were family.

Lou would tell you about his family, if you asked him. Or about bricklaying. He had opinions on just about anything. Cereal boxes. Toyotas. Just ask. But he tended to avoid politics and shows on Netflix, because he found that nobody listens to you when you talk about that shit anyway.

Lou was married for 17 years. He met Gabriella at a basketball game in high school. Bishop Kenrick was playing West Catholic, and kids from each school mingled at halftime and after the game. Lou, then a senior at Kenrick, had his eye on the tall girl with dark eyes and dark red hair that fell almost to her waist. She was watching the game with three girlfriends, and seemed more interested in the basketball than in socializing. Lou thought that was unusual.

Not being shy, Lou approached her after the final buzzer and said, "Hi, I'm Lou." Gabriella responded, "Why didn't you come say 'hi' at halftime, I have to go home now." Lou pulled out a book of matches and a pen – it never hurt to be prepared – and said, "Let me have your phone number, I'll give you a call. What's your name?"

Gabby was in a mischievous mood, who knows why. She wrote "Karen O'Reilly, 215-827-4866." Karen O'Reilly, Gabby's best friend, stood at her left shoulder, smiled slightly, and otherwise withheld all reaction.

When Lou called Karen's number early the following week, Karen asked him to call back in 15 minutes. That gave Gabby enough time to get over to Karen's house. Lou called again. Karen followed the script that Gabriella and she had devised. Karen explained to Lou that she couldn't go out on a date that week because she had to go see her obstetrician next Monday for a prenatal checkup, and she could only eat certain foods during the week before the appointment. Gabby stifled a laugh, as the two girls listened head to head through the earpiece. For his part, Lou's brain processed the possibilities like an IBM mainframe: a baby. Simple truth? Cry for help? Joke? She had a boyfriend. She didn't have a boyfriend. Give her a serious, supportive response. Change the subject. Ask her doctor's name. Hang up. What he settled upon, just as Karen finished explaining her circumstances, was "I hope you'll consider naming the baby 'Lou.'"

Both girls burst out laughing, and Lou knew he'd guessed right. "OK, let's start over. I'm Lou. And youse are?" Through laughs, he heard "Gabby," and "Karen."

Gabby and Karen had just provided him the opportunity for the easiest first date in history. "Why don't the three of us go down to Wanamaker's on Saturday, and I can figure out who's who?"

The date went well. Lou Incaviglia formally introduced himself to Gabriella Revella. They could talk to each other. Lou learned that Gabby was a junior at West Catholic, and already had a job lined up in her uncle's pastry business after graduation. She didn't have a boyfriend. She liked to write. "Write what?" asked Lou. "I write letters," she replied. Lou had never written a letter in his life, but he sensed the possibilities. "That's good," he said. "Living 20 miles apart, we have to stay in touch if, you know, we're gonna stay in touch."

Lou and Gabby fell in love, the way you can only fall in love when you're falling in love for the first time. They were devoted to each other. They talked on the phone daily and wrote letters back and forth. When they hurt each other, it was because one of them was acting young and dumb. Malice or unconcern toward the other would have been impossible for either of them. They knew they were lucky – they saw the horrible dysfunctional relationships that various adults and some of their friends endured – and they were grateful for each other's company.

When Lou graduated from Kenrick, he went into the Bricklayers. Gabby finished high school, learned bookkeeping part time at Peirce Junior College, and joined her uncle's business full time as she was turning 20. Lou and Gabby talked about getting married all the time. They wanted to save a little money first, and so they did. Lou was 23 and Gabby was 22 when they finally got married. Their wedding, paid for by Gabby's parents per the custom of the time, took place at St. Agatha's in Southwest Philadelphia, Gabby's home parish. The wedding, together with the reception at the Knights of Columbus, lasted about five hours. A year later Lou couldn't remember five minutes of it – he was in a nervous fog the whole time. Gabby remembered every guest, every toast, and every conversation, so between them they had rich and happy memories of their nuptials.

The young couple moved into an apartment in Norristown. Lou drove a couple of miles to the union hiring hall every day, and Gabby hopped on the Red Arrow Line trolley to get to her uncle's business in West Philadelphia. They kept saving, now for a baby. When Gabby got pregnant, they made an offer on a rowhouse on Walnut Street in Norristown, a few doors from Lou's parents. They moved in at the end of her first trimester, and by the time their daughter Olivia was born, her home was ready for her.

But Gabriella fought preeclampsia throughout her pregnancy – she had developed diabetes before she got pregnant — and her obstetrician ultimately advised her to think carefully about whether getting pregnant again was worth the risk to her health. Lou and Gabby talked about adopting, but Lou was concerned about Gabby's health, and together they ultimately decided to give all of their attention to Olivia as she grew up.

Olivia was a joyful little girl who loved people. She was curious about everything, and involved her parents in all of her obsessions – butterflies, dinosaurs, word puzzles, wild animals. Gabby cut back on her work schedule and home-schooled Olivia before anyone called it that. The homeschooling was after school and during the summer, but Olivia learned twice as much from her mother in two hours than she did from her teachers in six.

On a Tuesday afternoon when Olivia was barely 15, Gabriella passed out on the living room floor a half hour before Olivia was due to come home. A neighbor, looking through the screen door, saw her and called an ambulance. The diabetic coma was irreversible and, within two days, fatal. Lou and Olivia found themselves with only each other, a two-person family living in a Norristown rowhouse.

CHAPTER 3

"Hi Dad."

"Hi Honey." Lou shifted his cigar to his right hand and his phone to his left – the good ear side. Olivia's voice always gave him a lift. "How you doin'?"

"We're good. The heater guy came."

"You call Romano, like I tol' ya?"

"No, Greg called a guy recommended by somebody at his golf club."

"Aw shit. Did he fix it, at least?"

"Well, he said he needs a part, so he has to come back. But he started."

"Honey, heaters don't need no parts, and if they do, Joey Romano would have one in his truck. Are you sure it's not too late to call him?"

"No, this was up to Greg. He wanted to network."

"Networking's good. But the idea is to get better help, not worse."

"I hear you, Dad. Trouble with your advice is, it's always good. Makes me feel like an idiot when we don't take it." He could feel the smile in her voice.

"You are an idiot," he replied. "Did I tell you how much of an idiot you are? You're an embarrassment, a complete failure. When are you going to make something of yourself?"

Olivia laughed. "Are you coming for dinner on Sunday?"

"I'll be there. What are you making?"

"Unless you call in a chef, we're making whatever carry-out you want. Plan on 5:30, we'll have a glass of wine."

"That's the best offer I've had in a while."

Lou liked making plans to see Olivia and her husband Greg. It was always a good week when they were all able to see each other.

CHAPTER 4

"Aw, fuck. Go home, you're not welcome here." Lou's friend Vinny saying hello as Lou walked into the club.

"Bite me, you fuck. I was thinkin' a staying, till I saw you. Now I'm not so sure." He sat down and waved for Tommy Benelli at the other end of the bar. Tommy was the regular bartender, and also a member. The job paid minimum wage, plus OK tips. That worked for Tommy, because he would have been there anyway.

"S'new Ink?" asked Tommy.

"Think I got a good horse today. Have to see. Has Carmine been in?"

Carmine DeLuca knew more about horse racing than anyone else in the Italian American Citizens Club of Norristown, Pennsylvania – even more than Lou Incaviglia, who knew an awful lot. Problem was, Carmine's hours at the club were limited by his girlfriend, Martina, and you could never find him. He didn't pay his bills, so he didn't answer his phone.

"Nah, he won't be in," said Tommy. "Or maybe he will be. Who the fuck knows?"

If he couldn't find Carmine, Lou would have to evaluate the seventh race himself. No problem. A mile on a fast track at Pennsylvania Park. Greatly Able was probably going off at 5 to 1, or maybe 9 to 2. Lou had heard he ran a practice mile at 3 seconds quicker than the fastest time any of the other starters had ever *raced* a mile. With the whole field pushing him, he ought to be able to run it wire to wire and win by a couple of lengths. Or at least that's how Lou saw it. If he was right, and if he backed his conviction with a C-Note, he'd pay his bar bill for a couple of months. Where the fuck was Carmine?

Tommy placed a PBR draft in front of Lou, with a shot of VO. He picked up the ten that Lou had laid on the bar and made change. "Are you signing up for the beef and beer next week?" Tommy asked.

"Yeah, give me the sheet," Lou replied, reaching for the clipboard. He wrote "Lou 1019" on the next available line. The "1019" meant that he was the one thousand nineteenth person admitted to membership since the club was formed in the 1920's. Because there were always two or three Tony Rizzo's, and because most of the other last names were four- or five-syllable Italian surnames, it became standard practice for a member to record his presence or indicate interest or assent by signing his first name and his member number. "Lou 1019" was Lou's mark for anything he signed within the walls of the Italian American Citizens Club of Norristown.

Those walls were unremarkable. The main room in the club was a rectangle, with the bar on one of the long sides. There were three small windows on the wall across from the bar, but not much sunlight, even in the middle of the day. There were some tables and chairs in the middle of the room, and a dartboard and pool table in two of the corners. A large Italian flag and a large American flag were hanging on the back wall next to the kitchen. The kitchen was small, and served sandwiches, French fries, and a soup of the day. Nobody pretended the club was a restaurant.

Lou continued thinking about the seventh race. His train of thought was interrupted when he noticed a cigar sticking out of Tommy's shirt pocket. "Yo, Tommy, you don't smoke cigars. What's up?" asked Lou.

"I'm holding it for Enzo. He dropped it over at the pool table."

"You know, there's a lot of things most people don't know about cigars," Lou began.

"Hmmm," said Tommy.

"If you got a good one, you can burn a nice long ash and it won't fall on your pants. You only have to get up and walk over to the curb to drop your ash maybe four times. But whether it burns good depends completely on the wrapper. Good wrapper, good burn. Cigars want to burn in a nice circle. Can't always do it, a course, but they try."

"Hmm mmmm." Tommy replied. He knew better than to offer any substantive comment, to which Lou would have responded at length.

"I think six bucks is the sweet spot for a cigar," Lou continued. "Arturo Fuentes Corona, maybe. You can afford to smoke one, and you can't really tell it apart from one of them twenty dollar cigars."

"Yeah," said Tommy.

Lou then thought about whether he wanted to head for the Off-Track Betting parlor in Plymouth Meeting or go directly to the track. Pennsylvania Park – once known as Philadelphia Park, and then Parx Racing, and then, under new ownership, Pennsylvania Park – was twenty miles away in Bensalem, Pennsylvania. A long drive, with no decision yet made about how he would bet the seventh race. The worst outcome would be to drive that distance and then conclude that he didn't want to bet. That happened sometimes.

As he was mulling his options, Carmine called him back. "Greatly Able is a good bet," said Carmine, without preamble. In Lou's phone message to Carmine, he had inquired about Greatly Able. Carmine didn't feel any need to explain his views further.

"Do you want to bet him?" asked Lou.

"Yeah, put twenty on him for me," Carmine responded.

"OK, I'm headed for the track," said Lou. "See you later, and thanks."

Lou arrived at Pennsylvania Park 45 minutes later and settled onto his bench near the finish line. The track wasn't crowded, maybe 500 customers. It was almost free to get in – the track wanted you to bet, and most of the patrons didn't consider horse racing a spectator sport. But it is, and Lou never got tired of the spectacle.

Lou watched a few races without betting, and then bet a hundred and twenty dollars on Greatly Able to win the seventh race. Which he did. That meant that Lou left the track after collecting $465 for himself and $93 for Carmine. He drove back to Norristown happy.

CHAPTER 5

Sal Paglia was from Norristown. His company, Sal Paglia, Inc., began in Norristown and eventually did business everywhere in southeastern Pennsylvania. Quaker Heights Township, Upper Cornwall Township, Guilfoyle Township, Penn Manor Township, at least fifty others. If you were managing a municipality in the Philadelphia metropolitan area, you hoped to hire Sal Paglia to pave your streets, or maybe somebody else won the bid for one round, before Sal took it back. He also did private housing developments, shopping centers, you name it. Quality asphalt, great service, clean trucks.

The company had 900 employees, eight asphalt plants, two rock quarries, and more than 100 trucks. And not just any trucks – they had their signature 40-ton dump trucks with three rear axles, galvanized steel load beds, shiny black paint jobs, and sparkling chrome. All Kenworths. "Sal Paglia, Inc.," in big script on the door. It was impossible to drive to the grocery store without seeing at least one. More important, Sal Paglia, Inc., had $150 million in annual gross revenue.

Sal Paglia started the company in Norristown in the 1980's. Back then, all he had was a Ford F-350 pickup, a shovel, a rake, and a used asphalt pour pot. Sal was a big man – six feet, 210 pounds, strong – who didn't mind hard physical work. He sealed a half-dozen driveways a day, invested his (untaxed) cash proceeds in more equipment, and sold, and sold, and sold. You gotta sell if you want to eat. Sal wanted to eat.

Hancock Township, in Montgomery County, was his first big break. They were building a new township building – Township Supervisors, police, and a small library, all in the same place – and they were bidding the site prep, lighting, and parking lot separately. Sal heard about the parking lot piece from a friend, who suggested that he put in a bid. Sal had never bid a municipal job, but he was a quick study. He formed a corporation – Sal Paglia, Inc., was born – and talked to Arena Paving about being his (undisclosed) subcontractor if he won. Hancock Township awarded him the contract, and four other townships had him doing pavement jobs within the next year.

Sal bought out Arena Paving three years later. At the time, Arena Paving owed a few bucks more in loans than it owned in assets. The loans were owed to the owner's extended family, and the family was getting antsy – they wanted their money back. Sal persuaded the owner to give him all of the stock in the company in exchange for Sal's agreement to guarantee the debt. The owner jumped on the offer because he wanted out. Sal said, "let's leave lawyers out of this," which sounded to the seller like a reasonable plan. So far, so good. But the seller neglected to document Sal's guarantee of the indebtedness, and signed over the shares anyway. Sal promptly told all of the lenders that the company was under new ownership and didn't owe them a dime – a bold lie that they halfway believed. Sal lined up a bank loan for 40% of Arena Paving's debt, and offered each one of the lenders forty cents on the dollar. Take it or leave it, and you should take it because the company isn't going to pay, and we'll see you in bankruptcy court if you don't like it. So they agreed, and Arena Paving was merged into Sal Paglia, Inc.

Porter Township was his next big break. He was doing a job repaving the township's main roads when the Township Engineer put him in touch with a private developer building The Estates at Townsford Mews. Eighty-five houses, three-car garages, and a mile of paving, from the dirt up. The developer liked the fact that Sal's trucks were already in the neighborhood; the Township Engineer OK'd the paving in the development without blinking an eye; and Sal offered a good price. One stop shopping. And just like that, Sal Paglia, Inc., was working for private developers, in the middle of a housing boom.

The next opportunity for growth was Lincoln Financial Field – the stadium seats, not the parking lot. The "Linc" in South Philadelphia – home of the Philadelphia Eagles – opened in 2003. Sal Paglia, Inc., bought the occasional ticket for a developer customer, of course, but Sal had a bigger and better idea. He created a shell company to invest a small fortune in five four-seat sets in the lower level, all between the 40 yard lines, and all subleased from existing season ticket holders at three times the face value of the tickets. Plus, each season ticket holder had the right to occupy one of his seats for one game a year, so he wouldn't feel shut out. Sal had lawyers draw up the deals, and did not trouble the Eagles for their approval, inasmuch as the names on their season ticket contracts never changed.

Sal talked to his two sisters' boys – Locatelli and Cattaneo, not Paglias – and said, "How would each of you like to go to eight or nine home Eagles games a year?" All they had to do was invite a few of their closest friends to each game. And Sal helpfully provided the names of those friends from time to time, from whom his nephews could expect phone calls.

State and municipal procurement codes in Pennsylvania include stringent anti-bribery provisions. But, come on, a friendly heads-up about an unused ticket isn't bribery. Sal mentioned to Township Managers and Township Engineers of his acquaintance that "a friend" knew "some rich guy" who "wasn't using his ticket on September 18" (or October 9 or November 27). He gave them a cell phone number for one of his nephews. Very quickly, the township people realized that Sal could be counted on, somehow, to hear about empty seats every year, and later learned that they could, and should, call his nephews directly if they wanted to hear about those empty seats earlier and pick up a free ticket or two. There would be no paper trail or unhelpful phone records.

Jeez, if rich people don't want to use their Eagles seats, and friends of friends are telling you they're otherwise going to go to waste if you don't use them, and if no township contractor appears to be involved, why wouldn't you say yes? And maybe when it comes time to approve bid specifications for paving work, our township should specify techniques that Sal Paglia, Inc., is uniquely equipped to provide. Modern paving is challenging work, after all, and not everyone can do it well. Sal Paglia, Inc., always provides great value, and when we need to make small changes to the work, they are always prepared to do those changes for a reasonable price. Hiring a good road contractor is only good sense and good government. So Sal Paglia's business grew large.

Are professional football tickets really that important? Sal Paglia's most important competitive insight was that, yes, they are. At least in Pennsylvania.

Notwithstanding the changes in his life as his business grew, many of Sal's closest friends remained those he had grown up with in Norristown. He remained a member of St. Francis Parish, and lived his life as the shot-and-a-beer kind of guy he was – a shot of Seagram's VO and a pint of Yuengling Lager. Not everybody liked Sal, but few disliked him.

But Sal always wanted more. He liked running things, and his takeover of Arena Paving gave him a taste for other acquisitions. He saw no reason he shouldn't be running more than just his paving company. He didn't have the time or energy to start any new ventures, but he liked the idea of investing in other peoples' start-ups.

It was low risk, and high reward. Sal would buy shares in small companies and make such a nuisance of himself that the owners would have no choice but to get rid of him somehow. He first employed his strategy against a small, privately owned manufacturer of pipefittings and connectors out in Chester County. He had heard about the company from a guy at his golf club who owned a few shares. Sal badgered his friend for a couple of months, and the guy finally agreed to sell his shares.

The moment Sal received his shares, he began to pester company management for all of the information to which he was entitled as a shareholder under Pennsylvania law. He had his lawyer write a letter per week asking for different documents – a profit and loss statement from two years ago, a copy of the shareholders' register, a state tax return from three years ago, a copy of the articles of incorporation. He objected in writing to the fact that the annual shareholders' meeting was scheduled with inadequate notice, and demanded the full ten business days specified in the by-laws. The meeting was duly rescheduled, with everybody receiving a fresh notice. Sal proposed twelve questions to be voted on by shareholders at the meeting, and made a speech during the meeting about every issue he had raised. After three hours, most of the other shareholders had gone home.

Management hated Sal within a month, and were looking for ways to get rid of him within a year. They suggested that perhaps he should think about selling his shares, and he responded by telling them they wouldn't be able to afford his price. But he would listen, he said.

The majority owners of the company had a problem. They would have liked to have used company funds to purchase Sal's shares at two or three times what he paid for them – whatever it took. But under state law they couldn't redeem Sal's shares at a given price without offering the same amount per share to all of the other shareholders. The company didn't have that kind of cash available.

But there was another option. The company's president and largest shareholder, a grandson of the company's founder, owned a 35% stake in the company. If he offered to purchase Sal's shares for his own account, he was not obliged, as an individual shareholder, to make the same offer to other shareholders. Given that many of the problems that Sal was creating wound up on his desk, he figured he could either go crazy or find the money to meet Sal's price.

The deal was not easy to negotiate – Sal was a tenacious bargainer – but they finally got it done. Sal walked away with more than three times what he paid for his shares. In return, he signed a confidentiality agreement keeping the terms secret, and he promised never to purchase shares in the company again. Both sides welcomed the resolution, although the company's owners felt like they'd just survived a locust swarm.

Sal stashed the proceeds into a bank account he considered fun money, a slush fund for hostile takeovers. He liked this new sport.

The third or fourth time Sal Paglia bought stock in a small-ish company – a farm equipment distributor – he scooped up his five percent interest from the estate of a deceased minority shareholder. When he demanded documents the company promptly complied, and Sal put his lawyers and accountants to work. They discovered some serious accounting irregularities – or at least they were prepared to *say* they were serious. Sal confronted the majority owners about what he'd found. After a year of accusations and counter-accusations, the majority owners – three brothers – realized they were spending more time fending off Sal Paglia than running the business. Litigation seemed imminent.

At that point, Sal resorted to a tactic that would have been familiar to his Roman ancestors – divide and conquer. He struck a deal, at a price he liked, to buy the shares of the youngest brother. Both he and the brother kept their deal secret while Sal continued to negotiate with other shareholders. Sal's five percent, plus the youngest brother's twenty percent, gave him control of a quarter of the shares. He just needed to pry some shares loose from other investors to get himself to 50% plus one. He painted them a picture of a company propped up with accounting gimmicks, and he persuaded several investors that they needed to get out while the getting was good. He struck a deal for the last two percent he needed by offering to pay four times what the shares were worth – a true "premium for control." On a rainy Sunday afternoon, he gathered all of the selling shareholders into a room at his country club and gave them certified checks in the amounts each of them had agreed. He had gained control of the company by paying a fraction of what it was worth.

Sal really enjoyed Monday morning. He called the two older brothers and advised them that he owned 51% of the company. He was no longer interested in buying their shares, and they should consider themselves relieved of their managerial duties.

As satisfying as it had been to win, Sal had no interest in farm equipment. So he hired somebody to run the business while he shopped for a buyer. Everybody likes a cash cow, and he sold his stake to one of the company's competitors within six months. Sal doubled the amount he had paid for his shares, not a bad return for eight or nine months' effort. And he was doubly happy that the buyer was prepared to tolerate the two brothers' remaining minority interests, so the older brothers didn't see a dime from the deal – they were stuck. Sal liked the last laugh whenever he could get it.

CHAPTER 6

The sun was peeking through puffy clouds, and the wind was a little stiffer than he would have liked, but late April was warm enough for a cigar. Lou pulled up to Olivia's house – he tried to think of it as Greg and Olivia's house – in his 2010 Mercury Grand Marquis. He loved his car. It was sold as the luxury version of the taxicab, cop car, Crown Vic thing that Ford sold for, what, twenty years. Leather seats, quiet V-8, metallic silver paint, soft ride, big. An old man's car. That was OK, because Lou was an old man – sixty-two. When Lou was a kid, if you were sixty you were ready to be dead. Now it was, "Sixty is the new forty." Bullshit. Most mornings, Lou felt old in every joint. It probably didn't help that he ate anything he wanted, smoked too many cigars, never exercised, and usually forgot to fill his blood pressure medication until the bottle had been empty for two weeks. See, Lou believed that your life was measured out in advance. If it was your time, it was your time. His grandfather had lived to ninety-two. Fuck it. Just be happy in the meantime.

Lou didn't need to worry about his weight because it was always 185. At 5'7", Lou was exactly the height he was meant to be. His hair was meant to be white – for the past 10 years, anyway — and his Sicilian good looks were exactly the way they were supposed to be. Lou had no idea how Buddhist he was, but if you told him, he would have listened politely and then told you you're full of shit.

Lou's daughter, Olivia, lived in Villanova in a big house. Her husband, Gregory C. Morris, Jr., had found the house online, when they weren't even looking for a house. It had five bedrooms, a yard, and a big three-car garage. Way too much house for two people.

Lou was wearing a shirt with a collar, because Olivia asked him to. But it was one of those big short-sleeved shirts you don't ever tuck in. Like a bowling shirt or a Hawaiian shirt. They probably had a name, and Lou had ten of them, but he didn't know what they were called, if anything. Why does everybody think everything has to have a name? And how come everybody else kept track of names, except Lou? What do you call that thing you put your feet on? Hassock, Ottoman, footrest? Who cares?

Lou was about to tap on Olivia's front door when Olivia opened it. "Hi Daddy!" She reached out and gave him a hug. "Where's your jacket?"

"Don't need no jacket, it's almost May." He tilted his head up. "Smells good, what a we got?"

"We called out for Thai. But it'll wait, I promised you a glass of wine."

As they were passing through the house to the back patio door, Greg came out of the kitchen. "Hi Lou."

"Hi Greg."

"You probably won't like the curry, but the wine's Italian." And then to Olivia: "Hon, I'm going to make a call."

"On Sunday at dinnertime?" She shook her head, almost imperceptibly.

"Have to make a living." Greg was the president of a high-tech manufacturing company that he had founded, and like most start-ups, it required constant attention. As Greg often put it, "If I'm awake, I'm working." No use complaining.

Greg turned up the stairs. As Olivia watched him go, she imagined she saw smoke coming out of his ears. Stress. She tried, whenever she could, to yank him away for a long weekend or a short vacation, but their hours remained brutal, and free time was non-existent. Olivia sighed, and took her father by the elbow as she led him out to the deck. She was holding a bottle of red in her other hand. "I looked for this all week. It's a Chianti Classico.

Apparently, you have to make a super high quality wine to qualify for the name. Something to do with the Italian government."

"I was likin' it till you mentioned the Italian government."

Olivia laughed. "Shut up and drink it. And you'd better say you like it."

Olivia began to pour two glasses as Lou settled into a padded chair on the deck. He reached into his shirt pocket for a cigar. Olivia's face changed.

"What's the matter?" asked Lou.

"Greg was going to ask if you wouldn't mind smoking your cigar in one of the lawn chairs on the outer patio. He says the ashes and smell are noticeable here on the deck."

Lou was speechless for a moment. "I don't unnerstand. You been borrowing puffs from my cigars since you were sixteen. You love the smell of cigars."

"Well, Greg lives here too. I need to respect his feelings. I told him I'd talk to you."

"Why doesn't he talk to me?"

Olivia hesitated. "Well, he was going to. But I told him I'd talk to you about it."

Lou just shook his head. He wished he and Greg got along better. They both made efforts, and they both understood the importance of making those efforts, but Greg grew up in a rich family in Connecticut, and Lou grew up in the Italian neighborhood in Norristown. Worlds apart. Both of them worked hard to bridge the gap, for Olivia's sake, but it wasn't always easy. Big Italian families Lou knew mostly enjoyed each other's company, just because. Even the in-laws. Working at it was different for Lou.

"I'm sorry Honey. I can smoke my cigars out on the lawn chairs."

Olivia smiled. "It's almost summer," she said, finally. "Another thing we can do, we can go for a walk next time you're here, and we'll share a corona." And then, "I love you Daddy." She got up, leaned down, and gave him a hug.

CHAPTER 7

Vinny was at the bar playing with his phone.

"You never take your nose outta that thing," said Lou as he arrived at the club.

"Bite me," Vinny responded.

"You know why Sicilian men are so handsome?" asked Lou, sitting down at the bar.

"No. I don't care," Vinny responded. "But I'm sure you're gonna tell me."

"Because we can't help it," said Lou.

"You made that up?" asked Vinny.

"No, it's an eternal truth. Can't make up no eternal truth. It's chiseled right there in the columns of the Coliseum in Rome – Sicilian men are handsome."

"Get the fuck outta here," Vinny replied. "Nobody in Rome ever said nothin' nice about Sicilians."

"I meant the Amphitheater in Catania," said Lou, improvising quickly.

"I don't disagree with you," said Vinny. "We are very good lookin'. But that don't explain *why* we're so good looking."

"I think it's our North African blood," said Lou. "And our French temperament. Arab-Norman Sicily, a thousand years ago."

"Thing is, you're only half Sicilian. And me too," said Vinny. "Like Frank Sinatra. Yo, Tommy, why are half-Sicilian men so handsome?"

Tommy Benelli, behind the bar, looked up from his cash register. "You mean half of all Sicilian men? Because the other half are in jail?"

"No, you fuckin' moron, why are men who are half Sicilian and half Italian so good lookin'?"

"Because of course they are," replied Tommy.

"Good answer," said Lou, as he opened his Daily Racing Form.

"Did you hear the Deputy Mayor might get locked up for molesting a 16 year old?" asked Vinny.

"I hear everything," Lou replied. "A course I heard that. Why'd ya ask?"

"Because I wanted to know if it's true."

"A course it's true," Lou replied. "My neighbor Anna is friends with the girl's mom. Anna says the mom is all upset about it. I would be too. I'd kill the cocksucker. Nice and quiet at night, I'd sneak into his house and shoot him. Anyway, the cops are takin' statements, and supposably he's gonna be locked up before the end of the week."

"Lou, do you want somethin' to eat?" asked Tommy.

"Nope, thanks. I'm gonna eat at the track. Have you heard from Carmine?"

"Of course not," Tommy replied.

Lou studied his Daily Racing Form and tried to remember whether he needed gas in his car. If so, he needed to leave a few minutes earlier. Lou liked to be on time.

CHAPTER 8

Olivia was carefully arranging the silverware and dishes. Over-arranging, for that matter. She was OCD before OCD was a thing. Most foods were red, green or yellow, so she was preparing a food tray for her guests separated into red, green, yellow and "other." She had fun with bell peppers, especially, because she could always find a red, a green and a yellow. Then she sliced them up and separated them by color, just to see whether any of her guests would notice that two of three colors were not anywhere near the dip. After she deployed the food and wines in the living room, she straightened the chairs and checked the openings in the drapes for the fourth time. Then the doorbell began to ring.

The evening with friends went well. No one commented on the food tray. Olivia almost asked the group, "Hey, do you notice anything interesting about the food tray?" But she knew that her OCD was more amusing to her than it was to others. When she made an OCD joke at her own expense, sometimes people laughed and sometimes they didn't, and when they didn't, they tended to look at her oddly.

The guests were gone by 11:00 – something of an early evening. Greg and Olivia cleared the living room, put most of the dishes in the dishwasher and climbed the stairs to their bedroom. As they were peeling off scruffy jeans and expensive shirts, Olivia asked Greg, "Did you have fun?"

Greg thought for a minute as he threw his wristwatch on his dresser. "Sort of. It seemed a little subdued, I don't know."

"Everybody's tired from working all the time. You can tell that people liked being here, and our friends like each other. That's huge. But we should probably invite a clown or a magician every time we have a party. People need to laugh."

"Yeah, exactly," said Greg. "We weren't laughing tonight."

"We'll get 'em next time," said Olivia, as she collapsed into bed. She wondered for the millionth time why she could tell a joke reasonably well, but could never remember any.

CHAPTER 9

Growing up, Olivia's personality quirks were invisible – kids don't notice subtle behavioral tendencies, and, anyway, Olivia presented her friends with the Pretty Girl Problem. From the age of 12 onward she was stunning – tall, lean, long beautiful dark hair, hazel eyes – and quiet. The other kids, especially the boys, were terrified of her. Conversations in which Olivia was involved were stammered, on both sides. As a teenager, she had no earthly idea how kids talked, and, because of the communications barrier, her friends had no earthly idea what she was really like. The fact that she was very, very smart didn't help either.

And then her mother died suddenly while Olivia was a sophomore. Having had no time to prepare or say goodbye, Olivia simply froze in place. She wasn't a rebellious kid and she didn't take her pain out on Lou. Even then she understood that he wasn't the reason she felt so awful. Not depressed – in some odd way it was even deeper than that. She was traumatized. During her last 2½ years of high school, her existence was robotic and joyless, and her OCD began to develop and take hold. She became very quiet. The few friends she had weren't able to coax her into much of a social life. She studied hard to take her mind off her loneliness.

She could talk to her dad, of course. And Lou could talk to anyone, even his daughter. Despite his tendency with other people to advise first and listen after, he was patient in hearing Olivia out. He wanted to understand the problem before he counseled her about it. His advice was usually pretty good, and he always seemed able to cut through the anxiety and simplify her decisionmaking.

Three years after her mother died, Olivia left for Princeton. She didn't exactly blossom at Princeton, but she found her footing a little bit. Princeton was Geek Central, and it was easy to fall into long conversations about big ideas. Her loneliness eased, and she began to look forward to social gatherings. The kids who stammered were the same kids who were designing rocket motors, or, in Olivia's case, majoring in macroeconomics. She made friends and kept them.

Gregory C. Morris, Jr. wasn't a geek – far from it – but he wasn't cool, either. He was intense. He could persuade anyone to do anything. Although his personality wasn't big or fake enough to be a campus-wide celebrity, he knew a lot of people. He was widely regarded as "focused." While most undergraduates would admit to themselves and each other that they had no frigging clue what they wanted to do with their lives, the undergrads at Princeton knew that Greg Morris would either be the manager of a large hedge fund, or, failing that, a U.S. Senator from his home state of Connecticut.

Greg began to pursue Olivia Incaviglia after Winter Break of their sophomore year. Olivia had a lot of her father's stubbornness, and it was more than a year, till the spring of their junior year, that Olivia finally agreed to go out on a real date. But Olivia placed Greg on more-or-less permanent probation. Olivia was used to being treated with respect by her father, and she demanded it from her boyfriend. So while it was Greg's preference to cajole people into doing favors – even when he could have had the same thing for the asking – he wouldn't cajole Olivia. Persuasion didn't work with Livvie. She would do something with him, or for him, or instead of him, when she had concluded it was the right or best thing to do. Time spent alone in high school had taught her to rely on her own judgment, and she was one of the few people who were largely immune to Greg's talents of persuasion.

They decided to stay together after graduation. Both headed for New York City, Greg to Goldman Sachs, and Olivia to graduate school in Economics at Columbia. It was an unsettled period for Olivia. Greg was paying the rent and the grocery bills (they lived in a small apartment on West 109th Street), and the best Olivia could manage was to pay for a pizza every once in a while from her TA stipend. She didn't enjoy feeling dependent. Neither of them talked about getting married – yet.

Olivia loved her work at Columbia. Like a few other junior academics around the country, Olivia was fascinated by the apparent applicability of the Heisenberg Uncertainty Principle to macroeconomics. Professor Heisenberg posited that it's impossible to measure both the position and the momentum of a sub-atomic particle simultaneously. Olivia wondered whether a rule applicable in quantum physics might have an analog in market theory. She took note of the fact that many economists lamented their inability to use the same equations to describe where the economy was and where it was going. Maybe, she reasoned, it is literally impossible to find hints about our economic future by examining an economic present that is, by definition, always in equipoise at the end of a business day, neither expanding nor contracting. Her doctoral thesis argued that you might have been able to spot some hints of the coming Great Depression by tracking annual economic reports from across the Roaring Twenties— only in retrospect, of course — but all the data you could possibly have mustered from private and governmental financial reports on October 28, 1929, was not going to reveal anything about October 29, 1929, or 1932, or 1936. If she was right, macroeconomic prognostication was more a guessing game than its practitioners would ever be prepared to concede. On the subject of economic forecasting, Olivia liked to quote Yogi Berra: "Predictions are hard, especially about the future."

Olivia earned her PhD in four years, fast for a Columbia economist. Lou was present when she received her diploma, and two weeks later he was present when Olivia and Greg were married at St. Vincent's in Norristown. It was a traditional wedding, and Lou gave Olivia away. When the wedding weekend was over, Olivia and Greg headed back to New York City, vowing to take a honeymoon that they never really got around to. New York is only 90 miles from Norristown, but to Olivia it sometimes seemed like a million miles. She missed her dad a lot.

Olivia decided not to pursue a post-doc, and opted, instead, to try the private sector. After considering a handful of offers, she went to work in Manhattan as an economist for the Commercial Bank of New York. Within two years, the bank had collapsed, ignominiously, for an odd reason. The bank had almost entirely neglected its compliance obligations, and faced shut down threats from the New York State Department of Financial Services, the New York State Department of Labor, and the New York State Department of Taxation and Finance. They even received a hefty fine from the New York City Department of Sanitation for failing to recycle. A big, solid, respected institution collapsed because nobody was filling out the required forms. It seems that every business, even the successful ones, has its skeletons.

Thus, two years after she began with CBNY, Olivia found herself looking to make a career move. And Greg, still at Goldman Sachs, was itching to start his own business. For both of them, Philadelphia looked like the perfect choice. Greg knew he could start his own hedge fund anywhere, and he liked Philly's size and business climate. Olivia wanted, finally, to go home. So Greg rented space in downtown Philadelphia, and Olivia took her ideas to Biddle & Co., Philadelphia's oldest investment bank.

Olivia's job at Biddle was to act as the resident contrarian. If one of the partners was selling a deal internally on the basis of rosy economic assumptions (or, occasionally, dreary ones), it was Olivia's job to run the same numbers and explain all of the reasons the assumptions were probably wrong. Olivia marveled occasionally that Biddle was willing to pay her a mid-six-figure salary just to serve as the Devil's Advocate, but she knew that Biddle's ROI and default rates were the envy of the industry, and she believed she was helping to make that happen. She was seven years into her tenure, and looking forward to the next phases of her career. That and having kids.

Although she didn't like to admit it, not getting pregnant was anxiety producing. And when her aunts and uncles and friends told her it didn't matter, it made her feel worse, not better. Of course it mattered. Her dad, to his credit, never told her it didn't matter to him, because it clearly did. She knew he wanted grandchildren, because he often said so. "We go back six generations in Sicily, it would be nice to go forward four or five generations here." Olivia was an only child, so if those four or five generations were going to happen, she had to step up and become a link in the chain. Greg, too.

A baby. God, it was difficult. Emotionally, practically, you name it. It didn't help, of course, that they hadn't tried at all during their first four years in Philadelphia – too busy at work. And when they finally decided to have a baby, they tried the old-fashioned way for a couple of years, without success. Their first visit to the fertility clinic was confusing. The clinic wanted her to consider in vitro fertilization, or IVF, right away, because it was their best shot and Greg and Olivia could afford the cost. But Olivia took her Catholicism seriously, and she was squeamish about creating lots of extra embryos. She preferred to try other methods first. So her first prescription was for six months of Clomiphene, which was supposed to stimulate ovulation. It didn't work.

The next attempt was a prescription for Greg for Anastrozole, a breast cancer drug that is often prescribed off-label to raise testosterone levels in men. It seemed kind of dumb, since Greg's testosterone levels were within the normal range, but the doctors thought it might help. It didn't.

Next up was Letrozole, which Olivia took for four months. The drug is particularly useful if a woman has polycystic ovary syndrome, or PCOS. Nobody could tell Olivia whether she had PCOS, but, by then, she had concluded that the fertility industry ran on the principle, "What the hell, let's try this – or maybe that."

So they were still trying.

CHAPTER 10

Sal Paglia's latest project was finding an investment in health care. His financial advisor pointed out that Baby Boomers were slowly becoming end-of-lifers, and their medical expenses were mounting. Can't miss, as far as Sal was concerned.

The challenge, of course, was that Sal was not looking for an investment as much as trying to spot prey. He needed to find a company that had developed promising technology; it needed to be privately owned; and he needed to be able to identify some minority shareholders who could be persuaded to sell. Finding the right company might take some time. Sal was not a patient man, but he wasn't impulsive either. He tasked his financial advisor with finding candidates, and he spent time online himself. He figured he'd turn something up if he kept his eyes and ears open.

A few weeks after he'd established his investment criteria, he heard somebody at his club talking about a company that was testing a new artificial knee. He was immediately interested – being as how one of his golfing buddies had gone through a knee implant three years earlier and came out of it hitting the ball farther than he ever had before his surgery. Sal looked the company up on the internet, and asked his financial advisor to see what he could find. His advisor came back with a packet of documents that one of his clients had reviewed before deciding not to invest, and, *presto*, Sal could read the company's offering circular and all of the other promotional materials they provided to investors as they were raising funds.

Sal liked what he saw in the offering circular and online. The technology looked interesting, and one of the company's press releases said that their knee was already in clinical trials. But Sal wanted to hedge his bets. He decided to buy some shares in Century Medical Technologies, a publicly traded company that was the industry leader in titanium knees, and worked up a plan for establishing a connection with management. He figured that if he managed to take over the smaller company, and they weren't making enough money to suit him, he could sell the technology to Century, and close the newer company down. Win-win.

He also instructed his financial advisor to find some more private placements in medical technology so he could compare them to the artificial knee opportunity. Sal was starting to have fun with this.

His advisor promised to bring him back a "myriad" of options. Sal liked that word – it sounded like a unit of crypto-currency. They agreed to meet again in a month or so to talk about possibilities.

CHAPTER 11

Lou and Olivia were food shopping on Saturday morning, a ritual they never missed if they were both in town. "What's the difference between an economist and a dementia patient?" Lou asked, half way up Aisle 3.

Olivia laughed.

Lou waited a beat. "Every once in a while the dementia patient will admit he doesn't know what he's talking about."

"What's the difference between an old, opinionated Italian man and the dusty cans of soup in the back of your cupboard?" she shot back.

Lou laughed.

"Once a year you'll pull something useful out of one of the cans of soup," she declared, triumphantly.

"Not if you're a young Italian economist who's never figured out how to use a can opener," said Lou. Checkmate. Olivia tossed a loaf of bread at him.

Food shopping was one of Lou's talents, and an opportunity for father and daughter to spend time together. Lou usually stopped by her house for a cup of coffee, and then they would go together in his car to the supermarket. On the way back to her house, he asked, "What do you need fixed?"

For a few years, Olivia had struggled with her answer to that question – she didn't want to take advantage of her dad's good nature. But her uneasiness had faded, gradually.

"I have a list as long as your arm," she replied. "Where do you want to start?" Olivia understood family even better at 35 than she had at 25.

"OK, I'll start with the gutter by the back bedroom, and then I'll do a couple of these other things," he said, pointing at the list. "My fee is gonna be a very nice lunch."

"Fine, as long as you pay for it," she replied.

They both smiled. It occurred to Lou that Olivia would hold her own in the Italian American Citizens Club of Norristown. It was a good thing she showed no interest in that idea.

CHAPTER 12

On Monday, after a cigar and a look at the Daily Racing Form, Lou thought about whether to call Anna Marino to have coffee that week, maybe catch up a little. Lou felt like the reason he got along good with Anna was that she was nice. Nicer than he was, certainly. Anna was nice to everybody. She almost never got angry, and she took people exactly as she found them. With Anna, there was never any of this "you should," or "if I were you," or "you let me down again." She was one of those people who could be kind to everybody, but nobody seemed to take advantage of her good nature. She was Lou's age, and had a lot of friends she made over the years. She was 60's-ish plump, 5'3", beautiful eyes, still-mostly-blond hair (her mother was Irish), and always smiling. Intelligent, without having to remind you all the time. Happy, mostly all the time.

Anna was a friend, but not a girlfriend. She lived around the corner from Lou and had a job as a bookkeeper for a good company, a nice house, and a dog. When Gabby was alive, she and Anna were friends, and Anna was a lot of help in those early months after Gabby died, when Lou and Olivia needed it the most. Anna and Olivia were still friends, despite the age difference.

Lou had thought every once in a while about why Anna was a friend but not a girlfriend. As far as he could recall, he had never had a female friend before Anna. The best he could figure was that he liked how simple it was that she was just a friend and couldn't imagine how complicated it would be if she were his girlfriend. And she seemed to feel more or less the same way. So Anna and Lou were friends without benefits, but with other benefits that were way more important.

Lou and Anna never had any problem talking, even when Gabby was alive. Anna would talk to Lou about "feelings" every once in a while – not all that often — and then would helpfully tell Lou what his feelings were. That might have driven Lou nuts, except she was almost always right. She knew him well.

Anna was married when she was in her twenties, but it didn't last. No kids. Later, when she started dating Crazy Al Morgan – that was what Lou called him, because he was – she asked Crazy Al if he had any problems with Lou being a good friend, and Al said he didn't, which was probably true. She didn't seem quite as happy during the two years they dated. But Lou never forgave Crazy Al when he dumped her. He was one of those mahafs who got drunk and called her twice a year to ask her to come back. There were a couple of times when Lou thought she was considering the possibility of getting back together with Crazy Al, but, to her credit, she turned him down.

When Lou dated – well, he never really dated anybody for more than a couple of dates. Except for Patty, and that was a few years ago. Long story. But Anna was always very respectful of anyone Lou introduced her to, and actually kind of encouraged him to date more.

Lou and Anna never went on dates together, except maybe the Christmas party at the club, if you count that. But once a week or so they binge-watched something at her place or his, and a lot of times they went to Sunday breakfast somewhere. Sometimes they made a meal, especially if one of them bought too much of something and needed somebody to share it with. Once a year, Lou would let Anna drag him to an estate sale, and once a year she would let him drag her to the racetrack. That kind of thing.

Lou treated people pretty well, except for when he was busting somebody's balls, but then again, that wasn't really serious. Anna, for her part, always got the best Lou had to give. He loved her unconditionally.

CHAPTER 13

Sal had kept his investment accounts with Alabaster Financial Group in King of Prussia for more than 20 years. He was tempted to move his money when the markets fell in 2008 and 2022, but concluded that those disasters were Wall Street's fault – neighborhood financial advisors in Pennsylvania were not the problem.

He liked Alabaster for mostly one reason – when he said "Jump," they asked him "How high?" The principal advisor assigned to his account changed periodically, but everyone who worked there was equally obsequious. Thus, when Sal requested private placement memoranda and offering circulars – two labels denoting pretty much the same thing – for small companies specializing in health care technology, the staff at Alabaster got busy.

Among the universe of financial advisors, lawyers, accountants and brokers, financial advisors are uniquely situated to possess copies of private placement documents – offers to sell shares in privately-owned companies – because their clients often seek their advice on the investments as they become available. Sometimes a client will participate in the offering – *i.e.* buy some of the offered shares – and sometimes not. In either event, the private placement memorandum is tossed into a filing cabinet and largely forgotten after the offering is closed. But the paper doesn't go away. It holds a treasure trove of information about the subject company's structure and prospects.

Alabaster was able to locate offering circulars and private placement memoranda in its files for six companies involved in health care technology.

Five of the six stock offerings were successful, and the companies were still in business. But it was almost impossible to identify shareholders in a private company through online searches – in the vast majority of cases, the information simply wasn't available online. So Sal decided to put off finding shareholders with whom he might strike a deal until he decided which company interested him the most. To do that, he had to read offering circulars, or have somebody read them first and then explain what they said.

"Why are these documents so full of unnecessary bullshit?" asked Sal to no one in particular during a meeting at Alabaster.

One of the junior advisors spoke up. He had been to law school for a year. "You're right, Sal, it is bullshit. The reason these things exist is that state and federal securities laws require any seller of stock to disclose all facts about the company that would be material to the buyer's decision about whether to purchase the shares."

"Why isn't Johnson & Johnson in this pile of paper?" Sal asked.

"Because if a company's stock is publicly-traded on one of the securities exchanges – like the New York Stock Exchange or the NASDAQ – the company files its disclosures with the federal Securities and Exchange Commission and those documents are available online. But when a company isn't publicly traded and it wants to sell stock – in other words, a private company like we're looking at – it usually puts the disclosure in a private placement memorandum or offering circular. Surprisingly, if you're an individual owner of stock in a company, and you want to sell some of your shares, you still have to disclose material facts to your buyer if you want to stay out of trouble. There's no set method for doing that where it's individual-to-individual, but if you're the seller, you have to figure out a way to get it done. Often an individual seller will just give the buyer the private placement memorandum that he received when he was buying the shares in the first place."

"Do most people really read all this stuff before they buy the shares?"

"No. Some do, maybe, but most don't. This is all just window dressing to avoid liability later. The idea of an offering circular is to try to disclose every fact and every risk about the company that some investor might consider important. Then if the investment craters, the investor might not have much of a basis to sue, because all the risks were disclosed."

"Sue who, and for what?" asked Sal.

"You'd sue the seller for your money back," said the kid, "based on a claim that he failed to disclose something that was material to the risk. It's legalized extortion, but there you have it."

Sal nodded, and mentally filed the information away. He had spent a fair amount of time looking through the five piles of documents that had been placed in front of him, one pile for each of the five companies that were still in business. Two of the companies had purchased rights to drugs that had been tested in clinical trials but didn't do well enough to sustain the interest of the drug companies that had commissioned the trials. A third company was selling wellness plans directly to consumers online. Another was manufacturing a patented childproof cap designed for easy manipulation by seniors. And the last one was a digital imaging company that was going to produce and market a new machine that it claimed would be better than an MRI for most purposes. But the machine existed mostly on paper. None of the companies had enough near-term upside to interest Sal.

So Sal was back to 3Device, the Philly-based artificial knee company that he heard about at his club. The market for those knees – Baby Boomers – was huge; the technology the company was developing looked great; and he already knew who at least one of the shareholders was. He could buy in, make a pest of himself and sell his shares at a profit. Or he could figure out a way to take the company over, and then he could either market the product or sell the whole company to a competitor – Century Medical Technologies in this case.

The company's knees were already being tested in clinical trials. The offering circular disclosed where the trials were going to be conducted, and Sal had one of his golfing buddies, who was also a doctor, call one of the surgical centers that was conducting part of the trial. The word he got back was that the new knee was doing great – no problems, no injuries, no complaints from doctors. Sal saw some risk, obviously. The product wasn't approved by the FDA yet, and it wasn't being sold. But Sal thought the upside was tremendous, and Alabaster agreed.

Sal was going to think about it a little bit longer, but he was about ready to put the wheels in motion.

CHAPTER 14

It was Mothers' Day, and Lou and Olivia were visiting Gabby's grave in St. Stephen's Cemetery. They brought a large bunch of carnations which they laid carefully on her headstone. Gabby always loved carnations.

Neither spoke for the first couple of minutes. It was a beautiful spring day, and a light breeze was coming in from the west over a nearby tree line. Bees were buzzing quietly.

"I wonder why Mom and I have had so many issues with pregnancies," Olivia said. "Different issues – mine is getting pregnant, and Mom's was being pregnant – but Aunt Angela never had a problem. Two boys, no problems getting pregnant, no problems while she was pregnant."

"I think your Mom was willing to take the risk of having a second baby," Lou responded. "The doctors told her about the risks, and I was the one who didn't want to do it. I didn't want to lose her that way. And then we lost her anyway. I shoulda let her do what she thought was right."

"Mom *always* did what she thought was right," responded Olivia. "And I don't think it was a matter of her listening to you. She told me once – maybe a year before she died, I think I was 13 or 14 – that when I was little you both talked about giving me a brother or sister, but she didn't want to risk leaving me without a mother. I think that was the reason for her decision. I think it was me and not you who made up her mind."

Lou nodded slowly. "I'm glad she talked to you that way. She thought of you as an adult. It's nice you got to know your mom like that. The way you would have if she had lived longer. Adult to adult. You would have stayed very close."

"It's been twenty years, and it still hurts as if it happened yesterday. I can't . . ." Olivia began to cry quietly, and Lou put his arm across her shoulder. He didn't risk saying anything, or he would have been crying too. As they turned to leave, he thought, once again, that some things in life are what they are, and you can't fix them. That knowledge didn't make them hurt less. Neither Lou nor Olivia was a quitter, and broken hearts heal. But part of Lou died with Gabby, and he never tried to hide that fact from himself or from Olivia, even if he rarely talked about it with anyone else.

CHAPTER 15

L ou didn't spend a lot of time online. When it came to horse racing, there was nothing he could find online that wasn't laid out better in the Daily Racing Form, which was printed on paper and sold for a buck fifty a day at the Mexican bodega down the street. He got the weather from Channel 6 in the morning. And he got his sports news mostly from ESPN, which he watched at the club.

He didn't have much use for politics. He was a Democrat, of course, but the good thing about being a Democrat was that nobody bothered him about politics, at least in Norristown. Everybody else was a Democrat, too.

But everybody has something. Lou's something was that he was one of maybe six people in Pennsylvania who made at least $20,000 a year betting on horses, year after year. Parimutuel betting was designed to offset everybody's bet against everybody else's bet. That's how odds were determined, and the odds would change as additional bets came in. If a lot of bettors favored a particular horse, the odds on that horse would go down, and the people betting on the horse would earn a smaller return if the horse won. A pool was created by the bets placed on a given race, and that pool – minus the track's cut of the handle – was distributed to the win, place and show bettors, whose returns, plus the track's cut, equaled other bettors' losses.

The problem, of course, was that bettors as a group all lost money, on every race, because the track took its cut. So horse racing was a lot like the Pennsylvania Lottery. The state or the racetrack took a huge chunk of the proceeds, and then redistributed less than was actually paid for tickets. Lou's neighbor Gloria, for example, knew that the lottery was a bad bet, but she didn't care.

Lou cared. He knew that he had to be a lot smarter and better informed than the average bettor at the racetrack if he wanted to turn an annual profit. Very, very few people did. So Lou made it his life's goal to design a system that beat the system.

He started with bootlegged summaries of the betting systems developed by Bill Benter and Alan Woods. Benter and Woods made a billion dollars at racetracks in Hong Kong and elsewhere by identifying the variables that were most important in any given race, and betting on the basis of the presence or absence of those variables. And Alan Woods was a Pennsylvania guy.

All betting systems begin with the basic math. Favorites win 33% of all races, and finish first or second – win or place – 53% of the time. They finish first, second or third – win, place or show – 60% of the time. Second favorites win 21% of all races and finish first or second 42% of the time.

Lou understood that faster horses usually beat slower horses – it wasn't rocket science. He had concluded, however, that the size of the field was an under-appreciated variable in the most popular systems. In a field of 16 horses, 15 of them are hoping to run a great race and to beat any strong favorite. But determining *which* slower horse is going to break out of the pack and win is much more difficult when the field is large. So Lou always hesitated to bet a large field, because there are too many long shots to predict which one might break out of the pack.

Conversely, smaller fields reduce the number of variables. If all of the horses in a race are evenly matched – which almost never happens – the addition of one starter decreases every other starter's chances of winning. Any "scratch" – the withdrawal of a single horse from a race before it starts – *increases* every other starter's chances of winning. Lou liked the races where a scratch increased everybody else's chances.

On average, seven and a half horses go to the post in any given race in the United States. Because half horses don't exist, a smaller-than-average field will usually consist of seven or six horses. Lou looked for seven or six horse fields with a weak favorite – not weak in an athletic sense, but in a betting sense – odds of 3 to 1 or thereabouts (a 2 dollar bet to win will return close to 6 dollars if the horse wins), rather than, say, 4 to 5 (the same 2 dollar bet will return almost $2.50). He then tried to eliminate one horse based on health issues – you have to keep your eyes and ears open when you're down at the paddock. Then he would apply the basics of the Benter-Wood system. And, finally, he would pick one horse out of the healthy horses remaining and bet it to win – if, and only if, the horse had run consistent times in his previous five starts.

He had to be patient; sometimes there wouldn't be a single race on the day's card that fit his system, so he wouldn't bet at all. Losses hurt as well, and sometimes, chance being what it is, he would go a few days losing money. But on average, his system worked. His winnings at the track often matched what he was getting from Social Security and his union pension, and he wanted for nothing.

More than that, he loved the sport. Anyone who has stood at the rail of a racetrack as a dozen thoroughbreds thundered by understands the feeling. If there were anything in life quite as beautiful, Lou wasn't sure what it could be.

CHAPTER 16

Lou was on his way to the track on a Tuesday afternoon, giving Carmine a lift. "That's my brick," Lou said as they passed the Bensalem firehouse. He mentioned it because Carmine and he didn't often ride to the track together – nowadays, Carmine usually Uber-ed over to the OTB in Plymouth Meeting — and he wasn't sure he'd ever pointed it out to Carmine.

"I know," said Carmine, "you told me before."

Lou took no offense. Lou was proud of all of his brickwork – having spent almost 40 years doing it — and was perfectly happy to claim it every time he passed one of his buildings. Didn't matter if he'd said it before. The brick wasn't going nowhere, but when Lou was dead, nobody else was gonna give a damn who put it there. Point of pride.

Carmine was reading the Daily Racing Form. "I think the 3 horse is gonna win in the fifth, probably late."

Lou had noticed the 3 horse too, but didn't pick him out as a late closer in a race that long. Three-year-olds just starting to run farther. He was therefore keenly interested, as he always was, in Carmine's reasoning. "Why do you say that?"

"This is the first time he's ever run a full mile. But you look at what he's done at six and seven furlongs, he's always speeding up when he finishes. I don't think a mile is gonna bother him a bit. He'll keep running right into the grandstand, give him half a chance. His sire was Never a Doubt. Same deal with him, he always closed late."

Lou had read the same numbers Carmine had. "He speeds up, but he doesn't catch nobody," said Lou. "I don't know whether he's figured out how to win yet."

"He won his last race as a two-year old, against a tough field. Trust me, I'm gonna take care of you on this one, Lou."

Lou recognized that tone, having heard it reasonably often over the years. "Whaddaya mean, you're gonna take care of *me*?" Lou replied. "You're not gonna bet him?"

"Nooo. I got two reasons. First, Angel Jimenez is riding the 2 horse. I would never bet against Angel if it's a close call. And second, the 2 horse's name is Luke. Can't be named Carmine DeLuca and not bet on Luke."

"The 2 horse's name is All the Angles," Lou replied. "So forget reason number two."

"You know better than that," said Carmine. "All the Angles is his *racing* name. Down in the stables they call him Luke. Every racehorse gets a name from the people who love him. Angel told me he's 'Luke'."

There was a backstory to Carmine's affinity for Angel Jimenez's rides. Angel Jimenez had once helped Carmine jump start his car in the parking lot after the last race, back when Carmine still had a car. Helped him for most of an hour in November cold. They still said hello and traded insults when they crossed paths.

"Don't do it C," said Lou. "You're bettin' with your heart, not your head." The very worst thing any bettor could do. Carmine was notorious for that. He knew more about handicapping a horse race than anyone at Pennsylvania Park, Lou included. He had magical instincts and an encyclopedic memory, and he could've won more bets and more money than Lou in any year you could pick. But he was a romantic at heart. He would rather support a horse, jockey, trainer or owner that he liked than go home with a lot of money in his pocket. And God knows, he needed money, and couldn't afford to be throwing it away on dumb bets. To Lou, it didn't make no sense. But that was Carmine.

Lou had a very good day, and bought food and beers. Carmine lost all of the money he brought. The fifth race was Carmine's and Lou's friendship in microcosm. At Carmine's suggestion, Lou bet the 3 horse, which won on a late close. Carmine bet Angel Jimenez and the 2 horse to win – but horse and jockey finished second. Carmine took it in stride. He never, ever resented Lou's success at the racetrack, because Lou was Lou. And watching Lou let Carmine see how he would have made out betting with his head, if he had ever decided to do it.

CHAPTER 17

Sal's due diligence was complete. He was sure he knew as much about 3Device, Inc., as any of its shareholders, and probably more. It was time to talk to his lawyer.

The problem with lawyers, as far as Sal was concerned, was that they tended to get preachy if they thought you were getting close to crossing a line. He figured that's why they paid so much for malpractice insurance – they were scared their clients were going to steer them into illegal stuff they couldn't see coming. Sal didn't think they were any more honest than anybody else – on the contrary – but they were experts at covering their own asses.

"I want to buy some shares in another small company," Sal began, as he adjusted the blue tooth in his ear.

"What's the name of the company?" asked Palmer Eastman, Esquire.

"It's called 3Device, Inc. They make knee implants."

"How do you spell that?"

"The number 3, no space, capital D, lower case e-v-i-c-e."

"What are the financial terms? And how many shares?"

"I don't know. I haven't negotiated the deal yet."

"All right. How about if I open a file, and we'll start work when things are farther along."

"Well, that sort of brings up the reason I'm calling. I wanted to know if I need to get you involved at all. What would the seller and I need to do to transfer ownership of the shares if we wanted to keep lawyers out of it?"

Eastman hesitated. "Are legal fees the issue?"

"No, not at all. I just expect that the seller is not going to want to have lawyers involved."

"All right. Well, it's pretty easy. As the buyer, all you need to do is pay whatever amount you and the seller have agreed. The company will take care of the process of preparing and issuing a certificate for your new shares. If you're buying directly from the company, you pay the money and they'll issue you a certificate for the number of shares you bought. That would be the end of the process. If you're buying from an existing shareholder, the company will retire that shareholder's share certificate and then issue you a new certificate for the number of shares you're buying. If the seller is keeping some shares, the company will also issue a new certificate to him for the shares he's keeping."

"OK, that sounds pretty simple. As always, Palmer, thanks for your time. If you would, just bill this time to my personal account. Just describe it as 'legal advice' and I'll remember what we talked about. I'll let you know how all of this works out."

CHAPTER 18

Greg Morris sat with his back to the wall, facing his partner David Stein across a small cocktail table. They were having drinks at a new bar on the forty-fifth floor of one of the Comcast buildings in downtown Philadelphia. The waitress was about thirty-five and casually beautiful, and she looked more prosperous than either of her clients. Which was no mean feat, because Greg dressed very well.

Greg and David were not only partners but close friends who had worked together at Goldman. When Greg formed his hedge fund in Philadelphia, David kept in touch and kibitzed about investment strategies. As sometimes happens in the hedge fund world, Greg's fund invested in a small company, and then Greg decided he liked what the investment target was doing better than what he had been doing. He liquidated his fund – with a healthy profit for his investors – and voted himself onto the board of the company he had financed. He wound up buying control at the age of 33, and immediately invited David Stein to partner with him. David jumped at the chance. Working together, they expanded the original company's market share, and then raised additional funds for a subsidiary that was also showing a lot of promise.

Greg ordered a second round of drinks. They had a lot to talk about. One of the subjects on Greg's mind was Lou – not the first time he had been the topic of discussion between the partners.

"You know the guy is important to Olivia and me – he's family, what can I say? But he makes me crazy, I don't know what to do. He has an opinion on everything. He thinks he can jump into any conversation he wants, and take it over. If he were here now, he'd have an opinion about why people jump into conversations. Most of the time I see him, he's got a four-day growth of beard, and what's left of his hair has been all blown around at the racetrack. He wears a wife beater most of the time, unless Olivia asks him to dress up. And the cigars. Jesus."

"Nothing you're telling me is that bad. When I met Lou, he just seemed a little eccentric. But I guess I don't have your nerve endings."

"Every time we drive anywhere together, we'll pass some brick building or other, and he'll say 'That's my brick.' It really gets tedious." Greg took a sip of his Grey Goose. "I should have known what I was getting into. When Livvie and I were at Princeton, he would come up every once in a while in some old car and park illegally on Nassau Street. We'd go out for lunch, and when one of my friends stopped at the table to say hi, I'd introduce Lou, and he'd say to the person he just met, 'Yo, how you doon?,' the way he does. 'Good to meet you. You wanna sit for a beer? It's on me.'"

"That doesn't sound that bad."

"He hit on a horse the day before. Of course he was buying."

David Stein was concerned about his partner. Greg's level of agitation didn't match the words he was hearing. As the back-office person, David didn't routinely intrude on the development or sales functions. But he was sensing something.

"How did it go with Blue Tech?"

"They were non-committal," replied Greg. Non-committal was not good. Non-committal meant that the consulting firm handling the FDA application for 3Device's knee was not feeling warm and fuzzy about recent developments. For ten months they had been assuming that the FDA was the least of their problems. They knew they needed to persuade their investors that the product worked. In the meantime, they had kind of been taking the FDA's approval for granted. Maybe not, as it was turning out.

Greg and David thought of themselves as problem-solvers. They had guided 3Device through product development, a private stock offering, and early clinical trials. But they weren't doctors or scientists, and managing the work of MD's and PhD's during a clinical trial was a stressful, exhausting process for both of them. And endless. If they were awake, they were working . . .

CHAPTER 19

Tony Abruzzi liked good calamari. There were a lot of ways to make it, but he liked fried. He could have it as an appetizer at Chez Wally on Rittenhouse Square for fifty bucks, or he could have it at the South Broad Diner as a main course for twelve, but either way he loved it. He never got tired of it, which was good, because Tony lived with a lot of stress, and he didn't drink. So food was his pacifier.

Now, you would think he was stressed about the possibility of violent death. There was Angelo Bruno in 1980, and Philip "Chicken Man" Testa in 1981. There was a stretch of time where Philly's bosses didn't have much of a life expectancy. But, truth be told, Tony never gave any thought to that possibility. He told his Capos that all they had to do to get rid of him was ask him to retire, and he would. "Don't pay for no out-of-town button man," he would say. "I'm 72 fucking years old. Why risk goin' to jail and spend all that money for something you can have for free? Tell me to leave, I'm in Boca 24 hours later." So Tony's stress was more prosaic – how do I properly administer an organization that's growing 8%, year-over-year-over-year? And at my fucking age.

Tony's principal insight, and the key reason for his success, was that violence doesn't solve nothin', even for the Mafia. He had a high school teacher at South Catholic during the Cold War who used to talk about nuclear "deterrence," and while Tony had no particular interest in geopolitics, he was interested in human beings, and what motivated them. His teacher's lesson stuck – people won't fuck with you if they think they're likely to get hurt in the process. While he was working his way up through the mob, first as a soldier and then as a Capo, he learned that three guys on the sidewalk with body armor and (fully licensed) shotguns, defending a dice game, were more effective than tracking and shooting someone for having fucked with your dice game. So he built prostitution and escort rings around fortified central facilities. Armed personnel protected all of his titty bars and speakeasies. The homes of his men were reinforced with bullet and blast protection, and like cops, they always worked in pairs.

So nobody fucked with Tony Abruzzi's thing, not because they didn't want to, but because they didn't want to get hurt in the process. And Tony became Don Abruzzi in a peaceful ascension to power when the previous boss died in his sleep. Tony won the job because he made money for his people, and he had been fully in charge for 18 years now.

One problem with abjuring violence, as Tony certainly appreciated, was that loansharking and protection were made more difficult. Who would pay vig or protection money if they weren't going to suffer physical harm upon default? Tony accepted that fact of human nature – as he accepted all facts of human nature – and worked around it.

People borrow from loan sharks because they can't borrow from banks or payday lenders. They just want the money, and they understand they're going to pay higher interest to compensate for the fact that they're a shitty risk. And Tony saw that every one of these mahafs had 40k in credit card debt, at 23%. So he saw a market opportunity – why not charge them 23%, flat rate, sort of like the credit cards, instead of 100% per month like the New York families?

Here's how it works. You borrow $1,000. You pay Tony back $1,230 when you have it. Just like your credit card, except simpler and easier. No minimum payments, no annoying phone calls. Tony won't lend to you if you're a junkie, but you're not, so no problem. Collateral? Yes, of course. You give Tony's lending officer copies of your house key and your car key. If you don't repay $1,230 within a reasonable time, Tony's boys will give you a polite reminder. If you still don't pay, they'll chop your car for parts, or empty your house while you're at work.

See, people liked that. No credit checks, and Tony's lending officers were helpful and courteous. No anxiety as the balance on a loan mounted, because you knew your payback number when you borrowed the cash. The borrowers only needed the money to tide them over, they knew the repayment amount they needed to scrounge up, and they didn't want to lose access to future credit by failing to pay back the loan. And they needed to have a car. So while they were perfectly willing to tell MasterCard to go fuck itself, they were eager to pay Tony back. Tony's default rate was under 5%.

Protection money? Easier still. Just provide protection. Tony would have his guys patrol his restaurant blocks every Friday and Saturday night – certainly the cops weren't interested in doing it. Free valet parking with armed drivers. Cars, some of them very expensive, parked in fenced and locked facilities nearby. Customers *loved* coming to South Philly and finding the streets safer and better lit than the inner-ring-suburb dumpy places they could have gone to in Upper Darby or Lower Who-the-Fuck-Knows-Where.

Protection money? Hell yes, Tony, thanks for having your guys stop by my place. Great value for the money. What do you have in the way of upgrades?

Of course, nobody on one of Tony's commercial blocks had what you might call a choice about whether the protection money was due, or to whom. Which made those blocks no different from any other Downtown Improvement District in Pennsylvania, as far as Tony could tell. A cost of doing business is, well, a cost of doing business.

Tony also worked with unions. For example, he joint-ventured with the Warehousemen's and Produce Workers International Union, Local 882, in controlling excess inventory in local warehouses. Philadelphia is a major port, and South Philadelphia has lots of large warehouses. The Warehousemen managed billions of dollars of inventory per year, and some of it, unfortunately, was damaged in handling. Not very damaged. Maybe not damaged at all, but reported as damaged. In all events, inventory found its way to side doors and into Tony's trucks. Whereupon, Tony's people sold it through channels they'd established with independent retailers. A third of the proceeds went back to the Warehousemen's Christmas Fund, and everyone was happy.

So Tony didn't need to worry (much) about violent death. His soldiers and Capos – and ordinary independent contractors parking his cars and collecting his loans – were making serious coin, and they revered their Capo-di-Tutti-Capo as a result. The last thing they wanted was to see him dead or retired, and they protected him well.

Tony also understood, of course, that you could overdo sweetness and light, and like the Wizard of Oz, he knew bad things could happen if people stopped fearing him. So he had one trusted guy – and he wasn't proud of this, it was a little creepy – who would find a recently dead body every so often, shoot it in the head with a shotgun, and dump it near the old Navy Yard or by the river in Camden. The cops and the Philadelphia Daily News would be notified anonymously and simultaneously, and the reporter would receive a detailed tip about what mob score was being settled. If the Medical Examiner ever figured out that any of the victims was dead before he was shot, that conclusion never made it back to Tony's ears. More important, the Daily News never mentioned anything like that.

The result was that the public had no reason to question whether its Mafia remained violent. Of course they were, what are you, kidding? Don Abruzzi is a fun guy, but if you cross him, he'll hurt you. It was still exciting to go to restaurants in South Philly to see whether a scary mobster would be sitting at the next table. Relations between the mob and its public could not have been better.

His pacifist tendencies notwithstanding, Tony Abruzzi was no choir-boy. Every leader has his quirks. Tony's quirk was how much he hated these motherfuckers who operated non-union. Philly is a union town, and Tony's arrangements with most of the unions on the waterfront, in the big hotels, and in the warehouses were harmonious and profitable. But if Tony heard that some Greek or Russian fuck was trying to roll produce through his space behind a non-union driver, he'd go fucking ballistic. Assuming somebody was available to do the job, that trailer's contents would be all over the street before it hit the next stoplight. Or at worst, Tony would get him the next day. Unions are important. People have to stick together. If you're a little guy, there are forces in this world that want to destroy you, whether you run a dice game, or drive a truck, or work a shift as a nurse. Tony felt profound solidarity with the working people in his town, and he acted on that commitment. If only he could find some working people to staff his valet parking on Thursdays — but he didn't want to overpay, and couldn't do the impossible.

This Friday, Tony and his wife Angela were going to Chez Wally to celebrate their 48th wedding anniversary. Angela Abruzzi was born Angela Revella, and grew up in Southwest Philadelphia (not to be confused in any way, shape or form with South Philadelphia). She met Tony at the Ben-Mar Bowling Lanes in South Philadelphia while her younger sister Gabriella was teaching her how to bowl. Tony, a little older and as good looking then as he is now, came over and made a couple of polite suggestions, and the rest was history. Together, Tony and Angela raised a family and fretted over the ups and downs of Tony's career. Angela and Gabriella stayed close until Gabby's death, and both Tony and Angela stayed in touch with Gabby's husband, Lou, and, of course, with their niece Olivia. They didn't see Lou a lot now, what with the press of business in South Philly, but it was always good to see him when they could make it happen. Lou made them laugh, and reminded Angela of the days when her sister was still around.

CHAPTER 20

It was a Thursday in May at the Italian American Citizens Club of Norristown. There were maybe 12 or 13 people at the bar.

"Hey Sallie," said Lou in greeting, as Sal Paglia climbed onto the next barstool.

"Yo, Inky, what's up?" Sal replied.

"Not too much. How you been? How's work?"

"Busy. The paving season started, so like every fucking year we find out we don't have enough trucks, or we have too much asphalt, or something else isn't right. Takes a month for everything to even out."

"That's good. If you don't have no problems, it just means you're dead."

"I don't wanna be dead. I just want it to be June, when all this shit starts to get organized."

"Playin' any golf?" asked Lou.

"Some. Not much. Twice so far this year. I'm playin' this weekend."

"Where at?"

"Martha's Vineyard."

Lou started to laugh, and then stopped. "Isn't that's where Bill Clinton bought stuff for Monica Lewinsky? Or maybe she bought something for him. Who the fuck remembers that far back?"

"I just remember thinking that if he's gonna take a risk like that, he oughta aim higher," said Sal. "Hollywood or something. He was a fuckin' idiot with all that."

"Yeah, and Epstein didn't kill himself," said Lou.

Sal laughed. "A course he didn't."

Tommy brought Sal a VO and a Yuengling, without having been asked. "Me too," said Lou, "I'm ready." Tommy didn't need to be told that Lou would have a VO and a Pabst Blue Ribbon. "And Sal's is on me." Tommy nodded, and deducted two shots and two beers from Lou's cash on the bar.

"Thanks Louie. How's your son-in-law's business doin'?" asked Sal. Sal was leaning in closer to Lou, on purpose. Sal was a big guy.

"I don't know," Lou replied. "Depends which one you're talkin' about. The thing where they're making casts for broken bones is doin' fine, it looks like. He says he's waitin' on some kind of approval on the other thing, the artificial knee."

"He's got you invested in the knee thing?"

"Fuck, were you in here the night I was talking about that? You must a been. I didn't invest a dime. I got shares from my daughter as a Christmas gift, and it was just, like, one percent of the company. You know, I love my Olivia, but I'd a had more use for a coffee mug."

Tommy brought Lou his VO and a Pabst.

"Saluti!" Lou and Sal upended their shot glasses.

"I been thinkin'" said Sal. "If you don't want 'em, would you consider selling me your shares in the knee thing? I'm lookin' out for investments in health care . . ."

"Jeez, Sallie, I don't know. It's a private company. I don't know whether I'm allowed to sell you shares. And then I don't want to hurt Olivia's feelings. And I don't know what they're worth, I don't have no idea. I wouldn't wanna cheat you."

"Well, first, just tell me again what the company does," said Sal. "I'm a big boy, I can make my own judgments. And you don't have to decide tonight."

"Best I can tell, they're printing artificial knees on a 3D printer. The idea is, if you're havin' a knee replacement, they can put you on the table, knock you out, and then fit the new knee to your body, and to the space they have to put it in. Like puttin' a lintel in a run of brick. The knee fits tighter, it's less painful, and cheaper than a lot of the machine-made parts they been using." He paused. "I don't unnerstand, Sallie. Why would you be interested in a little company like this that isn't doin' nothin' yet? You already have a big business and enough headaches already."

Sal thought quickly. He didn't want Lou to suspect he'd been studying 3Device and its prospects for weeks, and he didn't know what information about his past investments would be discoverable if Lou's son-in-law started looking into his prior dealings. His proposed purchase had to appear impulsive.

"Health care," said Sal, in response to Lou's question. "It's not complicated. Health care is a huge market. I like a good investment as much as the next guy, and I don't have anything invested in health care. So just give me the scoop on what you *do* know about the company, and that's all I'm asking about. How big is the market? Are we talkin' 100 knees a year, or a million?"

Lou sighed, and looked down the bar. "Tommy, help us out here. How many knee replacements do they do a year, and how much does it cost?" Tommy was the quickest hand in the Italian American Citizens Club when it came to finding stuff out on Google. His phone was always in his hand, because his customers always needed point spreads for their sports bets. Lou and Sal waited while he clicked.

"OK," said Tommy, "here's what I got. Six-hundred-thousand-plus knee replacements in the U.S. per year. Average price of the operation is fifty grand. So people are spending, let's see, I gotta open the calculator . . .

. north of . . . Fuck, how many zeros is that?" Every ear in the bar was now tuned in while Tommy counted zeros. "North of thirty billion dollars."

"Whoa, slow down," said Lou. "My son-in-law isn't doin' the operations. Tommy, how much do they sell a fake knee for — not installed, just the part? Like if you were buying brake pads?"

This time, there was a general buzz as Tommy worked. Speculation ranged from $500 to $10,000. This one took him longer.

"It says here $3,000 to $10,000," announced Tommy.

"OK," said Sal, "let's split the difference. Figure your little company wants to give better quality for the same price. Let's call it $6,500 per part, just talkin'. Tommy how much is 600,000 operations times $6,500?"

Tommy clicked. "I get 3.9 billion."

"OK, let's call it four billion a year," said Sal. "Does that sound right, Louie?" Sal seemed to want Lou to agree with the math.

"The math sounds right," Lou replied. "Depends on whether Google is right, I guess."

"So then we get into hips," said Sal. "Lou, wouldn't you say that if you can print knees you can print hips?"

"Yeah, I suppose."

"Tommy, how many hip operations per year?"

They waited while Tommy asked Google. "It says here 450,000."

"OK, that's three quarters the number of knees," said Sal. "If the total market for hip parts is three quarters of what it is for knee parts, you get another three billion. Still OK with my math, Lou?"

"Well, the math, yeah. But I've owned these shares for half a year, and I haven't seen a dime," said Lou. "If my son-in-law is chasing after seven billion bucks, he hasn't tol' me about it."

"Look, Louie, that's why this stuff is so exciting," said Sal. "You hafta time it right, don't get in too early, don't get in too late. Let's figure he's lookin' for a twenty percent profit, and he grabs a quarter of the market. That would be about . . ." – he calculated in his head – "1.75 billion in revenue. And 20 percent of that in profit is $350 million a year. One percent of that – that's your stake — your earnings on your shares could be three and a half mil. A year."

Lou turned to Sal. "You're out of your fucking mind."

"Louie, no offense, but that's why I'm flying on a private jet to Martha's Vineyard this weekend, and you're gonna be in here watching the Phillies on TV." And then quietly, so that only Lou could hear. "Will you talk to your son-in-law for me? See if you can sell me shares. I'll make it worth your while, I promise."

Sal wasn't worried that he was driving up the price he was going to have to pay for Lou's shares. He knew the company had sold the shares ten or eleven months ago for $1,000 per share, and not much about the company's prospects had changed since then. He also knew he only needed a few shares to get his foot in the door, and he could do the deal with Lou with seed money. The bigger plays for shares of 3Device would come later.

CHAPTER 21

"So tell me a little about Sal Paglia," said Greg. He and Lou were having Sunday morning coffee in the sunroom in Villanova.

"He's the big paving guy, road projects, does work for townships," replied Lou. "You see his big dump trucks all over the place, 'Sal Paglia, Inc.'"

Greg visualized for a second. "Yeah, absolutely. I see one of those black trucks every time I'm at a stoplight. He's a member at the Italian American Club?"

Lou ignored the implied suggestion that no rich person would ever want to join his club. "Yeah, I know him good. He doesn't mind being the only rich guy at the club, and most of the time he doesn't act like he's got money. Maybe that's why it seemed so fucked up that he was asking me to sell him shares. It was completely out of the blue."

"How did he know about 3Device?"

Lou hesitated. "I got buzzed one weekend and wanted to brag about Livvie's giving me some of her shares. Sal was there."

Greg rolled his eyes. "Lou, you have to be careful. Private companies are called private for a reason. You can't be talking about owning shares at a bar."

"That may be obvious to you, but nobody told me nothin' like that. I was proud she wanted to do something nice for me for Christmas. I tol' my friends, that's all."

"Well, look, water under the bridge," replied Greg. "Let's deal with the issue. First thing is — there's a shareholders' agreement. That agreement says that any sale of shares to anyone except a current shareholder requires approval from 75% of all of the voting shares. The idea is to restrict ownership to people we've vetted, people who understand what we're doing, and who understand the risks. There's an exception for transfers to family – that's why Olivia was able to give you some of her shares – but you'd need shareholder approval before you could sell shares to Sal Paglia."

"Well, OK, that settles it," said Lou. "I don't have approval, and I can tell Sal that."

"Well, let's talk about it," said Greg. "Sal Paglia is obviously motivated to invest, and he has plenty of resources. If we have to go back to our existing shareholders for additional funds, or even if we open it up to new investors, having Sal Paglia as an existing shareholder could be an advantage. It's not unusual for a small shareholder to increase his investment if he likes the way the company is being run."

Lou nodded. "Makes sense."

"Getting shareholder approval wouldn't be difficult," continued Greg. "We would just have a Zoom meeting of all the shareholders – I think we have twenty right now, and they're due for a quarterly update. We'd describe Sal's business and his interest in our company, and ask for shareholder consent to the transfer. This would be the first time anyone has asked for that kind of consent, and so there might be some shareholders who would like to piggyback on your request and ask for the same approval. But truthfully, I think most of our shareholders are in for the long haul, and are looking forward to seeing how it turns out."

"Well, how much should I charge him if I'm gonna sell him some of my shares?" asked Lou.

"I think that's an easier question than you would expect. 3D Prosthetics owns 50.1% of 3Device. The other 49.9% of 3Device is owned by twenty shareholders who all invested at the same time. We did what was called a private placement, where we valued the company at three million dollars. We explained to prospective investors what 3Device, Inc., was doing, and we charged them $30,000 for each one percent interest. We raised a million and a half dollars, basically all of which is being spent on the FDA approval process."

Greg's email bell rang on his iWatch, he checked it, and turned back to Lou. "So Olivia invested $60,000 for a two percent interest – she wanted to support what I was doing, and she liked the product – and then she gave half of those shares to you, which are worth $30,000. If you sell half of yours to Sal Paglia, you can charge him $15,000. That's the rate that everybody else paid."

"How many shares is that?"

Greg thought for a second. "I think we capitalized 3Device with an initial issuance of 3,000 shares, and valued the company, as a startup, at $3,000,000. So we sold just under 1,500 shares in the private placement, at an even $1,000 a share. You'd sell him 15 shares at $1,000 each."

"Look, Greg, I'll do what you tell me to do. I haven't given no thought to those shares since Livvie gave 'em to me. But I would wanna know that she's OK with this too."

"That I'm OK with what?" asked Olivia as she came into the sunroom with hot coffee.

"I have a buddy at the club who wants to buy some of my shares in 3Device," Lou responded. "I was just asking Greg what he thinks about it. I'm on the fence. It seems like a lot of trouble for nothin'."

"It seems like a nice opportunity," said Olivia. "You could do some things to the house that you've been wanting to do. I think it's going to be a while, still, before 3Device proves that it's going to work. If it does, you would still be able to make a nice return on whatever shares you keep." She turned to her husband. "Greg, what do you think?"

"I think it sounds like a nice opportunity as well. But I have a little bit of a conflict of interest. I think it would be good for the company to have Mr. Paglia as a shareholder, and so I'm biased in favor of Lou doing the deal. But the Company doesn't have any shares allocated for sale to new investors, and the shares would have to come from Lou." Greg turned to Lou. "Lou, listen, I don't want you to sell if you don't want to. It's your call, your decision."

Lou blew out some air. "Aw, hell, I don't know. I need a new head gasket in my car. And my water heater is leaking. I can find some things to do with the money. If it could be good for your company to have Sal involved, I'm happy to keep talkin' with him." Lou looked up. "Anybody up for Olive Garden?"

Greg and Olivia exchanged a glance. Normally they would have found a polite way to say no. But Lou had driven all the way over from Norristown, just to talk to them about Greg's company. This Sunday, late in the morning, they said "yes" and turned to find the car keys. As the three of them were heading out of Villanova toward Bryn Mawr and Ardmore, Lou pointed to the McDonald's on Lancaster Avenue. "That's my brick," he said. Olivia smiled. It was, perhaps, the tenth time her father had mentioned the brick in that McDonald's. She hoped he never stopped mentioning it.

CHAPTER 22

O livia was sitting at her desk in her office at Biddle & Co. She looked out at the Delaware River, as a big ship was going by. Normally, she loved the view, but it was cloudy today, and she was feeling unsettled. She picked up the phone to call the clinic. After two transfers, she explained what she wanted.

"Let me see, I'm pulling up the file," said the unidentified back-office person, after asking Olivia for her date of birth. "The tests from last week were fine. Your prolactin is 19. Your estrogen is 180. Your husband's total testosterone is 620 and his free testosterone is 115."

"OK, thanks. Can I speak to Maggie?" Maggie Portnoy was one of two Physician's Assistants at the clinic, and the person with whom Olivia interacted most often.

"I'll see if she's free," said the voice. Olivia waited for three or four minutes, and checked her emails while she waited.

"Hi Olivia," said Maggie, as she came on the line. "I looked at your test results. They're still fine. Dr. Evans put a note on the chart suggesting that we talk to you about tweaking the dosage on your Cabergoline. I was actually going to call you today. So, Cabergoline lowers your level of pro-lactin, which is a hormone produced by your pituitary gland. High levels of prolactin are associated with infertility. Your prolactin when we started the Cabergoline in January was 22, which was high normal. But high normal for one person can be abnormal for someone else. And now you're down to 19. She thinks that maybe if we can get your prolactin down a little bit more, it could really help. But the medication has some side effects – not for everyone, but for a lot of people – and we want to talk to you about them again before we increase your dosage. You're likely to have questions, and we should talk about it in person."

"OK, give me just a second to check my calendar." Olivia pressed "mute" and began to cry. She grabbed a tissue, wiped her eyes and her nose, and took a deep breath. She came back on the line.

"Maggie, it sounds to me like we're just throwing spaghetti at the wall to see if any of it sticks. I don't want to increase the dosage on a drug with a bunch of side effects if it's not likely to help. Is this really the best option?"

"It really is, Olivia," Maggie replied. "You're doing well with Cabergoline so far – no side effects – and we think you'll be OK. We just want to give a refresher on the side effects in case any show up. Look, infertility has a lot of causes, and they tend to disguise themselves or overlap. The best clinical practice – and what we do – is to patiently address the most likely possibilities, based on test results, physical exams, age, weight, a hundred other factors. We're good at what we do, and you and Greg are both healthy. I believe we'll get there, and I doubt we'll have to go as far as IVF. Hang in there with us. Can you do that?"

Olivia sighed. "OK, we'll talk about Cabergoline again. Can I have one of your late afternoon consultation slots? Late afternoons look pretty good for me next week."

CHAPTER 23

Lou and Olivia rang the doorbell of the rowhouse on Diamond Street in South Philadelphia. The bell was answered by a large man wearing an overcoat, out of season. "Yo, Pete, how you doin'?" said Lou. "He's expecting us."

"Yeah, he is, come on in," replied Pete Fraterrigo. "Lemme tell him you're here."

Pete disappeared down a long, wide hallway leading from the front door. Tony and Angela Abruzzi had combined three two-story rowhouses into a single town home, and there was room enough for an entrance hallway, a first floor sitting room, a big dining room, and a kitchen that stretched almost all the way across the rear of the original three houses. Olivia looked into the front sitting room and recalled crawling under the sofa when she was six, trying to catch Angela's cat. Nice memories. She realized it had been too long since she'd been here, almost two years. Life was too full, and went by too fast.

Tony Abruzzi came up the hallway from the kitchen with his arms extended. "Uncle Tony!" cried Olivia, "You look great!" She gave him a long hug.

"Aw, you know, if I look good, it's 'cuz I don't eat no pasta no more," Tony replied. "Louie, how you doin'?" as he turned to Lou and shook his hand.

"Good, Tone, can't complain," Lou replied. "How 'bout you, it don't look like the hip is still bothering you."

"No, it don't hurt. Glucosamine. Miracle drug, and, like, twenty cents a pill. Come on in, Angela's ready for youse."

Lou and Olivia walked with Tony down the main hallway, past porcelain vases and expensive paintings. Aunt Angela knew her art, and the overall impression was one of quiet affluence.

"Hi, Honey!" Angela called out to Olivia when they reached the kitchen. "And Lou! How is the most handsome man in Pennsylvania? You look great, really you do."

"I feel good," replied Lou. "I'm blessed." And then, "How are the boys?"

"Joey should be here later, maybe for dessert," replied Tony. "He's doing great, he's really helping me keep things going at work. Benny is in California this week, for work. His company is buying a factory or something."

"Do you know what kind of factory it is?" asked Olivia.

"They make the little lights that blink in the dashboard of your car," replied Tony. "You know, just stupid shit. And Benny's company is paying 500 million bucks to be able to do that. The world's gone nuts."

Olivia nodded in agreement. "We had a client who paid almost that much for an app for smart phones. Half a billion dollars for something that will never exist in the physical world. It's just software, a bunch of ones and zeros. Amazing. At least Benny's guys can touch what they're buying. A factory is real."

"You know what else is real?" said Lou. "Veal Piccata, it smells like. Angela, can I see what you're doin'?" The group conversation broke into two, with Lou talking about cooking with Angela, and Olivia talking business with Tony as the two of them sat on high counter stools.

"My problems are all flesh and blood," said Tony. "I wish I could buy some software and fix 'em."

"What's up?" asked Olivia.

"Oh boy, how much time you got?" Tony responded. "I'd love to get your advice. I need an economist on this one."

Olivia smiled. "If you think an economist can help you with anything, you have a bigger problem than you thought you had. But tell me what's going on."

Tony took a breath and looked into the middle distance. He nibbled a small piece of cheese. "I can't find people who want to work. I pay good. Most of it's tax free, 'cause I pay cash. The work is easy. And I can't find nobody. They're all playing Nintendo on their couches." Olivia nodded. "So here's the problem," continued Tony. "I'm looking for people to man my valet parking on Passyunk Avenue on Thursday nights. Thursday is turning into a big restaurant and bar night all of a sudden, and we got more business than we can handle. I need to be able to park everybody who comes down the block to eat. With valet, we keep all the proceeds, and the guys keep all the tips, and there's a friggin' traffic jam of people who would like to give us their keys and step right from the curb into a restaurant. Fridays and Saturdays we're getting it done with students and moonlighters, and we're makin' good money. Thursdays, customers just wander around looking for parking themselves, 'cause we don't have guys on the sidewalk ready to help." He paused, framing the issue in his mind. "So here's the question. How do we find people to do this job?"

"Let me think for a second," Olivia replied. Tony just nodded. One of the many reasons Tony Abruzzi was a good boss was that he let his people think before they talked. He was a patient man, in all things.

Olivia looked at the ceiling fan in the kitchen as she pondered. Eventually, she lowered her gaze back to her uncle.

"Thursday night is a time when most people are not doing anything else, and you ought to be able to attract manpower if you create the right incentives," she began. "So I think you have a solvable problem. The question is, what are the available incentives? 'Cash' probably isn't the best answer, because I can't imagine your margins on valet are that great. And it takes a lot of cash these days to get someone off a couch. So let's look at mostly non-cash incentives."

Tony nodded, without interrupting.

"How many exotic dancers do you have working at the Sir Albert Saloon?" asked Olivia.

Tony was surprised at the question, but was able to come up with an answer. "Probably thirty."

"How many valet drivers do you need on Thursdays?"

"To be on the safe side, probably twenty-five."

"OK, here's my idea for creating the right incentives," Olivia continued. "Tell your dancers that you're looking for volunteers to work valet on Passyunk on Thursday nights. Let them know you'll guarantee the same average amount they would make dancing on a Thursday night, whatever that might be. You can tell them they're going to be traffic managers and dispatchers for Eddystone Logistics, Incorporated, and that they're welcome to put that position on their resumes. Let them know they'll be within view of armed security from restaurant to parking lot and back to restaurant. Customers and restaurant owners will love them, they'll have fun, they'll get to drive cool cars. They'll be starting to pad their resume for when their looks are gone, or when they're just sick of dancing and want to do something else. Dancing has got to be exhausting. Valet will be a nice change of pace. And they can sell Eddystone Logistics to future employers as if it's the next FedEx."

"That sounds good," Tony replied, "but I can't afford to lose the revenue at my club on Thursday nights."

"Here's the rest of the plan," replied Olivia. "Incentives. You create an 'Amateur Night' at Sir Albert's, where bachelorette parties talk each other into showing off exotic dance moves, on the pole or down on the stage. You sell a lot of drinks, and you don't need to pay your dancers for dancing on Thursday nights."

"This is brilliant," Tony replied. "I can make this work. But it sounds too 'all or nothin'.' I could cause problems for my valet service and for my club, and I'll have two problems instead of one."

"I might agree with you if this really were an all-or-nothing idea," Olivia responded, "but the whole plan, I think, is scalable. Suppose you only had eight or ten dancers volunteering. You bring them over to the valet service" – she made squares with her hands and moved imaginary workers between them – "and the other guys working Thursday nights see who their co-workers are. All of a sudden you don't have any trouble getting young guys off of couches to come work for you. All of a sudden they can't wait to get to work, because they're meeting pretty girls. You have a co-ed workforce. And back at the club, you don't necessarily have to do Amateur Night – you could do Amateur Hour. The girls who would rather dance than drive can stick around the club, while the amateur girls make up for the fact that you have fewer professional dancers."

Tony nodded. He couldn't find any holes in the plan – except maybe one. "How much is it going to cost me to guarantee each girl that she'll make what she usually makes dancing on a Thursday night?"

Estimating wage rates was part of what Olivia did for a living. She spent less than two minutes on her phone. "OK, Google says that exotic dancers average about $30 per hour for total time spent on-site, and valet parking attendants make about $20 per hour. That ten-dollar difference per hour, over maybe six hours, is about $60 per girl, per Thursday night. Times 25 girls is $1,500 a week. And times about 50 weeks a year is $75,000. Would you pay 75 grand to solve this problem and bring in another full night of parking revenues? I think you would. And it's not going to cost that much. The girls are going to make their personalities pay off. They're going to make a fortune in tips as valet attendants on Thursday nights, same as they do back in the club. You're not going to have to guarantee that much."

"I love this," said Tony. "I wouldn'a thought a this in a million years."

"It's a healthy approach to business no matter what the business might be," said Olivia. "You look for opportunities to let your people get good at different tasks within the organization. The auto companies learned all of this back in the 1980's. It turns out that if your people know how to do five different things, and can do what needs doing, when it needs doing, the whole operation runs more efficiently. An employee who only knows how to do one job on an assembly line gets to be very expensive when the line is down for maintenance."

"All right, I'm gonna put this in motion," said Tony. "But I need to keep you in the loop. Let Angela and me take you to a nice dinner once a month, till the problem is solved. Would you do that?"

Olivia hesitated — not because her uncle was the Don of La Cosa Nostra in Philadelphia, but because Greg and she were already stretched to the breaking point with various commitments.

"Oh, Tony, you know I could say yes. And then each of us will cancel once or twice because we don't have time. And once a month will turn into once every six months. But look, it's been too long. Family is just too import-ant to . . . we can't be taking more than a year between times when we see each other. How about this? We'll pick a date in August when we'll meet at Roberto's, and in the meantime, when you call me at home any evening, we'll take the time to talk this thing to death, if necessary. Does that work?"

"Perfect," Tony replied. "Whatever they're paying you at that bank of yours, it's not enough." He patted the back of her hand and smiled.

"Tony," interrupted Angela from across the kitchen, "what time did you say Joey is coming over?"

"He said he'd be here by dessert," Tony replied, "probably 8:30 or 9:00."

"OK, Lou and I can finish getting dinner ready in the next 15 minutes. You two can pick the wine and the music; the table's already set."

Dinner went by quickly, as the four of them caught up. As always when they got together, there were stories about Gabby. Olivia, in particular, loved to hear things about her mom that she hadn't known before. When Tony and Lou got up and went out back for cigarillos – the little Italian kind – Angela had an opportunity to talk with Olivia alone.

"How are you feeling with the Cabergoline?" asked Angela.

"God, I can't believe you can remember the name of the drug," Olivia replied. "They're all running together for us. Fine, no side effects."

"I write them all down when you tell me about them, and then I do some research online. I worry about both of you, and want to feel like I know where it's going, and how it's going. How long will they have you taking it before they try something else?"

"Cabergoline's a six month course of treatment," Olivia replied. "We're four and a half months into it, so we'll see."

"I was talking to Sister Sophia Francesca again last week," said Angela. "I mentioned you to her, and she's happy to talk. No pressure."

"I love you, Angela. Thanks. I'm probably closer to that than you think."

After ten more minutes, Tony and Lou opened the door from the back deck, and the four of them sat down in the kitchen for cappuccinos. At 8:45, Joey came in carrying a box of cannoli. Joey and Olivia were about the same age and had always been close friends growing up. The fact that Joey was deeply involved in the family business put a little bit of a strain on their relationship – Olivia didn't want to know too many details, and Joey didn't want to share them – but there remained a lot of life to talk about.

In particular, Joey asked Olivia about some investment ideas he was considering – with the added obstacle that Vanguard and Fidelity were obliged to report cash deposits larger than $10,000 to the IRS. That was a non-starter for Joey, owing to his unique circumstances. For Olivia, there were rules, and then there was family, and, where possible, family came first. Joey wasn't hurting anybody. "I think I have an idea. Open an IRA. Then buy gold at a gold dealer – they'll *only* take cash — and get the bullion dealer to transfer the gold to the custodian for the IRA. There are some good investment houses that will let you do that. Then change the form of the asset within your account – exchange the gold for an S&P 500 index fund, and keep the index fund in your IRA account. No cash transaction will be reported to the IRS, and your IRA account will grow tax free."

Joey asked questions, and Olivia had good answers. Both Joey and Olivia were more than happy to let the IRS figure out what Joey was up to, if they were that interested. And if they did, investing cash in financial assets wasn't illegal – yet.

CHAPTER 24

"The moderator is joining the meeting," announced the helpful videoconference robot lady.

"Hello everybody," said Greg, "thanks for making time to participate in this meeting of shareholders of 3Device, Inc. If no one has an objection, we're going to record the meeting, so that we won't have to appoint a secretary and over-formalize it, if you will. I think I've met everyone in person, but in some cases it was briefly and a few months ago, so let me re-introduce myself. I'm Gregory Morris, now serving as the President and CEO of 3Device, Inc. This is a special meeting of shareholders of 3Device, for the purposes we sketched out in the notice of meeting. I'm checking the list of attendees, and it looks like we have 18 shareholders on hand. We presently have 20 shareholders of record. We're missing Paul Miller and Avery Benson, so before we go much farther, has anyone heard from Paul or Avery?"

"Greg, this is Bill Ford, I have Paul's proxy. He's asked me to vote his shares."

"OK," responded Greg, "that's great. So everyone is aware, proxy voting is allowed, and if you can't make a meeting you can always ask someone to vote in accordance with your instructions."

"Greg, this is Mary Steiner. Avery gave me his proxy, we invested more or less together on this thing."

"OK, super, that means that all shares are accounted for," said Greg. "Before we get to the matter to be considered by shareholders, let me do what we do in every quarterly meeting. I'll give you an update on the business plan and how we think we're doing."

Greg turned from the camera and pulled up a loose-leaf binder. He took a sip of water, and turned back to his audience. He opened the binder and set it on the desk in front of him.

"You will all recall, ten months ago now, when we closed our private placement. That share offering raised $1.5 million in new capital for 3Device, Inc. As investors, you purchased 49.9 percent of the available equity, or basically half the company. We operate as a subsidiary of 3D Prosthetics, Inc., which owns 51.1% of the outstanding shares, and controls the day-to-day operation of 3Device.

"3Device was formed and exists to manufacture and market one class of products – medical devices created on a computer and a 3D printer. Now, 'medical device' is a term of art. It refers, generally speaking, to any object that is implanted in the body, or used on the body, for medical purposes, with the authorization of the United States Food and Drug Administration. When we talk about a 'device,' we're talking about something that must be tested in clinical trials, much like a new drug, which requires the approval of the FDA before it can be marketed.

"As you'll recall from your Private Placement Memorandum which you received before you bought your shares, 3Device is going to concentrate, first, on an artificial knee; then we hope to expand our effort to an artificial hip; and finally, we may think about implants used in spinal fusions and other orthopedic corrective or reconstructive surgeries.

"You may also recall that the first company that David Stein and I started together – 3D Prosthetics – makes custom-designed casts for fracture repair. Doctors can make a laser scan of a patient's limb and then create a hard plastic cast — which is actually open and honeycombed, rather than solid – and the resulting cast conforms perfectly to the patient's body. So it fits better, it's more comfortable, less itchy, and lighter than any plaster cast. And with a 3D printer available in the emergency room or orthopedic office, you can create a cast that will be ready within a few minutes after the bone has been set. Now, we have some competition in the market, but we think we have a better mousetrap because our software and printers are faster, and the business has been growing slowly but steadily.

"The reason that 3Device was created – in other words, the reason we didn't simply start a new product line within 3D Prosthetics – is that clinical trials and FDA approval are a different kettle of fish. Nothing we're doing with 3D Prosthetics involves clinical trials. It's one thing to create a product that doctors and medical professionals can use, and entirely a different challenge to get it approved by the FDA.

"So you'll recall that's why we solicited your investment. When we described what's called the 'sources and uses' of funds in your Private Placement Memorandum, we explained that we were going to raise 1.5 million dollars, and that basically all of that money was going to be spent on seeking FDA approval for our implantable knee. 3D Prosthetics already has the needed software, the 3D printers, and the design expertise, and that is what 3D Prosthetics contributed to 3Device. 3D Prosthetics has already built the first knees for the clinical trials.

"But clinical trials and FDA approval aren't for amateurs. Your funds are being used to retain Blue Tech Consultants, LLC, a consulting firm in Dallas, that does one thing and does it well – they shepherd applications for approvals of medical devices through the FDA review and approval process. They know the rules, they know how to set up clinical trials, and they know how to present the results to the FDA. And, fortunately, they agreed to undertake the application for our knee for a fixed fee of just under a million and a half dollars, which was a reasonable price indeed. They have given us the impression that they view 3D printed devices as the wave of the future, and they want to be able to demonstrate to their prospective clients that they know how to work with the FDA to get those devices approved. So we are as valuable to them as they are to us.

"At the moment, we're carrying on a clinical trial that will include 150 patients. 3D Prosthetics, on behalf of 3Device, is going to build up to 300 knees for the patients involved. We have a patent license from the inventor of the knee, which has been used successfully for years, so we have the basic knee technology nailed down. And actually, we expect to build two knees for most patients. We'll build the first one using specs for a standard knee that will be offered in six or seven sizes, and the surgeon will have that first knee in the operating room when the operation begins. And the possibility for a second knee is the really exciting innovation, and where we will be value-added. If the first knee doesn't fit or needs adjustment, the doctor will no longer be obliged to shape bone and tendons to make it fit. He or she can just turn to the computer tech and order a new knee, re-shaped by computer design. The surgeon and tech will talk about what adjustments are necessary for the knee to fit the patient better. The second knee will be ready within a half hour, which is well within the time range required by the anesthesiologists.

"The clinical trial is going very well. If all continues to go well, we will have enough data to pursue the application further. Blue Tech tells us to expect provisional approval within twelve to fifteen months from now, if our patients don't experience any major setbacks or complications.

"That's where we are. I don't need to tell you, nothing is guaranteed. 3Device could be a tremendous success, but there are a lot of things that can still go wrong. This entire venture is one big calculated risk, and we'll just have to see how it goes. David and I will be working our tails off to make it happen, but it's too early to tell. We're hopeful, let's put it that way.

Greg paused, and looked at the faces on his screen. "Before we go further, are there any questions?"

The level of enthusiasm in the meeting was gratifying for Greg and David. At least half of the shareholders contributed questions or comments, and support for the product was palpable. Greg ultimately had to cut the discussion a little bit short to get to the purpose of the special meeting.

"OK, we can talk offline with any of you who would like to discuss all this further. But now we need to get to new business. David, do you want to take over?"

"Thanks Greg," David replied. "You may recall that we had you sign a pile of documents in connection with your investment. One of those documents was our Shareholders' Agreement, which every shareholder was, and is, required to sign to become a shareholder in the company. We're a private company, and our Shareholders' Agreement has three clauses that are very common in shareholders' agreements. First, we have a clause that says you can sell or transfer shares to an immediate family member without obtaining permission from the company or other shareholders. All you have to do is notify the company. That clause is intended to facilitate estate planning and personal asset management generally.

"We have two shareholders who have already taken advantage of that clause. Art Hanstead transferred half of his shares to his wife, Peggy. And Olivia Incaviglia transferred half of her shares to her father, Lou Incaviglia.

"Second, we have a clause that says you can transfer shares between existing shareholders without approval from the company or other shareholders. The logic behind that is that we have already vetted and qualified all of our existing shareholders as being Accredited Investors for purposes of federal securities laws, and it's not disruptive for the shareholders to change their relative ownership percentages by buying and selling from each other.

"Which brings me to the subject of our only shareholder vote this evening. A third clause in our Shareholder's Agreement says that any sales to new shareholders must be approved by a super-majority of existing shares eligible to be voted, in this case, 75%. The reason for that clause is that none of us wants to admit shareholders who, for example, might want to steal technology or marketing ideas from the company, or who have criminal backgrounds, or whatever. We want to know who our business partners are.

And so, the shareholders have an opportunity to challenge the transaction, and debate whether it would be good for the company.

"With that said – Lou Incaviglia was recently approached by Salvatore Paglia, who would be interested in buying some of Mr. Incaviglia's shares in 3Device. Sal Paglia owns Sal Paglia, Inc., which is by far the largest paving and road construction company in southeastern Pennsylvania. Because the company does a lot of public contracting, its finances are fairly transparent. I've been able to determine that Sal Paglia, Inc., has about 900 employees, and annual revenues of more than 150 million dollars. Sal has received a variety of civic awards and tributes, and has been active in many local charities.

"Mr. Incaviglia owns 30 shares of 3Device, and proposes to sell 15 of them to Mr. Paglia. They haven't agreed on a price, but Mr. Incaviglia advises us, and all of you, that the only price he would be prepared to accept is exactly the price that all of you paid for your shares, namely, $1,000 per share. He won't accept more or less.

"Greg and I have talked it over, and we're planning to vote 3D Prosthetics' shares in favor of granting Mr. Incaviglia permission to sell shares to Mr. Paglia. We think Sal Paglia will be an asset to our company. To reach 75%, approximately half of your respective shares will need to vote in favor of the proposal, and obviously we're not telling you how to vote your shares."

Brief discussion followed on the question. Bill Ford posed the question that Greg and David were expecting from a few shareholders. "If this is approved, are we all going to have the same right?"

Greg replied promptly. "Glad you asked, Bill. The simple answer is either 'no,' or perhaps, 'it depends.' You won't have the right to just go and sell your shares to people who aren't existing shareholders. That would still be prohibited by the Shareholders' Agreement. But any shareholder will have the same right that Lou Incaviglia has just exercised, which is to come to the other shareholders, explain the reasons you want or need to sell, and ask for permission to make the sale. We're always prepared to call a special meeting of shareholders to let you make that pitch."

"OK, understood," said Bill Ford.

"Any other comments or questions?" asked David. No response.

"OK then, let's put the matter to a vote. We'll have a voice vote first, and then poll the shareholders if necessary. All in favor of permitting a sale of shares to Salvatore Paglia, say 'Aye.'"

"Aye," came the response from the little heads on the videoconference screen.

"All opposed say 'Nay.'"

No one was opposed. Sal Paglia would become a shareholder of 3Device, Inc.

The meeting adjourned with the usual pleasantries and platitudes. Lou had listened to the proceedings, although he hadn't spoken. When he clicked "off," he wasn't sure whether he was relieved or nervous.

CHAPTER 25

Lou Incaviglia was not a worrier, so he wasn't worried. But he was puzzled. He liked to think he understood what made people do the things they did, and when he didn't, he asked, and usually got an answer that made sense to him. But Sal Paglia wasn't adding up.

Lou had called Sal at his office – Sal was easy enough to find – and they agreed to meet at the club at 6:00. Lou was there by 5:00, and sipped on a shot and a beer while he thought. The best he could figure was that Sal's reasons were what he said they were. Maybe he was looking for an investment in health care. OK, but what the fuck was the matter with Pfizer or Moderna? One thing Lou had figured out over a lot of years is that, most of the time, people tell you what they're really thinking. All you have to do is listen. Now, "most" of the time meant, what, 85% of the time? The other 15% of the time people lied their asses off. So, five times out of six, you have your answer. Was this the five times, or was it the one time?

Sal's voice interrupted his thoughts. "Yo, Louie, *que pasa*?" Sal sat down on the next barstool.

"Good, Sal. How you doin'?"

"I'm doin' great. Look, I'm sorry Lou, I don't have much time tonight, my wife is already making dinner. So I gotta get right down to business." Sal waved to Tommy, and Tommy started pouring a Yuengling.

"I want to be a part of this company," Sal began. "I want to be a share-holder – and you're my opportunity to get my foot in the door. My idea is to buy as much as you'll sell me."

Lou hesitated, and considered his words. "OK, unnerstood. But I think I need to start by . . ." Tommy put Sal's draft on a coaster in front of him, and glided back to his seat at the other end of the bar. Lou and Sal were alone.

"I think I need to start by telling you about the company," Lou con-tinued. "I listened in on a shareholders' meeting the other night by Zoom or whatever, and I learned a lot. They been . . ."

"Lou," interrupted Sal, "I don't need to hear about that. It's not going to change my mind about wanting to buy in. Tell me again, how much do you own?"

Lou hesitated again. He didn't want to answer, and he didn't know why. He felt like he was giving away secrets. "My daughter Olivia gave me shares as a Christmas present. My son-in-law is the president of the com-pany. So it's just those shares. I never invested nothin'."

"So how much do you own?" repeated Sal.

"I own one percent of the company," Lou responded, finally. "Thirty shares."

"I'll take 'em all," said Sal.

"Whoa, Sallie, slow down, please. First thing is, I don't wanna sell 'em all. And second, we haven't agreed on a price."

"I tol' ya, I'm looking to get my foot in the door. If you don't wanna sell all your shares, how about half?"

In thinking about what he wanted to do, Lou had settled, in his own mind, on selling half his shares. So, one problem solved. "Yeah, I can do that. Fifteen shares. I want to stay a shareholder myself, so that would work for me."

"Good, we're makin' progress here," continued Sal. "All we gotta do is figure a fair price. What do have in mind?"

Lou knew exactly what he was going to say, and he hoped what he had to say would be unacceptable to Sal. "These shares have only ever had one price – a thousand bucks a share. That's what my son-in-law sold 'em to his investors for. When I got permission to do this deal with you, I agreed with my son-in-law that I wasn't gonna' have you paying less than everybody else paid, and I wouldn't want you to pay more. So there's only one price I can talk about. Fifteen shares for 15 grand. And you hafta sign the Shareholders' Agreement. Everybody has to sign that." Lou watched Sal for a reaction.

Sal thought for a second. "Sounds fair. If everybody else paid a thou a share, I'm willin' to pay the same. Do you know how this works, how to sell shares?"

"I have no friggin' clue," responded Lou.

Sal remembered his lawyer's explanation and repeated it to Lou. "It's easy. Go back to your son-in-law and tell him you'd like to trade your share certificate for two new ones, one for fifteen shares in your name, the other for fifteen shares in mine. Salvatore Paglia. In the meantime, I'll pay for the shares now, and we'll shake on it."

Lou held up both hands. "Whoa, Sal, you don't have to do that. Wait till you get the shares."

Sal shook his head, pulled out his checkbook, and began writing a check. "No, I want to do this now. OK, this should be easy. L-O-U-I-S. Then, what, I-N-C-A-V-I-G-L-I-A? Us and our fuckin' guinea names." Sal looked up with an aside. "I had a good friend in grade school, Vince Maragulia, he couldn't spell Maragulia until he was in fourth grade. His own fuckin' name! We overcomplicate this shit." Sal signed his name. "OK, good."

He tore the check out of his checkbook. "Here you go." As he began to hand the check to Lou, he stopped. "Oh wait, one more thing." He put the check on the bar and wrote, "15 shares, 3Device, Inc." on the memo line. "This makes it official my friend. Look, I gotta push off for dinner." He downed the rest of his beer. "This is a good thing we're doin'. It's good to be in business with you." He slid from the barstool and held out his hand.

Lou studied Sal's face one more time. "Good, Sal, yeah. See you maybe bocce night." He shook Sal's hand. Lou watched Sal leave, with as many questions as he had a few minutes before. He shrugged and pulled out his Daily Racing Form. Night racing tonight at The Downs in Wilkes-Barre. He was through thinking about 3Device for the evening, and maybe for the whole week.

CHAPTER 26

Sergio "Ziggy" Gallo was heading to the auto-teller to roll over his win in the sixth race when he spotted Lou Incaviglia at the snack bar ordering a beer. He crossed the seating area and yelled, "Lou!"

Lou looked up, saw who it was, and smiled. He left the beer he was being handed on the counter and walked over to his friend. They shook hands and hugged. "Yo, Ziggy! Why're you here on a Wednesday?"

"Water main break at the job," Ziggy replied, grinning. "It was time to take a break. Which race are you watching?" Ziggy understood that, in recent years, Lou often picked a single race. At this point, Lou was too good at finding horses to bother with the three-legged two-year-olds running in the early races. Too much uncertainty.

"Nothin' much," replied Lou. "Wanted to be here for the seventh race. What's up at work? Where's your job?"

"We're doin' the brick at the new performing arts center in Media. Beautiful building, it's goin' good."

Lou and Ziggy went back eight years, but it seemed a lot longer than that. When Ziggy first came on the job, he showed unusual talent for a young guy, and Lou liked his sense of humor, his work ethic, and his approach to life. Ziggy left the undergraduate business program at LaSalle University to join the Bricklayers, and, like Lou, he loved what he did. Lou remembered their first conversation, when he asked Ziggy where he got his name. Ziggy explained that his parents named him Sergio, but, according to the story he was told, his dad soon tried out a slew of nicknames. Being both a Ziggy Marley fan, and a David Bowie fan, his dad thought that twisting Sergio into "Ziggy" seemed a reasonable step, and the nickname stuck. Ziggy was tall for a *paisan*, and he had the sort of dark good looks that Lou imagined Olivia should have been attracted to.

Lou took Ziggy under his wing, and taught him everything he'd ever learned about laying bricks. Which was a lot. They busted each other's balls constantly, but there was an unstated agreement that they had each other's back. Foremen would assign them to work together most of the time, because the results were always great. But if any foreman gave them unnecessary shit, they would push back together. Ziggy was dismayed when Lou retired, but he stepped into Lou's shoes on a bunch of jobs, and always had work. The man could lay bricks, and he wasn't an asshole about it. Other guys watched what he did — the way they used to watch Lou – and there wasn't anybody who resented him just because he was young. Well, maybe they did, a little.

Bricklaying wasn't the only important thing Lou taught Ziggy. There was also the matter of horse racing. The first time Lou took Ziggy to the track, Ziggy just watched and listened as Lou laid out the basics of his betting strategy. There was too much to learn in one, two or ten afternoons, but Ziggy was hooked. And he was a quick study. By the time Lou retired, Ziggy was usually breaking even on a ten-race card, and he was getting to know a lot of the trainers and jockeys whose tips made the difference between winning and losing.

Lou still saw Ziggy fairly often, mostly at the track on weekends. They would swap ideas on various races, and then, more often than not, grab a beer in the casino lounge after the tenth race.

Lou walked back to the counter in the snack bar, picked up his beer, and walked with Ziggy to the auto-teller. Ziggy rolled his winnings over to the seventh race, and bet exactly as Lou instructed him. Lou knew that, in parimutuel-betting-land, his winnings (if they won) would take a haircut because of Ziggy's bet. But Lou was Lou — and while he wouldn't hand out race tips to strangers, he never hesitated to share racing intel with friends.

The seventh race was the best one on the card that day. Six horses had a chance to win coming down the stretch. Lou heard "vamos, vamos, vamos," and "go, go, go." An older woman was screaming for the 6 horse. She turned to — by all appearances — her hooky-playing 10-year old granddaughter and said, "See if he goes to his whip." As it happened, Lou and Ziggy were betting the 6 horse. With half a furlong to go, the jockey went to his whip, and the horse surged forward, winning by half a length. The young girl leaped to her feet and yelled. Lou had a lump in his throat, remembering days when he and Olivia lived the same experience. Lou found out – because of course he did – that the grandmother's name was Claudia, and her granddaughter's name was Bethany. Claudia and Bethany and Ziggy and Lou walked to the window together to collect their winnings. Lou loved the racetrack.

CHAPTER 27

"Paul Smythe, this is Sal Paglia, did I catch you at a good time?"

"Sure, Sal, my lawyer told me you might be calling."

Mr. Smythe's lawyer, Arthur Makin, had indeed called his client. But it wasn't as simple as that. Sal Paglia's principal lawyer was Palmer Eastman, a senior partner at Major, Boardman & Patterson, LLP, one of Philadelphia's largest law firms. Sal had asked Palmer Eastman to shake the tree a little to see if any of Major Boardman's lawyers had ever represented any of the shareholders in 3Device. It turned out that one of the firm's partners had reviewed the Private Placement Memorandum for one of the company's smaller investors. Palmer Eastman and his partner called their client, the 3Device investor, to ask whether he had met any of the other investors. Indeed, the client had rubbed elbows with four or five people who bought shares. They all met at a pitch that Greg Morris and David Stein had done at Merion Golf Club. The client remembered Paul Smythe, in particular, because he was a relatively well-known real estate developer in southeastern Pennsylvania. With that information in hand, Palmer Eastman went back to his firm's conflicts data base and turned up a reference to a land use appeal in which Paul Smythe and his lawyer, Arthur Makin, were on one side, and Major Boardman was on the other. The case settled amicably. And Palmer Eastman happened to know Arthur Makin from bar association work, so he gave him a call, and asked him if he would be willing to ask Paul Smythe to perhaps take a call from Sal Paglia. Arthur Makin forwarded the request, and Paul Smythe said, "Sure."

When Sal learned that his law firm had found another shareholder in 3Device, he told his lawyer, Palmer Eastman, that he was going to call Lou Incaviglia to see what, if anything, he could learn from Lou about Paul Smythe. He got busy with other things and never made that call, and when his lawyer followed up Sal replied, "Yeah, I had a long talk with Incaviglia, and he thinks we should talk to Smythe." He didn't want his lawyers to think he depended on them.

Sal could have asked Gregory Morris, CEO of 3Device, to put him in touch with other shareholders of 3Device. Under Pennsylvania law, any shareholder may see his or her corporation's shareholder list. But some small private companies were reluctant to share that information if they could avoid it, and Sal wasn't interested in reading anyone the riot act about his rights as a shareholder. At least he wasn't interested yet. And he didn't want Gregory Morris to know he was contacting other shareholders.

"Before I get to the reason for my call," Sal began, "it occurred to me we've probably worked together. I think we did your site development for Huntsman's Crossing out in Bucks County, what, maybe ten years ago."

"Yeah, I think that sounds right," Paul Smythe replied. "I think my general contractor probably worked with you. Sometimes we do site development as a direct deal with the site prep guys, but probably not on that one. But, come to think of it, I remember your trucks being there. Big, black and shiny."

"Well, it's always good to know who's doing what, and maybe next time you're looking for paving or site prep, give us a call, we'll talk. Or I'll come find you, I won't be shy." Sal shifted gears. "But that's not the reason for my call."

"OK, what can I do you?"

Sal played with the Bluetooth in is ear. He hated handsets because he liked to have his hands free to shuffle papers or take notes. "You probably know that I just bought some shares in 3Device. I got 'em from a buddy of mine, Lou Incaviglia."

"Yeah, I knew you were going to, because we had a quick shareholders' meeting to approve the transfer."

"That's great, and I appreciate the vote of confidence, or whatever you'd call it. So, I'm very excited about the product and the way the company is being run, and I think there's a possibility for a very nice return on these shares. Still a long shot, but that's the way it is with any startup. In any event, I'm lookin' to buy more shares. I hadn't heard about the company while they were raising funds, and now the offer is closed and they're not selling directly to investors. But we just looked at the Shareholders' Agreement, and it turns out existing shareholders can sell to each other without getting prior approval from the other shareholders, or from the company. So here's my bottom line question: Do you happen to know anyone who might be looking to sell their shares?"

"Hmmm." Paul Smythe paused for a moment. "The investment's only about 11 months old, and we've been getting regular reports from management. They're just getting into Phase III trials, or whatever they call them, and I suppose we'll see whether the knees are helping people or crippling them. I think everybody who initially invested is probably in about the same place they were 11 months ago. It seems like a great idea on paper, and we just need to see whether it works. There are 18 or 20 shareholders, and in any group of 20 people you probably have at least one or two who need money for whatever reason, and would like to sell some assets. But nobody has spread that word."

"OK, I hear you," Sal replied. "I'll be a little blunt. I'm a motivated buyer. Let me ask you this. Is there a price at which you'd be willing to sell *your* shares?"

"Boy, I don't know. I bought an investment, not an anniversary present for my wife. So, sure, there would have to be some number I could give you. But I haven't thought about it. I don't know whether you're aware, I'm the largest shareholder in the private investors' group. I bought 15% of the company for $450,000. I believe in what they're doing, and if I were going to sell, my price would certainly be above $450,000."

"Makes sense," said Sal. "Here's what I'm willing to do. You invested 450k a little less than a year ago. I think you deserve an annual return of 10% on your investment, which would be $45,000. And I'll include a $5,000 sweetener, to get you to a round number. I'll pay $500,000, all cash, for your shares."

"I'm going to have to think about it."

"I understand completely. Just two requests. Please keep this conversation confidential. And get back to me within a week, say, next Monday." Sal offered his cell phone number, and Paul Smythe mumbled the numbers while he jotted it down.

"Sal, thanks for reaching out. Wasn't what I expected, but I appreciate your being direct and above board about this. I'll give you an answer by Monday, either way."

"OK, Paul, thanks. Nice to talk to you." Sal thumbed his cell phone and pulled his Bluetooth out of his ear. "That cocksucker wants to deal," he said. "I can feel it."

Palmer Eastman, Sal's lawyer, had listened to Sal's side of the call. Both were sitting in Eastman's office. "I thought you handled it well," said the lawyer. "I'll keep working this from our side. Let me know as soon as you hear."

As it happened, Paul Smythe was true to his word. He got back to Sal within a week, proposing to sell 97% of his stake in 3Device — 435 shares – for $500,000. That price, if he got it, would represent a $50,000 profit on his initial investment, a return of 11% in less than a year. And, as a kicker, he would still own 15 shares and might profit some on the upside.

Sal agreed immediately. The money and shares changed hands quickly, and Sal now owned 15% of the outstanding equity in 3Device. He was the largest shareholder in the company other than its parent company. Sal liked being the largest of anything, and he told his wife Sallie she should be prepared to buy a villa in Aruba with the profits they were going to make. He believed he knew how businessmen thought. Doctors were businessmen, as far as Sal was concerned, and they were bound to like having more and better stuff near the operating room, stuff that they could bill to insurance companies at the end of an operation. 3Device couldn't miss.

There was the matter of FDA approval. But Sal was used to dealing with governments. Persuading a government to do what you wanted was, in the end, pretty easy. A formality, really.

And, of course, he would be looking for ways to increase his ownership share in 3Device. Ultimately, he was looking for operational control. A company is no fun if you're not controlling it.

CHAPTER 28

Greg Morris and David Stein were at the Vesper Boat Club on the Schuylkill River, carrying their shells down the ramp. Late afternoons in June were often given over to rowing, for both of them.

"Did you get that email from Paul Smythe?" asked David. "It looks like he sold more than nine-tenths of his shares to Sal Paglia. He wants us to log the transaction on the Shareholders' Register."

"What?" Greg was trying to process what he'd just heard. "Just like that? I thought Paul Smythe was our biggest fan. That makes no sense."

"I thought so too," David replied. "But I have to believe the shareholders are having conversations we don't know about. It's just weird that Paul sold his shares before talking to us. Sal Paglia must have made him a good offer."

"I admit I didn't see this coming," said Greg. "Lou didn't mention anything like this when he sold his shares to Sal. But it might not be a bad thing. Sal Paglia's a mover and a shaker, I gotta give him that. Paul is a lot more laid back, and I never had the sense he was looking for a huge killing when he invested with us. He was mostly just looking for value. In either case, that bloc of shares represents our largest minority interest, and we're gonna have to deal with whoever owns them. Sal is pretty out there, and he could be our biggest cheerleader. Or the Dark Lord. Who knows?"

"Emperor Palpatine, as far as I'm concerned. Something's going on." David checked his oarlocks and settled his shell in the water. "I think he picked your father-in-law as a plump target. If he were just looking to make an investment, he would have come to us first. 'Which of your shareholders might be interested in selling?', that kind of thing. And certainly, 'how's it looking, what are your prospects?' Who buys a hefty interest in a small private company before they've talked to management? It makes no sense."

"You're right, I agree," Greg responded. "Should we invite Mr. Paglia to dinner, brief him on what's going on and take his temperature a little?"

"We could. But there's also something to be said for keeping our distance. We voted our shares in favor of Lou's transfer to Paglia, but we didn't invite it. The reality is, we control all of the decisionmaking for the company, and we don't have any obligation to provide information to any single shareholder that we're not simultaneously providing to all of the shareholders. This guy bought in without talking to us, and he's a sophisticated businessman with sophisticated advisers. This decision to buy more is on him. I want to figure out what he's up to – if anything – before we show any of our cards. Maybe we should just wait to see if he reaches out to us."

"Waiting also doesn't feel right," replied Greg. "I don't like not knowing where he's coming from, even if the explanation is simple. Maybe he likes medical devices."

"Well, that could be another problem," said David. "Supposing he's just an enthusiastic amateur investor, and likes our product and our prospects, as far as we know he hasn't been briefed on all of the risks. If this doesn't work out, he could be coming after everybody he can find so he doesn't have to face up to his own lack of due diligence. A lot of successful people hate to take responsibility for their own mistakes."

"Yeah, you're right, and that's scary," Greg replied. "But look, he voted with his checkbook in support of what we're doing. I think we should plan for the best, even if we're hedging our bets. How 'bout I send him an email saying, 'Heard about your purchase of Paul Smythe's shares, thank you for your continued confidence in the company, blah blah.' Let him know he's on the radar, and that we're happy to have him as a shareholder. Let's just play it straight until we know more."

David considered Greg's point. Finally, he replied, "Makes sense. It really does. We'll play it straight till we know more." David was seated in his shell and facing upriver. He hollered to Greg, "Race you to the railroad bridge," as he pushed off from the dock.

CHAPTER 29

Greg Morris, David Stein and Dr. Mark Ableson, 3Device's Chief Science Officer, were gathered around a speakerphone talking with Boris Provolov of Blue Tech Consultants. It was Blue Tech's job to deal with the Food and Drug Administration during the clinical trial. Blue Tech was describing the latest communication from the FDA, and the news wasn't good.

"We didn't see this one coming," said Provolov, "and I won't sugar coat it – this amounts to an indefinite hold. It could be a month. It could be three years. However long it takes the FDA to make up its mind and issue some guidance."

"The part that's not making sense to me," responded Dr. Ableson, "is this idea that we're arguably presenting multiple devices. They know perfectly well we're using one knee design. I could reach behind me and pull one off the shelf and hand it to them. There will be a standard knee present for every operation, just in case it fits."

"We think that way because we've trained ourselves to think that way," said Provolov. "But remember a year ago when all of us talked about this problem. How do you get FDA approval for a device that will rarely be the same twice? We worried out loud to ourselves, 'If we do 150 operations during the trial, we've arguably used 150 different devices.' And then you'll recall we researched FDA guidance on that question. The FDA themselves acknowledged that devices are modified during trials all the time, and they just considered that one factor in evaluating safety and effectiveness. In other words, they've always factored in whether and how badly a tired doctor could screw up the result."

"So why were our assumptions wrong?" asked Greg.

"They weren't wrong – we understood the FDA's guidance correctly, as it existed then," responded Provolov. "They're essentially admitting to us that they're moving the goalposts. But the way they've explained it to us is that they've never reviewed trials on a device that is likely to be substantially modified every time it's implanted. They said, 'at some point, too much change to the device is just too much. We have to know what device we're approving.' And they weren't aggressive or obnoxious about it, the way they often are. I think they want us to succeed. But they want to take some time to create a policy on how they're going to review something like this. And until they do, we're in limbo."

"Goddammit," said Greg, "it's one thing to do this at the beginning, but we're right near the end of Pivotal Stage and more than a hundred operations into our trial. We should be grandfathered, and they can apply their new policy to the next applicant."

"Yeah, but it doesn't work that way," replied Provolov. "When they make policy, they don't worry about whether the new policy is going to torpedo an individual applicant. If they're going to create a new policy, they can't grandfather anybody, because, by definition, they'd be letting somebody slip through knowing that they're not meeting the new requirements. They can't do that."

"Well, wait a minute," said Dave Stein, "let's think about this. We know that during the trial so far, 80% of our modifications were intended to regulate contact pressure on the tibial insert. By definition, different patients are going to have different-sized tibias and medullary cavities, and our knee solves that problem better than anyone else. There are other FDA approved devices out there – not knees, but some spinal stuff – where the doctor is expected to shave the device to fit, at point of care. Maybe we can ask them for provisional approval for the 3D-printed knee, with the stipulation that, when we take it to market, only the tibial insert would be modified during surgery. We'll phase the other stuff in when the FDA makes up its mind."

"I know you're just thinking out loud, Dave, and that's good," Greg responded, "but I think it would kill our marketing effort if we could only offer one mod. Doctors can already choose from 50 different sizes and shapes of knee, and I don't see them preferring us just because we can modify the tibial implant. That's not enough incentive to try something new."

The phone meeting continued for another 45 minutes, as the four participants discussed options. There didn't seem to be many. When they hung up, Dr. Ableson rushed out to feed his parking meter. Greg and David were exhausted, and slumped in their chairs. It was 5:05 p.m.

"It's always somethin'," said Greg, as he exhaled. "Let's go get a drink."

CHAPTER 30

Lou was housesitting for Olivia and Greg while they were taking a long weekend in Boothbay Harbor. He was washing some dishes in the kitchen. Olivia's cat stood on the counter, waiting to stick his paw in the water every time Lou opened the faucet. There was a loud knock on the front door.

As he was crossing the living room to answer, he heard "Merion Township Police, open the door." Lou was not born yesterday, and understood that the last thing he was going to do was open the door before he knew why the cop was there.

"What do you want, Officer?" asked Lou, through the door.

"We want you to open the door and we want to ask you some questions," replied the voice.

Lou thought for a short second. The visit didn't sound friendly, and that made him nervous. And he was stubborn. "What's this about?"

Pause. "We want to talk to you. I don't have to tell you why."

"Do you have a warrant or something?" Lou thought that was a pretty reasonable question. Buy some time till he knew more.

"We don't need a warrant. We want you to open the door."

"I don't want to do that until I know why you're here."

The cop hesitated, apparently deciding how much he was going to say. "We're not going away until we establish that you're not trespassing or squatting. You need to provide us with some ID."

"My ID is locked in my car in the driveway." It really was – Lou didn't like sitting on his wallet when he drove, so he usually threw it in the glove compartment. He'd forgotten to bring his wallet inside. "The Mercury is mine, you can run the plate. That's who I am."

"You need to open the door and let me in, now."

"Officer, if you don't have a warrant, I think you need to leave the property. And I'm recording this conversation as of now." Lou pulled out his phone and started recording video. The picture would only show his side of the door, but the sound would be clear enough.

Another pause, longer. "A neighbor saw you entering the house. There are only two people living here, and the neighbor says she thinks they're on vacation. She doesn't know you, and has never seen you before. That's probable cause to search. If you want us to go get a warrant, we will, but you'll wind up in handcuffs, and you won't be getting much sleep tonight in the holding cell."

Lou couldn't believe his ears. He liked cops generally, but this guy was a mahaf. "Let's do this," said Lou. "Run the plates on the two cars parked in the driveway." Lou knew that the plates would come back "Louis C. Incaviglia" and "Olivia Ann Incaviglia" – Olivia answered to "Morris" if someone called her by that name, but she had kept her maiden name for business and for official documents. It was her BMW parked in the driveway. He also knew that her address would come up at her house, and his address would come up at his.

"Don't tell us how to run our investigation," said the cop.

Lou wondered who "we" and "us" were. The guy's partner was probably still in the squad car. "All right, I won't tell you what to do. But what are you gonna tell the judge when I tell him I tol' you to run the plates, but you ignored me, and arrested me, and wasted his time? And I got it all on tape."

"I want to see some ID. Hold it up to the window."

"I told you it's locked in my car," replied Lou immediately. "But I want to see your ID. Hold it up to the window."

The cop hesitated for another 30 seconds. Finally, he held his badge wallet against the window. "Clayton M. Smith," badge number 103, and in the picture he looked about 12.

"OK, thank you. My name is Louis Incaviglia. I live on Walnut Street in Norristown. Run my license plate in your computer. The car will come up registered to me. And if you run the plate for the BMW parked beside it, it'll come up as registered to Olivia Incaviglia. If I'm trespassing, that would be quite a coincidence. How many Incaviglias do you think there are in the world?"

"You're making trouble for yourself," said Officer Smith. "If we have to do this the hard way, we're going to do it the very hard way. How about we stake out the property and arrest you when you leave? Are you going to stay in there forever, tough guy?"

Lou was incredulous. "Arrest me for what?"

"Trespassing. I told you we have probable cause."

"Not after you run the plates, Officer. I'm not opening the door. Call your supervisor, that's what I'd do. I don't want to have this conversation any more, and I'm gonna go watch Jeopardy." Lou turned away from the door to do exactly that. He missed Alex – it just wasn't the same now. But he still watched.

After about ten more minutes, Lou heard the faint sounds of the police cruiser backing out of the driveway and heading up the street. Lou didn't dislike rich people, or their neighborhoods, or their police forces – well, actually, he did, sort of. He wished he were back home on his stoop. It crossed his mind that the cop was probably lying to him about probable cause just to get him to agree to the search. He wondered if he could sue the cop for threatening him. Maybe ask Nigel Branca about it next time he saw him at the club.

Lou didn't hear from the township cops again, but Olivia told him later that the cops had called her up and hassled her for not informing them she was going to have a house-sitter. After about five minutes of lecturing from a sergeant, Olivia told him to go look for criminals and stop bothering her, and hung up. In so many ways, the apple hadn't fallen very far from the tree.

CHAPTER 31

Whenever Nigel Branca twisted the cap from a new bottle of Jack Daniel's he would immediately pour an ounce and a half into a shot glass. As a matter of ritual – but not for any other articulable reason – he drank the first drink from a new bottle at room temperature and undiluted. A shot. Sometimes he would have a beer with his second shot. Or sometimes a second shot would be just a second shot. Nigel believed that most things happened for no reason at all, other than, perhaps, naked cause and effect. Gravity, for example. But there was no God, and He was not directing traffic. Whether or not Nigel had a beer with his second shot would not determine anything in his life, during the day in question or in any subsequent time period. Perforce, he drank as his impulses moved him, and was never superstitious.

He recognized some interesting corollaries to his basic belief. Sports were stupid, for example. Balls bounce oddly, so what? Also, if things happened for no reason, there was no reason to try to make them happen. Which meant that as long as Nigel showed up and said the right words, with or without passion or conviction, he bore no responsibility for a client's punishment. The client he was defending would either get a light sentence, or he wouldn't. *Machts nix*, as they say in Pennsylvania Dutch.

Nigel was fortunate that his clients didn't have much choice about whether to tolerate his general lack of enthusiasm for their causes. Nigel accepted court appointments defending poor people in misdemeanor cases – $300 per case. He accepted about three new cases a week, and, as the math would suggest, he grossed about $45,000 per year. Enough for Jack Daniel's and beer, a studio apartment a half-mile from the courthouse, a budget cell phone, and a gmail account. He rarely – that is, never – took a case to trial. His approach was to convince his clients to plead guilty whether they were guilty or not. As he patiently explained to them (when he felt like it), there was no space in the Montgomery County Jail in which to house a misdemeanant. A sentence of probation on any misdemeanor charge – at least one not accompanied by a serious felony — was essentially guaranteed. A guilty plea made each client's problem go away until next time. On occasion, Nigel was assigned the case of a hardened felon for whom a misdemeanor conviction would result in a violation of parole and serious jail time. Such felons normally demanded that their misdemeanor case be tried. Thus, in every such case, Nigel tendered the file back to the criminal court administrator, explaining that he had a conflict of interest. A bit like Yossarian's liver ailment, a lawyer's conflict of interest is a very bad thing that can be very hard to define, and the court administrator had little choice but to re-assign the case.

Nigel didn't start out that way. He was the son of an English school-teacher and an Italian-American soldier who met and married in England during the 1950's. His mother wanted to call him Nigel, and his father didn't care what she called him as long as his last name was Branca. After the service, Nigel's father hired on with the U.S. Post Office as a mailman, and his mother raised Nigel and his sisters in a rowhouse in Norristown. Nigel was an uncommonly bright student, albeit a bit of a recluse. He won a scholarship to Lehigh University, worked a couple of years after gradua-tion in the Bethlehem Steel plant, and finally paid and borrowed his way through law school at Penn. He graduated from Penn Law *magna cum laude*, and was recruited and hired as an associate at a large Philadelphia law firm. He performed well as a labor litigator for five years, but just as he was about to be considered for partner, he threw up on himself at a Friday night Happy Hour in front of nine of his fellow associates and four young partners. Drinking is one thing, but all agreed that Nigel had crossed a line that night. When it happened again the following Friday, Nigel's dreams of an early partnership were effectively over. He ultimately drank himself out of continued employment as an associate, as well.

Nigel's fall through the profession was precipitous. He couldn't get a job, because he was terrible at interviews and showed up looking like the disheveled drunk he was. Women didn't like him, so he had no support from that quarter. He opened his own practice in his hometown of Norristown, which happens to be the county seat of Montgomery County, Pennsylvania, and thus the site of its courthouse. But because he had no people skills, he was unable to attract clients. So it was that he ended up doing the only work in town that required a law license and little else – court appointments in criminal cases. It was a living.

But a funny thing happened to Nigel as he passed through his forties, and into his fifties – he fell in love with law. Not *practicing* law – he hated that. But he was coming to love the law that was already in the books. He would pull a Federal Reporter off the shelf in the law library and open it to a random case. He would read that case carefully, working to understand the arguments, the court's reasoning, and the underlying authority that influenced the result. He would do the same with U.S. Supreme Court cases, rulings by workers' compensation judges, and Federal Trade Commission decisions. He could tell you why the National Labor Relations Board was drifting away from strict application of the Successor Doctrine, and how a ship's cargo could be seized in Admiralty Court. Had he been practicing in a large firm, he would have been the distinguished senior partner whom everyone else consulted when they didn't want to look something up for themselves.

Nigel certainly wasn't distinguished. He was 5'6" in heel lifts, his still-dark hair grew in patches around his head, and his eyes were always red and bleary. But there was a certain intelligence in his eyes that was hard to mistake. Nigel didn't miss anything, and that awareness of the world showed in his demeanor.

A few people actually understood how much law Nigel knew. His brothers at the Italian American Citizens Club of Norristown, Pennsylvania, figured out that there was no point of law on which Nigel was unable to provide at least a basic understanding. "My sister wants a divorce." "My boss fired me because I turned 60." "I got a tax notice from the government." "My new car sucks." "I slipped at the Shop Rite." "The transit agency wants to see my text messages before they hire me." And a thousand more. Nigel was the consummate consigliere. He listened, he considered, he responded. He didn't drone on with useless detail, but he was never peremptory. He answered any question fully and concisely. And then he went back to his Jack Daniel's. If no one else brought up law, Nigel didn't mention it either. He sat quietly, for the most part, becoming animated only when people talked about religion. He knew a lot about religion for someone who didn't believe a word of it.

If you asked Lou Incaviglia whether he liked Nigel Branca, he would have said, "Yes." Lou liked almost everybody. If you asked Lou Incaviglia whether he respected Nigel Branca, he would have paused and thought about it. Nigel's attitude toward his clients concerned Lou a little bit. Nigel wasn't covering himself in glory there. But for a guy whose liver was probably not going to be joining him for his 65th birthday, Nigel remained composed and true to himself. He didn't mope about his drinking or his job, and he didn't indulge in self-pity. He didn't ask people for favors. "I respect the fact that he maintains his dignity," Lou would have said if you asked him.

"So, should I sue this motherfucker, Officer Clayton M. Smith?" Lou asked Nigel Branca one Wednesday evening at the club.

Sitting on the next stool, Nigel thought for a second. "You should never sue anybody for anything. It's a horrible experience, being in a lawsuit, and you don't want any part of it."

CHAPTER 32

"The Moderator is joining the meeting," said Zoom's electronic voice. Greg came on-screen and began to speak in a measured tone.

"Hello everyone, thanks for participating in this special meeting of shareholders of 3Device, Inc. As per our usual practice, we are recording the meeting, if no one has an objection. According to the list of attendees, we have sixteen of twenty shareholders present. David Stein, acting as secretary of the meeting, is recording all your names, and will email the meeting summary to all shareholders, both those who are attending and those who aren't, within a day or so."

David nodded to his camera and surveyed the names and faces on the Zoom call. He happened to notice that Lou Incaviglia wasn't attending, even though he still owned 15 shares.

"This is simply an informational meeting, and there will be an opportunity to pose questions to management at the end. We don't have any matters that need to be voted on, so we don't have to record who's here with a proxy for casting a vote on behalf of another shareholder."

"Greg, can I interrupt for just a minute?" said Sal Paglia. Zoom made his face larger. "I'm the newest shareholder, I think, in 3Device, and I just wanted to take a minute to tell you, and the other shareholders, that I'm excited to be a part of this, and very, very optimistic about the company's future. I built a sizable company of my own, and I'd like to think I know something about how that's done. And I have to say, this company looks great. I'm looking forward to getting to know it better, and learning more about the technology. That's all. Thanks for letting me say hello to everybody."

Greg paused for a beat. "Thank you, Sal. We appreciate the support."

Mary Steiner jumped in. "Sal, welcome. Maybe we can have a company picnic this summer, and we can all get a ride in one of your trucks, if you'll bring one along." A couple of shareholders chuckled.

"OK, let me give you all a quick update on current progress," Greg began, "and then I'll talk about the reasons we called a special meeting."

"The Pivotal Phase trial continues to go extremely well. Results have been spectacular, in fact better than we could have hoped. We haven't had a single adverse reaction or immune system rejection, by any patient, since we last talked to you. The reason for that, we think, is that the knee is working beautifully. It fits better, it moves better, and rejection has not been a problem in any way. The titanium-cobalt alloy we're using has been tolerated very well by all of the patients in the trial, and as you know, titanium is an excellent material for fast 3D printing.

"We're now at 125 successful implants, and only one implant has had to come out. That one rejection was not caused by our knee. What happened was that the patient twisted her knee stepping in a hole in her garden. She damaged the tissue around the knee while it was in the process of healing after surgery. It was a bad result, and the doctors still aren't sure when they're going to be able to replace her knee again. But they think it's a matter of time and healing, and she should be able to have another replacement knee implanted. Again, our knee wasn't the problem.

"But we do have a problem, and that's the one we want to talk to you about today." Greg was quiet for a long moment. "We received a letter on Thursday of last week from the Chief Review Officer at the FDA. We have been advised that review of our application for marketing approval has been placed on administrative hold until – if at all – the FDA develops guidelines for 3D-printed medical devices that are designed to be modified at the point of care. The letter advised us that the guidelines will define when a device designed to be modified at the point of care constitutes a single device subject to a single FDA approval, and when the technology constitutes multiple devices requiring multiple approvals. We are permitted to continue with our clinical trial, but they're advising us that there will likely be a hold-up when we get ready to submit our data and push for approval.

"In a nutshell, the FDA can't decide which category our knee falls into – one device or many — because they haven't created rules or guidelines that will help the agency tell the difference. It's a chicken or egg problem. They can't decide whether we're multiple devices, because they don't have rules in place to govern that decision. But they haven't put rules in place because 3D-printed devices can be modified so quickly, and so extensively, that they don't quite know what they're looking to regulate.

"And you can see their problem, although it's painful for us. Our trial has included 150 patients and 125 surgeries so far. In that group, only 12 have used our standard knee, unmodified. The rest – 113 patients – have each been given a knee that is unique, and different from everyone else's. All of those 113 knees have been modified to fit. It ought to be very reassuring to the FDA that all these 'different' knees have produced outstanding clinical results. But we don't know, frankly, how they are factoring that in to their rulemaking. Somebody within the agency is looking at the possibility that we have created 113 different devices, and has begun to worry that more rules are needed.

"So, we'll be waiting for new regulations to be drafted and approved by the agency. How long will that be? The simple answer is – we don't know. Months, certainly, rather than weeks. Whether it goes longer than a year, I guess . . . well, it could. We just don't know.

"One of our first reactions when we got the letter was to worry that this will give prospective competitors a chance to catch up to us. But on further reflection, we think the uncertainty created by the FDA will actually discourage other companies from spending money to develop 3D knees and hips that can be modified at the point of care. Why would they spend money on an idea if they can't be sure, yet, whether they'll ever be able to get approval for it? So, in a sense, maybe we'll continue to have the benefit of our head start. We're still in the lead, and nobody can really race to catch up until this gets settled.

"One question I'm sure all of you will have is this: How certain is it that our product will be able to comply with the regulations once they're drafted? The answer to that question, we think, is the real silver lining in all this. Not to put too fine a point on it — our software can do anything. We can build any knee or hip that we want to. However the FDA might define a single, 3D-printed device, we can create something that will comply with that definition.

"To sum up, we want you to know that this is a delay, not a death sentence. Our technology is not going away, and this company is not going away. We will be compiling our clinical results and shaping up our application for the day when the FDA is ready to look at it again. And when the regulations are issued, we will be first in line asking for marketing approval for our knee. But in the meantime, we'll be asking for your patience. Hang in there with us, and we'll all see where this goes. The upside is still there.

"I'll open up the floor to questions."

"Pres, David, this is Ed O'Neil," said one of the Zoom faces. "What is your monthly nut to keep the company running, and what are the chances that you're going to run out of money before the FDA issues its rules?"

"That's another silver lining, Ed. 3Device doesn't have any overhead, because under our Shareholders' Agreement, basically all of the back-office costs for running the company are borne by 3D Prosthetics. All of our shareholders' investments have been directly applied to supporting our application to the FDA. We believe 3Device has enough cash left to be able to complete the clinical trial and the FDA process. If the FDA's new rules, whatever they might be, make the remainder of the application more expensive, so that we run out of cash, our intention would be to try to borrow whatever we need to complete the process."

"This is Mark Avery," came another voice. "Has our accounting firm made any comment on all of this is."

"Yes and no," Greg replied. "No third party has asked them for an opinion, so they haven't been in a position to comment, or needed to comment. But because the FDA has only expressed an intention to issue regulations – and hasn't promised they will – it's theoretically possible that our application will never be reviewed. It could be in limbo forever. The partner in charge indicated that if our CPA's were asked today, they'd have to give whoever asked a 'going concern' warning."

"This is Sal Paglia." Everyone was quiet, and Sal took his time before he spoke. "How much did you guys know about this when you let me invest a half million bucks in your stock?"

Greg responded carefully. "We always knew, and made clear to all of our initial investors, that FDA approval was uncertain, and whatever the FDA decided would likely determine the ultimate value of 3Device shares. That is still true. As for when we learned about the FDA putting our application on hold – as we said, we learned that on Thursday of last week, a few days after you bought shares from Paul Smythe, and well over a week after you bought your shares from Lou Incaviglia."

"And you're telling me you had no idea this was coming?"

"We did not. Our FDA consultants, Blue Tech, advised us that we should shape our application to emphasize that our modifications at point of care would be similar in scope to other modifiable devices that have already obtained FDA approval. And our arguments for approval were consistent with what the FDA had said about the issue before. More important, we were prepared to respond to questions and challenges from FDA staff as they came up. The drill is, you work with FDA staff to get their concerns addressed and the device approved. But the idea that the FDA would suspend consideration of our application while they think about issuing new rules was on no one's radar screen."

"You let me make a big speech in front of twenty people about what a great company this is, and how exciting the technology is, and then you tell me, in effect, I'm an idiot," Sal responded. "I got played by you and your father-in-law. You can't do this, you can't run a company this way. I will say to every shareholder on this call – I'm gonna do something about this. I'm gonna talk to my lawyers tomorrow morning. If you're a shareholder on this call, and if you want to take some kind of action with me, give me a call at my office. I'm not gonna let this stand." Sal's screen went blank.

The call was quiet for a long moment. Greg finally spoke up. "I don't think David or I will make any response to what you just heard, other than the responses you heard me give to Mr. Paglia. Are there any other questions for us?"

"Greg, this is Mary Steiner again. Does this mean we won't get to ride in one of those trucks?" The laughter broke the tension a little bit. "Seriously, though, will you keep us posted? Will management commit to monthly communications letting us know anything you hear from Blue Tech or the FDA? We want to be in the loop."

"That's a promise," replied Greg. "We'll send you a report monthly, on the first of every month. And if there are any significant developments, we'll tell you about those immediately, whether they're good or bad."

"Any other questions?" Greg looked at all of the small screens and no responses. "OK, thanks in advance for your patience. We will be in touch."

PART II

CHAPTER 33

Lou was figuring out the eighth race at Delaware Park – the feature race that day – from his barstool at the club. It was two o'clock in the afternoon. Normally, he didn't spend much time in the club during the afternoon, but he wanted to catch up with Carmine before the race.

The main door opened and somebody walked in, but it wasn't Carmine.

"Private club, sorry," said Tommy. This guy was blond, wearing khakis and a blue windbreaker, and carrying an envelope.

"Just here to leave something for somebody," said the man. When he reached the bar, he turned to Lou and said, "Mr. Incaviglia, you are hereby served with process," and thrust the envelope into Lou's hands. On closer inspection, the guy's windbreaker said "Constable." The man turned and left without saying another word.

"What the fuck?" muttered Lou. His first thought was that Officer Clayton Smith had figured out a way to make trouble for him for trespassing. No limit to what those pricks will do when they're holding a grudge.

But the grudge wasn't Officer Smith's. Inside the envelope was a document of twenty or thirty pages. On the first page, Lou read, "Salvatore Paglia vs. Louis C. Incaviglia." A lawsuit. The case had been filed in the United States District Court for the Eastern District of Pennsylvania.

"Lou, what's going on?" asked Tommy.

"I'm not sure," Lou replied. "I gotta go home and read. I'll prolly see you tonight." With that, Lou got up from his barstool, found his way through the front door of the club, and shuffled home in a fog. He figured that the case must have something to do with 3Device – he hadn't had any other recent interaction with Sal Paglia – but he couldn't imagine why he was being sued.

When he got home, he threw the document on the table in the kitchen and made himself a cup of coffee. He thought about calling Olivia, or even Greg, but he didn't know enough yet. He started reading, but he couldn't make any sense of what the document said. And then he thought of Nigel Branca.

Lou called the club. "Tommy, did Nigel come in by any chance?"

"No, haven't seen him. Lou, what's going on, what's this all about?"

"I'll let you know as soon as I figure it out myself. Can you see if anyone has Nigel's cell phone number?"

"Let me see. 'Yo, listen up. Does anybody have Nigel Branca's cell phone number?'" Lou heard some mumbles, and finally Tommy came back on the phone.

"I got it, Lenny had it. 610-343-8013."

"Thanks, Tommy. I'll talk to you later."

Lou immediately dialed Nigel's number. He wasn't expecting to reach him, because Nigel wouldn't recognize his number, and probably wouldn't pick up. But at least he got as far as voicemail, and had a chance to leave a message. "Nigel, this is Lou Incaviglia. Please give me a call as soon as you can. My number will be in your phone log."

Lou took a deep breath, let it out, and busied himself making a cup of coffee. He picked up the document to read some more, but finally said, "Fuck it." He didn't process information that way. He needed Nigel to tell him what the papers said, and then, he was pretty sure, he'd be able understand what Sal was up to.

Forty-five long minutes later, Nigel called him back. Lou explained what had happened. "This thing says I sold stock to Sal Paglia and broke the law somehow. It says right on the first page that it's a 'Civil Action,' so I don't think anybody's trying to lock me up. Right at the top of page one it says, 'In the United States District Court for the Eastern District of Pennsylvania.'" Nigel said "mmm-hmmm" a lot, but not much more.

"OK, I gotta read what you have," said Nigel, finally. "Can you meet me at the Swede Street Diner in a half hour? Bring the envelope?"

"Sure, I'll be there," said Lou. "Buy you an early dinner. And thanks."

CHAPTER 34

Lou and Nigel were at a booth at the back of the diner. They ordered coffee and told the Greek waiter they'd probably order some dinner in a while. Nigel had been reading for ten minutes and hadn't looked up. He took four sips from a little metal flask, about two and a half minutes between each sip. Lou saw him flip the last page.

"Wow, this is fucked up," Nigel began. "Did you piss on his shoes or something? He is really looking to hurt you."

Lou nodded. "Yeah. But what's it say, what's it all about?"

Nigel collected his thoughts. "This is a complaint in a federal lawsuit for securities fraud. The plaintiff, Sal Paglia, is represented by Major, Boardman & Patterson, one of the biggest, most prestigious firms in Pennsylvania. It's been around for 150 years. The complaint says you sold Sal Paglia some shares in this 3Device company, and told a bunch of lies to persuade him to buy them. It also says you failed to tell him that the FDA was likely to disapprove the artificial knee, even though you had reason to know about that fact."

"None of that is true," said Lou.

Nigel ignored him. "I figured from what you told me on the phone that this was likely to be a normal federal securities fraud case, so I printed out a copy of the law that he's relying on. It's called '10b-5,' and it's short, I'll read it to you. 'It shall be unlawful for any person, directly or indirectly, by the use of any means or instrumentality of interstate commerce, or of the mails or of any facility of any national securities exchange, to employ any device, scheme, or artifice to defraud; to make any untrue statement of a material fact or to omit to state a material fact necessary in order to make the statements made, in the light of the circumstances under which they were made, not misleading; or to engage in any act, practice, or course of business which operates or would operate as a fraud or deceit upon any person, in connection with the purchase or sale of any security.'"

"I didn't understand a word of that," said Lou.

"Well, that's the basic federal rule," Nigel replied. "And then he makes a bunch of similar claims under Pennsylvania state law."

"What does this mean, exactly?" asked Lou. "Did a judge write this? When are they gonna let me tell my side of the story?"

"The complaint is written by the plaintiff's lawyer," Nigel said. "The plaintiff is the party bringing the case, and the complaint is the very first document filed. It lays out all of the facts that the plaintiff is claiming are true, and all of the damages that he wants from the defendant. But it's just a bunch of allegations. The minute you deny them – and you'll file what's called an 'answer' to do that — the battle is on. The complaint is then just another piece of paper. It may be the most important piece of paper in the case, but the court isn't assuming that anything in there is true. That's up to the jury."

"You said he's saying I told a bunch of lies," said Lou.

"He's describing two significant conversations he had with you about the shares. In the first one, he says you made a pitch to him to buy your shares. He says he asked you all sorts of questions, and you claimed 3Device was a private company, but you'd get him the answers to his questions and report back. He says you had a second conversation where you gave him all his answers, but he says just about everything you told him was false."

"I didn't give him *any* information," said Lou. "He didn't wanna hear it."

"He says you promised him a lot of things that weren't true." Nigel began to count on his fingers. "He says you told him that the company was going to be making three hundred and fifty million dollars a year within two years. He says you told him they had a patent on the knee, and apparently they didn't, it was apparently just a revocable license. But the big thing is, he said you said that FDA approval was virtually guaranteed, and that the company was going to go to market with its knee within a matter of weeks. He says you knew, when you told him that, that it was false. He says the FDA had already told the company that the FDA wanted to 'go slow' on medical devices created by 3D printing."

"All of that is bullshit," said Lou. "Did you notice the stuff about these other shares he bought, from Paul what's-his-name?" asked Lou.

"Well, yeah, that was kind of surprising for this kind of case," replied Nigel. "It says he bought shares from somebody else – this Paul Smythe guy – on the basis of the things you told him.

"The reason *that's* kind of weird is that the law says that if he's going to sue you for false statements, those statements have to be made 'in connection with' a sale and purchase of securities. Your shares in 3Device are securities. But he's kind of fudging the 'in connection with' requirement here. He says he told you that he was interested in more shares than you owned, and that you recommended that he talk to this Paul Smythe guy. He claims you said that Paul Smythe was going to be eager to sell, and that you would put in a good word for Sal with him. He said you'd look for a little commission from Paul Smythe if the deal between Paglia and Smythe ever happened. He also said you were doing all this to benefit your son-in-law and your daughter."

Lou shook his head. "Nigel, I don't know what to say. None of those conversations ever happened. He came to me about the shares, I wasn't trying to sell him. I don't even know what the FDA is. I didn't know anything about a patent. I don't know who Paul what's-his-name is, and I didn't recommend that Sal talk to him."

Nigel looked across the table at Lou for a long moment. "Stick with that," he said, finally.

"No, I mean it, goddammit. He's making up conversations that never happened."

"Well, he's described these imaginary conversations in elaborate detail. They say in my business that you always want a client to tell you the truth. That, my friend, is bullshit. Sometimes the truth isn't very helpful. So I choose to believe you, because 'these conversations never happened' will be a complete and total defense if the jury believes you. Just make them believe you." Nigel pulled out a pencil to write something down. "I think you need to talk to Martin Hampshire. His firm is called Stein & Hampshire. His office is right across the street from the Montgomery County Courthouse. His number will be on their website. I know he does this kind of work for plaintiffs, and I imagine he'll be willing to help you."

Lou's face fell a notch. "Does that mean you won't represent me?"

"I can't take a case like this," replied Nigel. "You need to find somebody who does this kind of work."

"Listen, Nigel, this don't seem to me to be a regular case," Lou said quickly. "He can't get blood out of a turnip. I got nothin'. I may not even fight the case. And if I do, I won't be asking you to do nothin' except the minimum amount you need to do to keep me in the case. It should be pretty simple for you. All I really want to do is tell the judge that these conversations never happened, and maybe he'll believe me."

"Judge could be a woman," said Nigel.

"Yeah, whatever. The point is, it doesn't look like Sal is suing the company, or my son-in-law." Lou paused. "By the way, do you have any theory on that? Why is he suing me instead of my son-in-law, or his company?"

"Because he didn't buy any shares from your son-in-law, and presumably never had any conversations with him before he bought your shares. That's the 'in connection with' requirement. But you raise a good point. He must have some kind of ulterior motive to be suing you, knowing he can't get anything from you. He's probably assuming your son-in-law is going to step up – that's probably why he mentioned him in the complaint. Maybe he's thinking he's going to settle with your son-in-law."

"That brings me around to what I been getting at," Lou replied. "I feel shitty enough about this already. My daughter and son-in-law are gonna want to pay for my defense, and I'm not gonna let 'em. They're trying to have a baby, and the last thing they need is to have to worry about this fucking thing. Nigel, here's what I have to offer. I have the $15,000 that Sal paid me for those shares, still sittin' in the bank. I'll give you that as a retainer. And you can have the other 15 shares of 3Device that I still own. Maybe they'll be worth something someday. I promise you if Sal's lawyers start to over-whelm you, we'll sit back down at this table and I'll let you withdraw from the case. I'll just surrender, or represent myself, or whatever. I don't care if I lose. But what this motherfucker is doing is wrong. I want him to have to testify to this bullshit under oath, and then I'm gonna prove, somehow, that he's a fuckin' liar. I need your help to do that."

Nigel knew that he was about to make a big mistake. His stomach might not survive a case like this without blowing out, not to mention his liver and his heart. But part of him thought about what he had pissed away when he was thirty years old, and this case represented one last opportunity, perhaps, to reclaim a little of what once was.

"Fuck it, OK," he said. "I want the $15,000 by the end of the week, and I'm going to figure out ways for you to help support your own defense. I'm going to make you go to the FedEx Office Store for copies, and stuff envelopes, and deliver stuff, even if you'd rather be at the racetrack. And I'll take those shares."

"Thank you, Nigel," said Lou.

"I must be out of my fucking mind."

They never did order dinner, which was fine by Nigel. He planned to go home, turn on the TV, and drink. He felt bad for Lou Incaviglia. Poor bastard, he didn't deserve this, even if he did probably shoot off his mouth at the club. Sal Paglia was a piece of work.

CHAPTER 35

Lou pulled up to the house in Villanova and turned into the driveway. He had told Olivia that he needed to talk with both of them, but he wouldn't say about what.

Olivia had sensed he was worried, and was terrified that he was on his way over to tell them about some sort of diagnosis he'd just received. She kept glancing out the front window, looking for his car. When he turned into the driveway, she walked over to the front door and stepped onto the porch. Greg was in the kitchen chopping some celery.

"Hi Honey," said Lou as he stepped onto the porch. "Are youse both here?"

"Yeah, Greg's in the kitchen. What's going on?" Olivia was clearly concerned, and Lou guessed what she might be thinking.

"I'm fine, don't worry. This is about Sal Paglia and 3Device. I'll explain to you and Greg together." Olivia noticed that he was carrying an envelope. She led him down the hallway to the kitchen, apprehensively.

"Hi Greg," said Lou.

"Hi Lou," Greg replied. "Livvie told me you wanted to talk. Sounds serious."

As Lou sat at the kitchen counter, Olivia opened a bottle of Pabst Blue Ribbon and handed it to him. She kept PBR on hand especially for her dad.

"Yeah, it's serious, and I don't even know where to start," Lou replied. "Can I ask you to read something, and then we'll talk about it?"

"OK, sure," Greg replied. Olivia nodded.

Lou pulled the complaint from the envelope and handed it to Greg. He handed another copy to Olivia. Both began to read. Each decided, independently, that commentary wasn't going to help. They read quietly, and finished at about the same time. Lou was watching the birds at the bird feeder outside the kitchen window. One of them was an Eastern Bluebird, back from wherever they had all gone to.

"I'm not surprised," said Greg, finally. "He pretty much warned us at the last shareholders' meeting that this might be coming."

Lou was surprised, and it showed. "Really? What happened?"

"We didn't want you to worry about it," Greg responded. "It wasn't your fault. Mr. Paglia got very angry when we told him that the FDA had put our application on hold. And it was worse than that, because he had just made a speech about how happy he was to be a new shareholder in the company because the company's prospects were so good. He was embarrassed, and I think he thought we had made a chump out of him. It wasn't pretty. But none of that had anything to do with you."

"I didn't want nothin' like this to happen," said Lou, glumly. "I'm sorry I just didn't say 'no' to begin with. It's my fault for bringing this guy to you."

"Lou, let me say this right up front," Greg replied. "I know you didn't say any of the things that this complaint says you said. We knew you were ambivalent about bringing this guy to us, and we knew you didn't do anything to try to persuade him – or us, for that matter. Why would you have? There was no upside for you – fifteen grand is not that much money. And you were worried about hurting Olivia's feelings by selling the shares she gave you. But the real kicker – and what shows he's just making stuff up – is this bullshit about Paul Smythe. Paul and you don't know each other, and the idea that you would have been hitting him up for a finder's fee is just ridiculous." Greg slapped at the back of twenty pages of federal complaint. "You didn't cause this."

"Daddy, I'm so sorry this is happening," said Olivia. "We'll get you out of this somehow. I'll find you the best lawyer in Pennsylvania, and we'll fight this thing. Greg is right, you didn't cause this. This is just an evil man who wants to hurt you — and us. He won't win."

Lou felt like an anvil had been lifted off his chest. He had dreaded their reaction, especially Greg's. He was as surprised as he could possibly have been. He took a sip of his beer and thought about what to say next.

"I love you both," he said. "And I'm sorry about this. I know you're gonna wanna argue with me about what I'm about to say, but I'm not gonna change my mind. I knew it coming over here. I'm not gonna let either of you get involved with defending this thing, and I'm not gonna let 3Device help either."

"But we want to be involved, Daddy," Olivia replied.

"That would be crazy," Lou replied. "Sal Paglia left Greg and the company out of this case, and Nigel Branca – he's my lawyer – he told me why. You didn't talk to Sal before he bought his shares, and there's nothing he can say about you doin' somethin' wrong. He *wants* you to get involved, so he can squeeze you. The best way to deal with that – the only way – is for you to stay as far away from this case as you can. I'm a turnip, and he can't get no blood outta me. Let's leave it like that. It'll drive him nuts."

Greg and Olivia looked at each other, and then at Lou. Neither could think of anything to say.

CHAPTER 36

G reg's administrative assistant let him know that Sal Paglia was holding on Line 1. Greg was surprised by the call, and briefly considered
refusing it. He was not looking forward to the conversation.

"I'm sure you've heard about my lawsuit against your father-in-law,"
Sal Paglia began.

"Yes," Greg replied.

"Well, I'm still a shareholder of 3Device," Sal continued, "and you
and Stein owe me fiduciary duties. One of those obligations is to consider
the good-faith offer I'm about to make you."

"I'm not sure I agree with that assessment of our fiduciary duties, but
I'm listening," Greg replied.

"I am about to tie you up in discovery in federal court. I have a right
to take your deposition, and Stein's deposition. I can review all records about
the knee and your application to the FDA, which amounts to just about
every document you have. I can review a lot of records of 3D Prosthetics,
because you're providing services to your subsidiary. While I'm doing that,
you're going to be so busy complying with subpoenas that you'll half way
forget what business you're in."

"So far, that doesn't sound like much of an offer."

"I'm getting to that. Your other problem with my lawsuit is that I'm
going to be taking depositions from your shareholders. They're going to be
a lot more pissed at you than they are already. I'm gonna prove that a lot of

your shareholders were given information about the company that I never got from your father-in-law. If I had known what they knew, I would have reconsidered the investment."

"You never asked for any information."

"Sure I did, I asked for it from your father-in-law, but that's not the point. My lawyer says that it was your father-in-law's obligation to tell me everything about the company whether I asked for it or not. And speaking of lawyers, bear in mind that you'll be paying a bunch of lawyers a lot of money to help you compile documents, and they'll need to prepare for and attend your depositions. It's going to cost you a fortune, for no benefit whatsoever."

"Well, that pretty much sums up lawyers in one sentence," Greg replied. "If you're going to do this, you're going to do it, I can't stop you."

"Yes you can. Here's my offer to make all those problems go away. You can have your choice. You can pay me one million dollars, cash, which represents what my shares would have been worth if everything your father-in-law said had been true. That's actually a bargain price, because if he had been telling the truth, I was going to make a lot more money than that. And I want my attorneys' fees reimbursed.

"Your second option is a lot less expensive, cash-wise. I want a little more than two thirds of your 51% stake in 3Device. Sign over 1,080 of your shares to me, which will give me about 51% ownership. I'll control the company. In the meantime, you keep doing what you're doing. If the company solves its problems, we all win. You will still own about 15% of the company, and I'll let you and Stein take a reasonable salary. But if the FDA doesn't approve the knee within, let's say, two years, you'll owe me my $515,000 back. That's how much I paid for my shares when I bought them from Incaviglia and Smythe. And of course I'll keep my shares, but they won't be worth anything, except whatever the company owns in intellectual property.

"And finally – and this might be the most important point for your wife – if you accept either option, I'll give your father-in-law a release, and dismiss my lawsuit against him.

"I can put all that in writing," Sal continued, "but I wanted you to begin to think about it. If you want to keep your little company above water, you really ought to accept one option or the other."

Greg was dumbfounded, and took a few moments to collect his thoughts. "Mr. Paglia, it is always a privilege to be able to discuss the business of 3Device with one of our shareholders. But I don't see how paying you a million bucks is a better deal for us than paying our lawyers less than a tenth of that to respond to your subpoenas. So, we reject both options."

"OK pretty boy, act like a tough guy. But tell me how you'll feel – and how your wife is gonna feel – when I've got a judgment against your father-in-law, and every month when his social security check hits his bank account, I'm gonna serve a new levy on his bank. I'll take his car, if he still has one. And he will never, ever be able to go to the racetrack again, because he won't have enough money to make a five-dollar bet. And did I mention, as a practical matter he won't be able to sell his house, because I'll be entitled to all the proceeds from any sale. And ask your lawyer – he won't be able to declare bankruptcy, because you can't get a fraud judgment discharged in bankruptcy. He'll be stuck with me and my lawyers for the rest of his life. Just think about that for a couple of days, talk it over with your lovely wife. My offer is going to look a lot better after you've thought about it." Sal hung up, leaving Greg staring at a silent handset.

Greg had no idea what he was going to say to Olivia.

CHAPTER 37

"So, an answer to a complaint is a really simple document," said Nigel. "We go through their complaint paragraph by paragraph – you notice that all the paragraphs are numbered – and we say 'admitted' or 'denied' in response to every one. Then we just file the answer with the Clerk of Court." Nigel was sitting with Lou in the Swede Street Diner. Lou was working on a bagel with cream cheese. Nigel had his flask. It was 30 days since Sal Paglia's complaint had been handed to Lou at the club, and the answer was due to be filed that day.

"OK, but why did you need to talk to me?" asked Lou.

"Well, because it's your answer. I'm supposed to check with you about whether a statement in the complaint is true or false. I write your answers down and file the answer with the court."

"This burns my ass to have to do this."

"Don't be such a baby," said Nigel. "I never said you wouldn't have to do anything. In fact, I told you there's a lot you need to do."

Lou blew out some air. "OK, shit. Let's do it."

Nigel took Lou through all 125 paragraphs of the complaint and wrote down Lou's responses. They would say "admitted" in response to the paragraphs alleging that Lou sold the shares, and they would say "denied" in response to all of the conversations that Sal's complaint described. In federal practice, Nigel explained, the defendant doesn't have to provide his own version of what the participants in a conversation actually said. All the defendant has to do, if he disagrees with any of the words described, is to say, "Denied." Easy. And half of Sal's complaint consisted of paragraphs describing Lou's alleged statements to Sal. Nigel's suggested response to all of those paragraphs: "Denied."

"Admitted" and "denied" were reserved for factual allegations. Where a paragraph described one of the plaintiff's legal theories, Nigel responded, "This averment is a conclusion of law to which no response is required. To the extent a response is required, the averment is denied." Fuck you, in other words.

Lou had barely finished his second bagel when Nigel put down his pencil. "OK, that's one through 125. We're done. I'm going to go type this up, and I'll meet you at your place after lunch."

"Can I go to the track this afternoon?" asked Lou.

"Nope. I have to go downtown to Sixth and Market in Philly to sign up for electronic filing," said Nigel. "I can't file your answer to the complaint until the court has my signature and a bunch of other information on file. And then I'll file a pdf version of the answer electronically. I need you to drive me." Lou paid the check, as per the universal American rule applied by lawyers and clients alike. Lawyers sometimes pretend to offer to pay, but Nigel liked the general rule the way it was.

As promised, Nigel appeared on Lou's stoop early that afternoon. "Let's go."

They got in Lou's Mercury and headed toward the Schuylkill Expressway. "That's my brick," said Lou, as they passed a Presbyterian church in Plymouth Township. He would have tipped his cigar toward the church if he had had one. But Lou had never smoked in his Mercury Grand Marquis. Instead, he chewed gum relentlessly as he drove.

"I saw Sal at the club the other day," said Nigel.

"I'm glad I missed him," Lou replied.

"He seemed uncomfortable," Nigel continued. "He would say a few words to people, and get a few words back, but he almost seemed like he was in a bubble. I wonder if this case is affecting how people treat him."

"A course it is," said Lou. "How could it not? People hate shit like this. They stay away. Just human nature."

CHAPTER 38

O livia couldn't sleep, so she woke Greg up. That was their deal.

"I'm afraid this is going to kill him," she said.

"Me too." Greg may have been half awake himself.

"Isn't there something we can do?"

"I don't know, Honey, I really don't. I've talked to our lawyers, but they specialize in health care and business law. To them, any litigation is a big dumpster fire. They see a lot of problems if we get involved, and they don't see any upside. They're looking out for 3D Prosthetics and 3Device, and from their perspective it's just common sense to stay away from this case. They're not being paid to worry about Lou."

"Suppose we stay below the radar. Why can't we give him money to hire a better lawyer?"

"If we gave him money from the company, we'd be breaching our fiduciary obligations to our shareholders. The lawyers are telling me the company is not supposed to get involved in disputes between its own shareholders."

"Well, why can't we give him money from our personal funds?"

Greg thought for a second. "We could, I suppose, but then we're back to Square One anyway. Your dad says he's going to stop defending the case if we try to pay for his defense, and, as far as I know, that's where he still is."

"I'll just change his mind," said Olivia.

"Good luck with that. It'll be the first time *that's* ever happened. And I have to believe Sal Paglia will know we're paying for the lawyers, and he'll try to use that fact against Lou. He's already threatened to take our depositions, and the first thing he's going to ask us is whether we're paying for Lou's defense."

"So what? How is that going to help him?"

"I think he's going to want to claim that we were all in this together, trying to bring Sal into the company for our own purposes. And we're paying for Lou's lawyers to try to cover it all up. His case looks a lot stronger if it's Sal Paglia from Norristown against the hedge fund people from Villanova. Our lawyers are saying he's probably looking for ways to bring us into the suit."

"Can you talk to the lawyers again? Ask them if I can pay for the defense."

"I can do that. But that still doesn't solve the real problem. Your dad doesn't want you anywhere near this case."

Olivia was silent for a long moment. "I can do something else. I think I'll talk to Uncle Tony to see whether his lawyer can give me some advice. He's going to be a lot better tuned in to this kind of stuff than your lawyers would be."

Greg raised an eyebrow. And shook his head slightly. It was dark, so Olivia couldn't see his face. "If you do that, please don't do anything else until we've talked about it. Bringing Tony and his people – and especially his lawyer – into the case might complicate it in ways we can't predict."

"All I would want to do is talk to his lawyer. I'm not going to ask any lawyer to get directly involved."

"When you think about it, Lou's instincts are very good," Greg replied. "He knows that Sal Paglia would have sued the company – and us – if he could have. If Lou keeps the case small, he frustrates everything that Sal is trying to accomplish. Maybe we can help your dad more after he loses – if and when he loses – than we possibly could while the case is still going on. Your father is a smart guy, especially when it comes to people. His instincts seem spot on right now."

"Sal Paglia may be able to find out if we're spending money on this," said Olivia. "I don't know. But that's not all we can do. He can't follow me around, and he's not tapping my phone. I can help in the background, even if my dad doesn't change his mind about the legal fees. What do you think?"

"Not yet," said Greg. "Let's wait and see. Please."

CHAPTER 39

Walnut Street in Norristown was quiet. When the weather gets hot, you hear window units trying to cool upstairs bedrooms — but you don't hear kids. The kids are staring at Youtube or TikTok, or whatever. Nigel walked down the block to Lou's house and rapped on the screen door. He was feeling sweaty and out of sorts.

"Nigel, how you doin'?" said Lou as he opened the door. "Come on in." Lou led Nigel through the living room and dining room and back to the kitchen. "Want a beer?"

"That would be great," said Nigel. "Thanks."

Lou pulled a bottle of Pabst from the refrigerator as Nigel unscrewed his flask and sat down at the kitchen table. Lou sat down across from him. Nigel poured a splash of whiskey from his flask into the beer, and took a long gulp from the bottle. Arbitrary sequencing of units of alcohol. He pulled a folded piece of paper from his front pocket.

"We got this from Sal's lawyer," said Nigel, placing the document in front of Lou. "His name is Palmer Eastman. I looked him up. His specialty is corporate law – contracts and stuff – but he used to be a litigator when he was younger, and apparently he still handles a lawsuit every once in a while. When you're a senior partner at a big firm, you can do whatever you want."

"What is this paper?" asked Lou.

"It's a deposition notice," Nigel replied.

"What's a deposition notice?" asked Lou as he opened his own bottle.

"It means they're setting a place and time for taking your deposition. They've scheduled it for 10:00 in the morning on August 23, down at Major Boardman's offices in Center City. They received our answer and then gave us five days' notice of the deposition date. Hardball."

"Can they do that? Do I have to show up?" asked Lou.

"They can, and you do," Nigel replied. "They should have given you more notice, but to get it postponed, I would have to file a motion for a protective order. You and I agreed that I'm not going to be filing any motions."

"What's a deposition?" asked Lou.

"Aw, man, where do you want me to start? It's complicated."

"I'm retired. I got time."

Nigel took another long sip. "A deposition is when they take your testimony about the case before trial. You'll be under oath, and the testimony will be recorded and later transcribed. Sal's lawyer will be asking you questions, and you'll be answering. There's no judge present, but there is a court reporter. It's all done by the lawyers, who are supposed to follow the rules. In practice, a deposition usually becomes a huge cluster fuck with lawyers yelling at each other, and the questioning goes on forever. Most lawyers get paid by the hour, and they have to build up their fees."

"What's the point?" asked Lou.

"Well, a deposition serves two main purposes in a lawsuit," Nigel replied. "First, it lets a party find out what a witness – usually an opposing witness – has to say about the facts of the case. You find out what the other side's story is going to be. The second purpose is to lock the other side into a position in advance of trial. The witness is *able* to change his story between the deposition and trial, but as a practical matter he can't. He would risk a perjury charge, and the judge or the jury is not going to believe much of the story he's telling at trial if he told a different story under oath at his deposition."

"Sal already knows what I'm gonna say. It seems stupid for him to be paying a lawyer to find out what he already knows."

"Of course it's stupid," Nigel replied. "Everything about litigation is stupid."

"Why do we hafta have a trial? Why don't they just take the deposition transcripts and give 'em to the judge?"

"Interesting you should say that," said Nigel, "because the transcripts get used a lot at trial. Anything a party says at a deposition – the parties here are you and Sal – can be used at trial by the adverse party if it's relevant. But there's a lot of stuff that comes up at a deposition that isn't relevant to the case and can't be used at trial. And a lot of other stuff at the deposition, even though it might be relevant, isn't admissible under the rules of evidence. Hearsay, that kind of thing."

"Is Sal gonna be there?"

"Yes, and you'll be present at his deposition, if we take it."

"We might take his deposition? Why?"

"Well, I haven't decided yet. Sal recounted both of the conversations you supposedly had right in the complaint. He had to do that because he's obliged to plead fraud 'with particularity.' He's already told us his story about what you supposedly said to him to get him to buy the shares. So I might just want to save my questioning until I cross-examine him at trial. If I question him at a deposition, he's going to know what to expect from me at trial. If I skip the deposition, he won't."

"Well then, why are you considering taking his deposition?" asked Lou.

"Same reasons I just mentioned. His whole case is based on his descriptions of what you said to him during two conversations in the club. I think it's impossible for anybody to remember conversations exactly, and I would be counting on the fact that there will be some variations between his testimony at deposition and his testimony at trial. That's good for us, because it undermines his credibility."

"He's got no credibility to begin with, as far as I'm concerned," said Lou.

"The jury doesn't know that," Nigel replied. "They'll be meeting him for the first time. Anyway, the other thing I'd be doing by taking his deposition is locking him in. I'd ask him six different ways, 'So, is there anything else Mr. Incaviglia said to you?' When he finally says, 'No, that's all I can remember,' we've got him. It makes it very hard for him, at trial, to testify about something else you supposedly said, because he would have to explain why he can remember it at trial but couldn't remember it at his deposition."

"Which way are you leaning?"

"I'm going to decide after your deposition. Right now, I'm leaning toward taking Sal's deposition. I want to see what kind of witness he'll make. But I might not. We can send them a deposition notice and withdraw it later if we decide not to."

"Is there any chance they'll decide not to take my deposition?"

"No. They haven't heard your side of the story. Our answer didn't tell them anything except that we deny what Sal is saying. They need to hear what you have to say."

"OK. But this is peak racing season, and there will be races I won't wanna miss. You and I won't have to get together before the deposition, will we?"

Nigel chuckled. "*Au contraire.* We'll have to do at least a couple of long prep sessions in five short days, and you're going to be sick of my face by the time the deposition starts. I need to hear your side of this before they do, and I need to give you a sense of what it's going to feel like when he's questioning you. If you can answer my questions in a prep session, you can answer his questions during the deposition. The deposition is Wednesday. Let's plan on sitting down on Monday and Tuesday."

"I feel bad about taking up all your time," said Lou. "Are you handling any of your regular cases while all this is going on?"

"No. But I hate those cases anyway."

Lou hesitated "Nigel, I appreciate what you're doin' for me. This has got to be wreckin' your stomach."

"It is, but only 'cause I want to win so bad."

Lawyers, thought Lou. All they care about is winning. But, come to think of it, why would you want your own lawyer to care about anything else?

CHAPTER 40

"Good morning, Olivia, your uncle told me you'd be calling." Enrico "Rick" Deterra was Tony Abruzzi's lawyer. He was happy to pick up Olivia's call when his secretary told him Olivia was holding.

"Mr. Deterra, good morning," Olivia began. "Thanks for making some time for me. I just need some advice, if that's OK."

"Sure, anything I can do to help. What's the problem?"

"In a nutshell, my father is being sued for securities fraud by Sal Paglia, the big road construction guy. Mr. Paglia claims that my dad lied to him in connection with a sale of stock that my dad held in a privately owned company."

"Who is representing your dad?" asked Rick Deterra.

"Nigel Branca, from Norristown."

"Oh my God, Nigel was a year ahead of me in law school. I remember he worked in a big firm in Center City after he got out. I lost track of him."

"He's a solo practitioner now. And he's up against Major Boardman. They're representing Mr. Paglia."

"Ouch. That's a mismatch, for sure."

"Well, that's why I'm calling. My dad doesn't have much money or property, and he wants us to stay away from the case. My dad and my husband think this Paglia guy is suing my dad to try to squeeze my husband

and me. My husband owns the company that issued the stock involved in this case."

"Is this a big company, a start up, or what?" asked the lawyer.

"It's a start up," Olivia replied, "and my husband has put some money in it."

"How about the two of you? Are you fat targets, so to speak?"

"We're not super rich, but we're doing pretty well. We think Sal Paglia would like to see us involved, maybe as defendants or something. The reason I'm calling is to ask whether I can pay for my dad's legal fees with a reputable firm without getting my husband and me involved in the case."

Rick Deterra thought for a moment. "I've been a litigator a long time, and basically all I can tell you is that I'm not sure. But if I had to guess I would say that Mr. Paglia would probably be entitled to find out during discovery whether people close to the company are paying for your father's defense. And if he finds out you are, he's probably going to claim that the fraud he's alleging in his complaint was the result of a conspiracy between your dad and your husband. As lawyers like to say, you can sue anybody for anything. Even if he hasn't sued you yet, he still might, and paying for your dad's defense could hasten that decision."

"Isn't there *something* I can do to help my father?" Olivia heard herself sounding more plaintive than she wanted to.

"Nothing specific. I think your dad's instincts are right, and if you haven't been sued you should stay clear. But remember that Sal Paglia is doing something really dumb right now. He's spending a lot of money – Major Boardman is a really expensive firm, and they bill by the hour. Even if he wins, it sounds like he's never going to get his money back.

"It's my experience that, during litigation, most clients can only sustain anger for so long. They begin a case furious that they're having to sue, or being sued, and they tell me, 'I don't care what it costs, I just want to have a trial to prove I'm right.' Six months later, they start to complain about the legal fees. A year later, they're mad because they're still spending massive amounts of money, the case still hasn't been scheduled for trial, and the other side is still digging into their affairs. Discovery can be really intrusive. And at the end of the day, they come into my office and they say, 'Please just settle this thing, I can't stand this anymore.'

"I don't have any magic formula. I don't know how you make Sal Paglia realize that his anger isn't worth what he's paying to sustain it. I don't know how you make litigation more unpleasant for him than it already is. But if you can think of something – anything to make him regret suing your dad – the litigation will end. It always does."

Olivia thanked Rick Deterra for his time and advice and cradled her landline at Biddle & Co. She found it interesting that she had asked for legal advice, and he responded mostly with thoughts about what made people tick. So Olivia began to think about what made Sal Paglia tick.

CHAPTER 41

Lou and Nigel were riding in Lou's Mercury again, on their way to Lou's deposition in Center City Philadelphia. The deposition was to be held in a conference room in the offices of Major, Boardman & Patterson, LLP, near Logan Square.

As they were passing a power company substation in Conshohocken, Lou motioned and said, "That's my brick." Nigel was impressed with the workmanship.

Nigel had met with Lou twice to prepare for Lou's deposition, but he had the sense that his efforts to prep his witness were not sinking in. The time together in the car – about a 45-minute trip during morning rush hour – was his last, best opportunity.

"Lou, I've been thinking about how to put your mind in the right place," Nigel began. "I think I've been too focused on the facts, and I haven't talked enough about how you should handle the questioning."

"OK."

"It'd be normal for you to figure that this is your big chance, finally, to tell your side of the story, and you're going to want to lay out for them all the reasons that their case is bullshit. You're going to want to defend yourself. So what I'm going to ask you to do is completely counter-intuitive. I'm going to ask you to limit just about every one of your answers to four possible responses: 'Yes.' 'No.' 'I don't know.' Or, 'I don't recall.'"

"Yes. No. I don't know. I don't recall," Lou repeated.

"Don't use 'I don't recall' if you really do remember. But if you forget something, or don't remember it clearly, just say 'I don't recall,' and I'll deal with it later. If we ever have to explain why you somehow remembered a fact after the deposition, we'll try to come up with a reason.

"Sal's lawyer's job today is to get you talking, so he can figure out what your response to their story might be. The more you say, the more they know, and the more they've pinned you down. They know you're going to deny everything. You already have, in your answer. But they also know it's Sal's word against yours, so your defending yourself and calling Sal a liar isn't going to bother them a bit. They want to get you talking so that when they get to trial, Sal can tailor all of his lies to the things they know you're going to say.

"Let me give you a concrete example of why those four answers – yes, no, I don't know, I don't recall – are going to give them fits. You're going to hear questions like this from Sal's lawyer: 'Mr. Incaviglia, did you give a copy of the company's Shareholders' Agreement to Mr. Paglia before you sold shares to him?' And you're going to want to say, 'No, but I told him he was going to have to sign some paperwork when he received the shares.' And he'll ask, 'Did you tell him that the Shareholders' Agreement restricted his ability to resell his shares to somebody else if he wanted to get out of the investment?' and you'll want to say, 'No, but I assumed he knew that, because he knew I had to get permission to sell to him.'

"So right there, they got a couple of things from you they can use. You knew there was this very important agreement he was going to have to sign, but you didn't even give poor Sal a copy before you took his check. What were you trying to hide, you swindler? And you dragged poor Sal into his deal without telling him he couldn't get out. You just 'assumed' he was going to guess something that you intentionally refused to tell him."

Lou nodded. Nigel was making sense.

"So let's look at how it works when you do it right. He asks you, 'Did you give him a copy of the Shareholders' Agreement?' You respond, 'No.' Just

'No.' And he'll ask, 'Did you tell him the Shareholders' Agreement restricted his ability to resell his shares?' and you'll say, 'No.' Chances are, he'll pocket those answers and move on to something else, because he thinks he's just proved a couple of non-disclosures in connection with the sale. And if he lets you keep talking, your answer may get worse for him. But he doesn't really know what you're going to say at trial about the conversations you had with Sal. He has to go first at trial, because the plaintiff has the burden of proof, and he's going to make a big deal about the 'non-disclosures.' He testifies, "Mr. Incaviglia failed to give me a copy of the Shareholders' Agreement before I paid him for the shares, and I didn't know I wasn't going to be able to sell my shares if I wanted to.'

"So then what happens? It's your turn to testify at trial. You say to the jury, 'Well, I knew the company was going to demand that he sign the Shareholders' Agreement before they would issue him a share certificate. And I knew he ultimately signed the agreement. He's a very successful businessman, so I'm sure he read it, and I'm sure he read that part that restricts his ability to sell his shares. If the company *hadn't* issued the share certificate, I would have had to give back his check, which, by the way, I didn't deposit until after he got his shares. And he knew that *I* had to get permission to sell *my* shares to *him*, so of course he knew he would need permission if he ever wanted to sell. This whole ridiculous 'non-disclosure' is just a made-up thing.'"

"So part of his case crumbles, he looks like a putz, and he walks into that trap, all because you answered 'no' instead of 'no, but . . .' So don't try to defend yourself. Admit anything that's true, and don't explain anything. I hope we can prove at trial that *he* pushed this deal, not you. The testimony from the guys at the club – I must have talked to ten of them – is probably going to be helpful. They saw Sal calculating his profits out loud, and they saw that you weren't saying much of anything. But I don't want Sal and his lawyer to know anything about our defense they don't need to."

"Thanks for talking to those guys," said Lou. "I didn't hear nothin' about it, which means they're being careful."

"They should be. The guys at the club don't want any part of this. So, anyway, Sal's lawyer is going to ask you some sort of catch-all question, like 'Is there anything you haven't told us about during your testimony, or anything you want to add?' And all you have to say is 'no.' If he wants information, it's his job to ask the right questions. Don't volunteer anything. So what are your four answers that you have to use every chance you get?"

"Yes. No. I don't know. I don't recall," Lou replied.

"Good. You're ready," said Nigel.

CHAPTER 42

Nigel and Lou stepped from the elevators at 9:55 a.m. on the 40th floor, and turned into an open reception area. The windows looked out over City Hall and, farther east, the Delaware River. Everything was mahogany, steel and marble. Lou wondered who did the stone work, and speculated that Eddie Caprese might have been up here – it looked like his work.

Nigel approached the receptionist and told her that they were there for a ten o'clock deposition. If the suit Nigel was wearing was his best, he didn't have much in his closet. Lou was wearing a Hawaiian shirt. He nodded to the receptionist and added, "How you doin'?" She tilted her head a little bit and smiled. Lou often had that effect on people.

Before they had a chance to sit down, a young woman appeared from a hallway and said, "Mr. Branca, Mr. In-sa-vigg-lee-a, we're ready for you." She pronounced Incaviglia with a sibilant "c," a hard "g," and a two-syllable ending. A rare three-fer, in Lou's experience. He wondered whether Sal Paglia put her up to it.

The deposition was to take place in a conference room that looked out over North Philadelphia. You could see for twenty-five miles. Lou had taken Gabby up to the top of City Hall Tower in the 70's, but he'd never been in a Philadelphia skyscraper before. He felt like he could almost see his house in Norristown.

Nigel and Lou were seated at the main conference table by the young woman who had fetched them. There were eight seats, all big leather chairs, and some coffee and tea on a counter at the end of the room. Pretty much like one of those movies about Wall Street. What looked like recording equipment was set up at one end of the table. It was not lost on Lou that Sal and his lawyer had decided to make an entrance after Nigel and Lou were seated. Sal was six feet tall, but mentally he was 5'3".

A blond guy with perfect hair – presumably Sal's lawyer – came into the room, with Sal trailing after. "Good morning, gentlemen," said the blond guy. "I'm Palmer Eastman, and you both know Sal, of course. There is coffee and tea on the counter if you need it." He sat down directly across the table from Lou, and gestured Sal into the next seat. They didn't offer to shake hands. "Just bumped into the reporter, she'll be back from the ladies' room in a minute."

No one spoke. Lou looked across the table at Sal, who pretended to be involved with some paperwork. Lou thought he understood lies. He tried not to make a habit of it himself, but whaddaya gonna do if you're in a real jam? What he didn't understand was liars – people who lied without hesitation or regret, just to see if they could get away with it. Lou understood that Sal was enjoying telling lies. He didn't understand why.

The court reporter came in and sat down at her station. "Swear the witness, please," said Palmer Eastman, Esquire.

"Please raise your hand," said the court reporter. Lou raised his hand.

"Do you swear to tell the truth, the whole truth, and nothing but the truth, so help you God?"

"Yes," said Lou. Lou glanced around the room. Everybody else seemed more nervous than he felt. Laying bricks in mid-summer is hard. This wasn't hard. But he wondered whether he was missing something.

"Mr. Incaviglia, my name is Palmer Eastman, and I represent the plaintiff Salvatore Paglia in the matter of Salvatore Paglia vs. Louis C. Incaviglia, now pending in the United States District Court for the Eastern District of Pennsylvania. I'm going to ask you questions this morning, and you'll be responding to those questions under oath. I would ask you to answer verbally rather than just shaking your head or making some other gesture. The court reporter can only transcribe words, and a gesture is not a proper answer. If you don't understand a question, just let me know, and I will be happy to clarify it for you. If you need a bathroom break, just let us know."

Eastman turned to his notes, all nicely typed.

"What is your name, for the record?"

"Louis Incaviglia"

"Is your middle initial 'C'?"

"Yes."

"What does 'C' stand for?"

"Carlo."

"Mr. Ink-a-veal-ya – am I pronouncing that correctly?"

"Yes."

"Mr. Incaviglia, are you taking any medications this morning that might affect your ability to understand or respond to my questions?"

Lou looked at him for a long second. "No."

"Where were you born?"

There followed fifteen minutes of questions about Lou's childhood, his education, his apprenticeship and his career as a bricklayer. Lou knew all the answers. Finally, the questioning turned to the reason they were there.

"Mr. Incaviglia, did you sell fifteen shares of stock in a company called 3Device, Inc., to Salvatore Paglia?" asked Eastman.

"Yes," Lou responded. Nigel was proud of his client. You could tell that Eastman was a little thrown by the simplicity of the answer, because he flipped to the next page of his questions, and then turned the page again. The room was quiet while he did that.

"Do you know what a 'private placement memorandum' is?"

"Yes."

Eastman pulled a thick document off of a stack of papers to his left and announced, "For the record, I am showing the witness what we've marked as Incaviglia Deposition Exhibit 1." He handed the document to the reporter, and then took three more copies off the stack. He kept one, and gave one copy each to Nigel and Lou.

"Mr. Incaviglia, do you recognize Incaviglia Deposition Exhibit 1?"

"Yes."

"What is it?"

"That's 3Device's Private Placement Memorandum."

"Did you provide a copy of this Private Placement Memorandum to Mr. Paglia before you sold him shares in 3Device?"

"No."

"Did you ask anyone at 3Device to provide a copy of this Private Placement Memorandum to Mr. Paglia before you sold him shares in 3Device?"

"No."

Eastman nodded, and turned a couple more pages. As Nigel had predicted, Eastman was prepared for Lou to evade his questions, and was able to skip a lot of the follow-up he had written out, just in case. He turned again to his pile of exhibits, and pulled off another thick document. Reading upside down, Lou recognized it as the Shareholders' Agreement for 3Device. Eastman recited the exhibit number and handed out copies.

"Mr. Incaviglia, do you recognize Incaviglia Deposition Exhibit No. 2?" asked Eastman, finally.

"Yes."

"What is it?"

"It looks like the Shareholders' Agreement that all the shareholders of 3Device had to sign."

"Did you sign it?"

"Yes."

"Did you provide a copy of this Shareholders' Agreement to Mr. Paglia before you sold him shares in 3Device?"

"No."

"Did you ask anyone at 3Device to provide a copy of this Shareholders' Agreement to Mr. Paglia before you sold him shares in 3Device?"

"No."

"Did you provide any other documents to Mr. Paglia in connection with your sale to Mr. Paglia of shares of stock of 3Device, Inc.?"

"No."

"Did 3Device issue a share certificate to Mr. Paglia, in his name, representing the fifteen shares that you sold him?"

"I don't know."

"Well, did you talk with Mr. Paglia about how he would go about obtaining a share certificate for the fifteen shares you sold him?"

"I don't recall."

Eastman didn't appear frustrated, exactly – he seemed to be getting what he wanted out of the witness – but, to Nigel, he looked a little unsettled. Nigel could see why. In his five years of big-firm litigation practice – many years before — Nigel had never seen a witness as calm as Lou Incaviglia.

Eastman continued. "Well, do you recall any conversation with Mr. Paglia in the Italian American Citizens Club of Norristown, during which you and Mr. Paglia discussed your selling shares of 3Device to him?"

"Yeah, I recall two conversations like that."

"Tell me what you recall about what was said during the first conversation."

Lou thought for a moment. "Sal asked me how my son-in-law's business was doing. I asked him, 'which one,' and he said he was talking about the one I owned shares in. I told him that was the artificial knee company. He said he had been reading up, and wanted to invest in health care. He asked me if I would consider selling him some of my shares in the artificial knee company. I told him I didn't know whether I was allowed to sell to him. And I told him I had no idea what price I would ask. He asked me what the company does, and I told him they made artificial knees, you know, for knee surgery, on a 3D printer. And then he went into a long thing about what the market for artificial knees was, and how many operations there are a year. And then he talked about how many artificial hip operations there are a year, in case the company started making those. He asked Tommy Benelli, our bartender, to look up a lot of stuff on Google about knee and hip operations, while we were sitting there. And then Sal did these calculations out loud about how much the company could earn if things went well."

"What did you say in response to that?

"I said, 'You're out of your fucking mind.'"

Eastman's eyebrows shot up. He thought for a while about his next question. The best he could come up with was, "What did Mr. Paglia say in response to that?"

"He said, 'No offense, but that's why I'm going to Martha's Vineyard this weekend in a private jet, and you'll be sitting around Norristown watching the Phillies.'"

"Do you recall anything else about that conversation between Mr. Paglia and you?"

"No."

"So is it your contention that Mr. Paglia first came to you about the shares, you didn't approach him?"

Lou turned to look at Nigel, and said, "Contention?"

Nigel held up a palm to Lou in a 'hold up a minute' gesture, turned to Eastman, and said, "Objection to the form. Mr. Incaviglia is the defendant in this case, and he doesn't have any 'contentions' about the stock transaction in question. Only the plaintiff has contentions, and the burden of proof, on that subject. Mr. Incaviglia, if you understand the question, you can answer."

"OK. My answer is 'Yes.'"

"If he supposedly approached you, do you have any knowledge or belief about how he might have learned that you owned shares in 3Device?"

During one of their prep sessions, Lou and Nigel had talked about this question possibly coming up. Lou was adamant that he was not going to mention Olivia unless he absolutely had to. "I talked about owning shares in an artificial knee company at the club one night, at the bar, and I believe Sal must have been there that night and heard me."

"Did you receive thirty shares of stock in 3Device, Inc., from your daughter, Olivia Incaviglia?"

An angry red flush rose up Lou's neck, from inside his shirt collar. "Yes," answered Lou evenly, after a short pause.

"Did Olivia talk to you about the company's prospects?" Eastman continued.

"Objection," said Nigel. "This case is about a completely separate transaction. I instruct the witness not to answer."

Palmer Eastman put on his best "I'm insulted" look. "Mr. Branca, this is discovery. You know that question was proper, and your instruction to the witness was wildly improper. If necessary, we will call the court for a ruling."

"Fine, you can call the court," Nigel responded. "We'll wait. But we have no . . ."

"Nigel, thanks, but I wanna answer," Lou interjected. Nigel's intervention had bought Lou some helpful time to think. "My answer is, 'No.'"

"You never talked to your daughter about the company's prospects?" persisted Eastman.

"I just told you. No."

Olivia had tried a couple of times, and so had Greg, but Lou always changed the subject. What'd he need with shares in a little company that wasn't selling nothin'? He thought his son-in-law was crazy to be launching into projects like that, and Lou changed the subject immediately whenever the subject of the company came up.

Eastman shuffled his papers again. "You said there were two conversations with Mr. Paglia about the shares."

Lou looked at Eastman impassively.

Eastman finally seemed to realize that he hadn't asked a question. Most witnesses were not listening carefully enough to know the difference between a statement and a question.

"Were there two conversations between Mr. Paglia and you about the possibility of his buying shares in 3Device?"

"Yes."

"Was the conversation you described earlier the first of those two conversations?"

"Yes."

"When and where was the second conversation?"

"It was a week or two later, also at the Italian American Citizens Club."

"Was the meeting planned, or did you happen to bump into each other?"

"It was planned. I called Sal at his office."

Eastman really seemed to *like* that answer, and he asked the witness to say it again. "Where did you call him?"

Lawyers are idiots, thought Lou. "At his office."

"What was said during that phone conversation?"

"We agreed to meet at the club at 6:00 that afternoon."

"Did you, in fact, meet at the club as planned?"

"Yes."

"What was said during that conversation?"

"I told Sal that the other shareholders had approved a sale of shares from me to him. He said 'I want to get my foot in the door,' and he said 'I'll take as many shares as you'll sell me.' I tol' him I had just attended a shareholders meeting by Zoom, that I learned a lot, and there were a lot of things I wanted to tell him about what was going on with the company. He said he wasn't interested in hearing about any of that. He said he wanted to buy all of my shares. I said no, I wanted to stay a shareholder, so I need to keep some. And then he asked me if I'd sell him half of my shares, and I thought about it and said yes. That was fifteen shares, out of the thrity shares I owned. So then he said we had to figure out a price. I told him the only price I would consider was $1,000 per share, because that was the price all of the other shareholders had paid for their shares, and I didn't want to charge him more, or let him into the company for less than other shareholders had paid. So he starts writing out a check for $15,000, and I said you don't have to do that until you get the shares. He said no, he wanted to do it right then, and he wrote on the memo line that the check was for the shares. He handed me the check and said he had to go, because his wife was making dinner."

"Was there anything else that was said during that second conversation?"

"No."

"Who overheard you when you supposedly told Mr. Paglia that you wanted to tell him about the company?"

"Objection to the form," said Nigel.

"I don't know," replied Lou. Great place for an "I don't know," thought Nigel. Keep the other side guessing.

"What did you do with the check that Mr. Paglia gave you?" asked Eastman.

"I waited for a while until I figured Sal would have gotten his shares. Maybe two weeks. Then I deposited the check into my savings account at my bank."

"Did you change the form of the asset – in other words, what, if anything, did you spend the money on?"

"I used it to pay my lawyer for this case," replied Lou.

Eastman shifted to a new page of questions – all typed in advance. "Do you know who Paul Smythe is?"

This was a carefully crafted question. Eastman obviously figured that Lou might claim that he didn't know Paul Smythe. Asking the question this way might lock in a helpful answer that could be exploited at trial.

"Yes," replied Lou.

Nigel groaned inwardly. It would have been better if Lou had replied, "Well, I found out who he was when you filed your complaint." But Lou's answer was correct, and, ultimately, Nigel was fine with that. No. Yes. I don't know. I don't recall. The four answers that would keep you out of trouble.

"Did you ever tell Paul Smythe that you would not accept a finder's fee in connection with a sale of shares by Mr. Smythe to Mr. Paglia?"

Lou had to think about what he had just heard. "No," he said, finally.

Nigel had to give Palmer Eastman credit for one thing. He knew how to pose devious, misleading questions. Sal Paglia would testify at trial that Lou admitted to him that he was likely getting a finder's fee from Paul Smythe – it said so right in the complaint. Lou didn't tell Paul Smythe that he *wouldn't* accept a finder's fee. *Voila*, Sal's testimony was plausible, or at least that's the way Sal's lawyer would argue it.

Eastman spent some more time probing a few of Lou's earlier answers, but he had liked most of those answers, and didn't want to muddy them up. He had expected to spend the whole day on the deposition, and he was finishing up in half a morning. Lou Incaviglia had admitted under oath that he failed to disclose anything about the shares that Sal was buying. The case wasn't over – far from it. But Eastman figured that when Sal testified to the conversations that were described in the complaint, his case was made, unless the jury somehow bought the completely implausible story that Lou Incaviglia told today at his deposition. Eastman concluded the deposition, happy with the way his case was going.

CHAPTER 43

The 1600 block of Passyunk Avenue was lit up with white lights on all the trees, neon signs blazing colors, and the emergency flashers on double-parked cars blinking. Mobs of people on the sidewalks and lots of smiles. It was a glorious Thursday night in August, and it could have been Christmas.

Lou and Olivia were inching up the block in Olivia's BMW – toward Roberto's Trattoria – and spotted Joey Abruzzi on the sidewalk looking their way. He was motioning with one hand for them to stop, and waving with his other hand to a pretty twenty-year-old blond. She waved back to Joey, and then made a face and hand gesture toward Olivia's car like, "Is this the one?" Joey nodded, and she came around to the driver's side and knelt down a little, framing her face in the driver's side window. "Hi, I'm Christie," she said.

Olivia smiled. "Hi, I'm Olivia, this is Lou. Are you our valet tonight?"

"You bet," she replied. "I'll be taking care of your car like she's my baby."

A driver behind Olivia beeped his horn. Christie, Olivia and Lou ignored him. This is Philadelphia, Pennsylvania, you moron, not Salt Lake City or somewhere.

As Olivia stepped out, Christie gave her a valet ticket and a big smile. Olivia asked, "How long have you been working valet with Joey?"

"This is my third week," replied Christie. "I love it! I'm meeting all kinds of people, and I get to drive great cars – you know, like yours."

"Wait till you see my Mercury Marquis," said Lou over the roof of the car as he got out from the other side. "Then you'll really be driving a great car."

Christie didn't miss a beat. "Well, duh! All of our customers drive great cars! *Especially* good looking men in their fifties and sixties." She winked at Olivia and they both laughed.

The guy beeped his horn again. They ignored him again.

Olivia had an idea. "Have you ever done any event hosting?" she asked Christie. "My husband and I are throwing a Sunday afternoon lawn party, on the day before Labor Day. I'd love to have somebody greeting the guests, offering them a glass of wine, and showing them how to find the backyard. We're out in Villanova."

Christie's smile widened. "I'm not sure I can do it, but I'd love to talk to you about it. Let me give you my number." She borrowed the valet ticket back from Olivia and jotted her name and number on it. Female networking at work. "Enjoy your dinner!"

Olivia and Lou stepped onto the sidewalk, and Joey hugged them both. "Lou, Livvie, glad you could see this." He gestured up and down the block. "Thursday nights have gone nuts for us. Thanks to Olivia."

"It looks great," Lou replied. "But you're about to lose some help. Christie and I are leaving for Tahiti for a year or two. She said she likes my car. We'll send you a postcard."

"You're an idiot," said Olivia. "Why would you trade mornings talking with Gloria in Norristown for evenings with Christie in Tahiti?"

"No, you're an idiot," said Lou.

"No, you're an idiot," said Olivia, laughing.

"You're *stugats*," said Lou. "That's my final word on the subject." He tousled her hair, because she hated when he did it.

"Roberto saved a table for us," said Joey. "And they have an Ossobuco special, you're gonna love it." He led them to the Maitre d', who led them all to their table. Joey tipped him two hundred bucks.

Tony had sent his regrets that afternoon, because he wasn't digesting very well that week. Angela thought about coming herself, without Tony, but had a feeling that, for once, Tony wasn't just being a hypochondriac. She was thinking about sending him to the doctor the next day. She called Lou and Olivia and Joey. Joey had been planning to join the group from the beginning, and had encouraged Lou and Olivia to come down anyway.

During dinner, the conversation flowed. Family who were friends. At one point, Lou asked Joey whether he was giving himself time off every once in a while, and Joey got very serious. "What I'm really trying to do is give my dad a chance to take time off. He still works every day. He's a great delegator, and between us we have everything covered. But he deserves a break. Problem is, he's worried that if he cuts down on his hours, things will slip, people will get sloppy. So I remind him that's why I'm there. And he gives me this fearful look, and I know what it means. He respects me, and my abilities. But he doesn't trust everyone else in the organization to see the same things in me that he sees. I think he thinks he'd be throwing me to the wolves or something."

"That's the thing with every father," Lou replied. "Ask Livvie. You think we try to tell you what to do because we like being in charge. Our kids are the only people who have to listen to us. Everybody else can ignore us. That's what it seems like, right? But that's not it. We're like mothers with three-day beards. We wanna protect you, and we can't anymore. So we try to give advice instead, thinkin' it'll help. It don't, because you're already smarter and stronger than us. But we try."

"The thing is," Joey replied, "my dad really is my boss."

"That's a good point," said Lou, "and it makes your situation different from most other grown up kids. But Tony is a very smart man. You said it yourself, he delegates. Which means he trusts his people, and he especially trusts you."

Lou leaned over a little toward Joey. "So do you want some advice?" He smiled at his own little joke. "Don't answer that — of course you do. Tell your dad you want to talk to him about how things will work when he's gone."

"The business school professors call it succession planning," said Olivia. "Everybody else calls it 'figuring out what happens next.'"

Lou nodded in agreement. "Let him know you want to talk about everybody who works for him. How will this guy act when Tony's not around? Does that guy secretly want Tony's job? Has this other guy ever done a lick of work in the last ten years?"

"I think he'd have that conversation," said Joey.

"And then ask him the questions you think he's been asking himself. Does he think so-and-so will follow when and where young Joe Abruzzi leads? His instincts on that should be very good."

"What if the answer for a particular guy is, 'no, he won't.' What am I gonna do when one of the Capos says, 'Fuck that, I'm not gonna do it?'"

All three were quiet for a moment. Then Lou said quietly, "There is nobody on this planet who will give you a better answer to that question than your father."

CHAPTER 44

Lou was on his stoop lighting a cigar and studying the eighth race in the Daily Racing Form when a tall guy, probably in his 40's, with sandy hair and a windbreaker came down the sidewalk. The guy was checking addresses at first, and then spotted Lou and headed toward him. He stopped about eight feet away.

"Are you Louis Incaviglia?" the man asked. He pronounced it "Ink-a-vigg-lee-a."

"Who are you?" Lou replied, standing up.

"My name is Alex Bivens. I'm an investigator with the Pennsylvania Department of Banking and Securities."

"Is that supposed to mean something to me?" Lou asked.

"That depends on who you are," Bivens replied. "You haven't told me your name."

Lou was silent. For somebody as talkative as he was, Lou knew a lot about how to be quiet when he felt like it.

Alex Bivens fidgeted. "The Department has received a complaint about Louis Incaviglia in connection with a securities transaction. I'm the assigned investigator." He reached into his windbreaker, pulled out a small ID wallet, and flashed it to Lou. He didn't think Lou, if that's who he was, was entitled to take any undue time to read it, so he put it back in his pocket.

"I didn't see what you showed me," said Lou. "Slower this time."

The guy reluctantly pulled out his ID again, and showed it to Lou. Lou didn't say anything further. After an interval, the guy put his ID away again. They looked at each other.

"I'm going to assume that you are Louis Incaviglia, because this is the address I was given, and you are present at that address. My first job in a case like this is to determine whether a person named in a complaint with the Department is willing to cooperate in our investigation. You can request that we deal with you only through a lawyer, and we'll honor that request. But if you waive the right to be represented by counsel during our investigation, you'll be dealing directly with me."

Lou was silent. Investigator Bivens cleared his throat and reached into his windbreaker again. He pulled out a folded two-page document.

"This is a demand for production of documents. You should give it to your lawyer if you have one. We are asking you to produce those documents within 14 days. If you don't, we can go to court and get an order forcing you to produce them." Bivens extended the document toward Lou.

Lou remained silent, and didn't reach for the papers.

Bivens was annoyed. He didn't know whether he was dealing with the right person. He wasn't being shown any common courtesy, much less cooperation. And the guy he was looking at didn't seem very deferential for somebody who might be in a lot of trouble. So Bivens decided to show this guy what was what. Educate him a little.

"We are an investigative agency. That means that I can, and will, subpoena people you know to testify and produce documents relevant to this complaint. I want you to think about who might be receiving some of those subpoenas – people who might have witnessed any of the conversations that led up to this transaction, people who are involved with the company that issued these shares. We're going to run a full background check on you, to see whether this might be part of a pattern. If it is, and if we find probable cause that you acted with criminal intent, we can refer your case to the

Attorney General of Pennsylvania for criminal prosecution. I've done that before, and you wouldn't like it."

Bivens smoothed down some hair that had moved around in the breeze. Lou noticed that the guy had a comb-over.

"It's a shame," Bivens continued, "because we were just going to invite you and your lawyer to an informal discussion session out in Harrisburg. You could have told your side of the story. But since I don't even know who you are, I'm not going to do that. You can just look for us to begin showing up in your daily life." He dropped the document request at Lou's feet, turned around, and walked back up the sidewalk the way he had come.

When the guy turned the corner, Lou picked up the paper from the sidewalk. Nigel would probably want to see it.

CHAPTER 45

Olivia and Greg took the elevator to the twelfth floor of a nondescript building near Jefferson Hospital in Center City. They turned left from the elevator into the small reception area for Evans Wentworth Fertility Associates, PC. Olivia was so sick and tired of entering this space that she no longer noticed her own reaction to it. It was August 29.

They checked in with the receptionist and sat down to wait. Maggie Portnoy, their Physician's Assistant, came out to greet them after about 10 minutes. "Olivia, Greg, sorry to keep you waiting. Come on back, I'll get Kate to draw some blood, and then I'll be in to explain what we have in mind." She motioned them back into a narrow, dimly lit hallway – another space that Olivia hated – and motioned them into the examination room.

After their blood was drawn, and after their nurse had updated their histories, Maggie came in with a small case and a smile. The smile seemed forced to Olivia, but maybe that was just the grumpy mood Olivia was in. She hadn't slept much the night before – and as her father Lou often said, "Don't confuse fatigue with a real emotion."

"The Cabergoline didn't work – I guess you knew that," Maggie began. "It doesn't always work, obviously. So we need to go on to the next option. It's late August. We should try to get a lot done in September while everybody's around. Let me tell you about hCG. The letters stand for human chorionic gonadotropin. We'll be giving it to you by injection in about two weeks." She turned toward Olivia. "But first we need to give you a series of

12 daily FSH shots, which we need to begin now, while you're having your period. FSH is a follicle-stimulating hormone. The follicles hold eggs as they mature, and the FSH helps them do that. Assuming you decide to do this, would you like to have the FSH shots here, or should we make up a kit so you can do them at home?"

Olivia was nonplussed by the rapidity with which a fertility practice could shift gears. Her gears. Greg's gears. But she was listening carefully, and understood the question. "I can do them at home before I leave for work," she responded. "Will morning be OK for this?"

"Sure, that works," said Maggie. "After 12 days of FSH, you'll come back here to the office for your hCG injection. That injection will stimulate ovulation within 36 hours, so you'll need to have sex two days after you get the shot. For example, if you get the shot on a Monday, you'll need to have sex on Wednesday morning."

Olivia and Greg both rolled their eyes, mentally. Most of the time, sex for procreation now felt like work to them. Certainly not fun.

Maggie turned to Greg. "Greg, we think you should get injections of hCG as well. In men, hCG increases testosterone levels and improves sperm counts. We don't always prescribe hCG for the male partner as well, but we often do, and we've had good results. You'll be doing three injections per week during the same two-week period, and your last shot will be right at the same time that Olivia gets hers. We can give you a kit for five shots, and then we can do the last one here."

Greg responded simply, and without much enthusiasm, "OK."

"What's your success rate?" asked Olivia.

Maggie knew the question would be coming, because Olivia had posed the same question about earlier treatments. "Nationally, the success rate with hCG is about 20%, one in five. But we do significantly better than that – closer to 25 percent – because we screen out patients who have lower chances for success, and who would prefer to go directly to IVF. You fall into a group whose chances are pretty good. This approach often works, and you know quickly when it does or doesn't. With hCG, we're not going to keep you guessing for months."

Olivia had a series of additional questions, but Greg and she had both already decided that hCG was worth a try. What was so frustrating was that they were investing this much time, money and emotional energy into a procedure that had a 75% failure rate. They would do what they had done for the last three years – take the meds, then block it all out, and carry on with their lives.

CHAPTER 46

The two-page document that the guy from the Department of Banking and Securities had given Lou was rolled up in Lou's hand. Lou entered the Swede Street Diner and spotted Nigel sitting in back.

"Hey Nigel," said Lou, as he sat down. "Any thoughts about my deposition?"

"Nah, I don't think about shit like that after it's over," Nigel replied. "You did well. Now you don't have to think about it either."

"OK, well I have a new problem. The State of Pennsylvania wants documents from me." Lou handed Nigel the piece of paper he'd been carrying.

"I don't want to be pedantic," said Nigel as he opened the document, "but it's the Commonwealth of Pennsylvania. Like the Commonwealth of Massachusetts, the Commonwealth of Virginia, and the Commonwealth of Kentucky. Here's why it matters. If you're in the State of New York, the caption for a criminal case – they call the title of the case the 'caption' – will be 'State v. John Q. Malefactor.' But if you're in Pennsylvania, we call it '*Commonwealth* v. John Q. Malefactor.'"

"Do I need to know this?" asked Lou. Nigel started reading, and didn't respond.

After he finished reading the formal demand for documents issued by the investigative staff of the Pennsylvania Department of Banking and Securities, Nigel tore the document in half, and then tore the two halves in half. "You don't have any documents."

"Couldn't it be a problem if I ignore it?" Lou asked.

"No," replied Nigel. "But here's what's going to happen. If he really wants these documents, the investigator – what's this guy's name, 'Bivens'? – he's going to have to talk to his lawyers. His lawyers are government employees just like he is, and they're going to bust his balls about wasting time on a case like this. He'll probably ask them to go to court for him, to make you comply with this demand. And his lawyers are going to say, 'give us a year, maybe it will get to the top of our to-do list.' And then when it does get to the top of their to-do list, before they go to court the lawyers are going to call you to see if you've reconsidered. Or died, they would like that. When you say 'no,' and tell them to fuck off, they will ask for your lawyer's name, which you will give them. Then they'll call me, and I'll tell them you don't have any documents. And I'll tell them they're welcome to go to court. Maybe they will. We're two years out now, understand. They file a motion in court. I answer their motion by saying, 'We don't have any of the documents they're looking for.' The government guys argue that we must have documents. I repeat that we don't – it wasn't that kind of transaction. The judge says to the Commonwealth's lawyer, 'They don't have any documents. What am I supposed to do with that? I'll enter an order telling them that if they find some, they need to give them to you.' And then the judge says, 'Next case,' and some other lawyers in the courtroom step forward to argue about their thing, and your case is forgotten already."

Lou nodded slowly. It sounded like Nigel knew what he was talking about. "Sounds like a plan," said Lou.

CHAPTER 47

L ou finished watching Good Morning America and poured a second cup of coffee. He patted his shirt pocket to make sure his first cigar was there, and scrounged around the kitchen for a box of matches. His cigar shop always gave him a box of twenty wooden matches – pretty nice ones, actually – when he bought cigars for the day. And then Lou promptly lost them – the matches, not the cigars – somewhere in la-la land. Matches, sunglasses, winter gloves, umbrellas – they all disappeared into Oz. Didn't really affect his life much, but it was annoying.

Lou opened his front door to let some sunshine in – the weather report was calling for sun – and there was no sunshine to be seen. It took Lou a full three or four seconds to register why there wasn't any sun – he was looking at a giant black dump truck parked directly in front of his house. It had to be twelve feet high. Lou knew what the lettering on the cab was going to say before he turned his head to look: "Sal Paglia, Inc."

Lou was surprised he hadn't heard the engine of the truck as it was being parked. He had a frozen breakfast burrito that morning – maybe the fan in his microwave was making the loud noise it always made, and he didn't hear the truck. Who knows? Who cares? The point was, Sal was sending a message. "I will make your life unpleasant." Lou had some choices. He could get angry, he could try to get even, he could be sad, or he could ignore the truck altogether. After about five minutes of considering his options, he concluded that Sal had won a round. A brilliant move, actually. It was a public street with open parking. There was nothing Lou could do about it. So nothing was what he decided to do. He sat on his stoop, smoked his first cigar of the day, pulled his Racing Form from his pants pocket, and studied the horses in the eighth race.

CHAPTER 48

Lou was in line at the ticket window at Pennsylvania Park, looking to place his first bet of the day. He liked the number 4 horse in the eighth race. The horse's exercise rider had told his trainer that the horse was ready to run, the trainer told his wife, and his wife told a friend of Lou's. That, and the crowd favorite had an ear infection. "Have you ever tried to do anything while you had an ear infection?" thought Lou. Out of the corner of his eye he saw Adam Collier, the General Manager of the track, motioning to him to step out of line. Lou knew the guy a little bit just from many years of coming to the track, but they weren't friends, and this was odd. Lou walked over to him.

"Lou, I need to talk to you," Collier began. He looked nervous. "I have some news that you're not going to want to hear."

"Angelina Jolie has stopped making movies?"

"No, this is worse. I have just been instructed by the other members of our board of directors to deliver this letter of suspension" – he handed Lou a typed letter – "which bars you from the premises of Pennsylvania Park Racetrack until further notice."

"What?" Lou was stunned. "Why?"

"It's all in the letter, but in a nutshell, a certain person who has to remain nameless – but who says he is a former Township Supervisor in Berlin Township, and now a Constable in Bucks County – swore out an affidavit. He says you're guilty of securities fraud, and that you're under active investigation by the Pennsylvania Department of Banking and Securities. He also says that you're accepting and placing illegal bets for other people when you come over here to the track."

"Anybody care what I have to say?" asked Lou.

"He says he served you notice of the charges himself."

"No he didn't," said Lou.

"Well, he copied the Horse Racing Commission on the letter, and we asked them whether they had any instructions on how to handle this. They said they were concerned about the allegations, but that the initial determination is up to us. They'll go along with whatever we recommend. Our board felt like we had no choice but to suspend you, out of an abundance of caution, on a provisional basis."

"Provisional?" asked Lou. "I don't know what that is."

"It means we're not making any kind of final determination. You can appeal the provisional suspension to the Horse Racing Commission while these investigations are continuing. They have the staff and procedures in place to determine whether the suspension should be lifted. We'll just wait until somebody notifies us that the Commission has allowed you to come back on the premises, or maybe someone in authority will advise us you've been found not guilty, or something like that. We're just going to stand by."

"Did this Constable guy show up here himself?" Lou figured it was the same asshole who visited him at the Italian American Citizens Club, and was curious whether Sal would risk having the guy show his face at the racetrack.

"I'm not sure," said Collier. "The affidavit was on my desk when I got into work yesterday."

"Can I see the affidavit?"

"No, I don't think I can show you that. Lou, you're going to have to leave now. I don't want to embarrass you, and I won't need to call Security if you'll let me walk you out myself."

Lou walked with General Manager Adam Collier down the exit ramp of Pennsylvania Park and all the way to his car in the parking lot. Neither spoke. For the first time since he received notice of Sal Paglia's lawsuit, Lou was discouraged. Really, really discouraged. Maybe terrible things could, in fact, happen to him as a result of all this.

And then he remembered. Racing at Delaware Park was due to start up again in about 10 days. Delaware Park was only an hour's drive from Norristown. Life wasn't so bad.

CHAPTER 49

Olivia and her Aunt Angela were sitting in a booth in the Magnolia Diner in South Philadelphia talking about shoes. Neither one liked high heels – at all – and each had just bought a pair. Go figure.

It was a Wednesday, and Olivia had had her hCG injection on Monday. She and Greg had stayed home from work that morning, as planned. Maybe Olivia was conceiving as they spoke. But there was no reason not to try to improve the odds.

A tall-ish woman in a plain black dress walked in from the main entrance and approached the booth. Her salt-and-pepper hair was short without being severe. She was flashing a warm smile. Angela noticed her, jumped up, and gave her a hug. "Sophie!" She turned to introduce Olivia. "Olivia, I'd like you to meet Sister Sophia Francesca; Sophie, this is Olivia Incaviglia."

"Hi Sister," said Olivia, "I've heard so much about you from Angela. It's great to meet you, finally."

"Likewise," Sister Sophia replied. "I've been following your career. I was heppy when you came here from New York. Good decision, I thought, for you." Her Italian accent was subtle, and Olivia thought it was charming.

"Here, let's sit down and order," said Angela. "Sophie, you sit next to me, and we'll gang up on Olivia."

Olivia smiled. "This should be fun." All three sat down and grabbed menus. A silver haired waitress – she was one of the new girls, having worked there for only 28 years – took their orders.

"Olivia, you know almost everything about Sister Sophia from all I've told you, but I need to fill in a few more details. Sophia is a sister in the Third Order of St. Francis, which is a 'secular order.' I never knew there was such a thing until Sophia explained it. Members of the order assume duties of reverence and service, but they don't take vows of chastity, and they're permitted to marry. Most don't get married, and in fact, most Sisters of the Third Order continue to wear habits. So what binds the order together, more than their vows, is their devotion to God and to service."

"Angela said the order was founded in Naples?" said Olivia.

"Yes, we're Napolitano from Day One," Sophia replied.

"Sophia has been in the U.S. since . . ." Angela turned to Sophia: "What, since 1988?"

"Since 1989, when I started my Masters at St. Joseph's University," Sophia responded. "I wanted to study psychology and counseling, and St. Joe's, they had a good program. I expected to go back to Italy after. But there were great opportunities to work with my degree here in the States – I wound up with an M.S.W. – and I did a lot of work in all of the schools of the Archdiocese. I retired last year, but what was I going to do, stop working? So I still do a lot at different parishes, and I take care of older nuns in the area. Not many left, you know."

"We're glad you stayed," said Angela. "It's nice how people come to Philadelphia, and then they don't leave."

Sister Sophia looked calmly at Angela. "So you know I worked in Naples attending the Miracle Chair with other Sisters of the Third Order. I want to explain to you what the Miracle Chair is, and what it isn't."

"Please, go ahead," said Olivia.

"More than anything else, the Miracle Chair is a place where God is," said Sister Sophia. "You feel His presence in that room more than in any place I have ever been on Earth. The women who sit in that chair believe in Him deeply – otherwise, they wouldn't have made the trip. And they come from all over the world. When they have babies, they send us pictures, and we put the pictures on the walls. So the walls are full of life. Parents and babies from everywhere. The chair and its powers were discovered by Saint Francesca of the Five Wounds of Jesus, and her presence is there always. She intercedes on behalf of women who call on her, as saints are supposed to do. She is now called the Patron Saint of Fertility.

"My job – our job as sisters – was to attend all of the women who sat in the chair, and pray for them. We make the Sign of the Cross on their stomachs, and help them reach out to Saint Francesca and to God directly.

"The chair itself – well, it's just a plain old wooden chair in a small apartment in Naples. If God hadn't chosen it as the place to work His miracles, nobody would ever have paid any attention to it at all.

"That's what the chair is. And let me tell you what it isn't. It isn't what makes you pregnant, if you get pregnant. Only God does that. So if God has other plans for you and your husband, the chair doesn't change those plans. But I do know this, Olivia: the intercession of the saints is real, and with Saint Francesca helping you, God will hear you, as he always does."

After lunch, they walked over to Sister Sophia's apartment, in a small building around the corner on Mifflin Street. As Sophia led them into her living room, Olivia saw a plain wooden chair with a bronze and glass inset.

"A splinter of the Miracle Chair in Naples is underneath that little glass window," said Sister Sophia. "God likes to open branch offices because of the high demand."

Olivia smiled at the sophistication of Sister Sophia's economic analysis. Women were having babies later, and, yes, demand was obviously high. Sophia motioned to her, and gestured for her to sit in the chair. Olivia sat down slowly and closed her eyes as Sister Sophia made the Sign of the Cross on her abdomen, and said a prayer in Italian. For her part, Olivia prayed as hard as she ever had in her life.

As Angela and Olivia were leaving, Sister Sophia said a last word. "Remember, Sweetheart, God has a plan. We just don't always know what it is. But He loves you." There were tears in Olivia's eyes as she and Angela walked down the steps of Sophia's apartment building.

CHAPTER 50

Sal Paglia leaned back in his chair, thumbed his phone, and began to catch up on some emails. He was sitting in the upstairs office of the Italian American Citizens Club waiting for Enzo Primera, the president of the club, to arrive from work. Eddie Esposito and Mario Beneventi, the other two members of the club's Executive Committee, were both on their phones in the far corners of the room. When Enzo came in the door ten minutes after the others had arrived, he greeted everybody by name, and the phones were turned off. All four pulled up chairs around the meeting table.

"Sal, we got darts starting in a half hour," Enzo began, "but hopefully that'll give us enough time to talk about whatever you wanted to talk about. What's up?"

"First, thanks for agreein' to meet with me," said Sal. "I think a half hour should do it. Let's just talk some, and we'll see how it goes."

"OK, that works," Enzo replied. All three looked expectantly at Sal.

"OK, here's the thing," Sal began. "This is kinda difficult. I just heard yesterday – and I emailed you guys right after, you know, asking to meet – I heard that Lou Incaviglia has been suspended by Pennsylvania Park, and he can't set foot on the property. They escorted him from the track to his car yesterday, and told him to leave. The reason was, as I hear it, he's under investigation for fraud by the Pennsylvania Attorney General and the Pennsylvania Securities Department – I think that's what it's called.

Anyway, it's the agency the state has to protect against stock fraud. And the state Racing Commission is looking into him."

"Where did you hear all this?" asked Enzo.

"One of my people talked to the general manager out at Pennsylvania Park, and he confirmed what I just told you about the Racing Commission and the racetrack. And I can tell you that an investigator for the Securities Department called my office and took a statement from me. I got the thing about the Attorney General from my lawyer."

"How does any of this shit involve us?" asked Mario Beneventi.

"That's kinda why I'm here," Sal responded. "You know I've been a member for 35 years, and I spent a lot of years in this room doin' what you're doin'. I was acting president after Vinny Conti died. I love this club, and I don't want anything bad to happen to it, especially if we can prevent it.

"I talked with my lawyer – at my expense, obviously – and he says we have at least three things we need to worry about. There may be more, but these were his top issues.

"First, our liquor license says that it's against the law to permit illegal gambling on the premises. You know that Lou and Carmine are talking about their bets in the club all the time, and Lou will take money from other members to go bet it at the track. The club isn't an Off Track Betting parlor. When Lou accepts money from somebody and promises to place a bet, that's illegal gambling. And now we have the Racing Commission nosing around to see if Lou is breaking the law. The next guest we have come in could be a state investigator. If he sees that, we could be looking at a suspension of our liquor license. And you know what pricks the Liquor Control Board are, 'cause they've hassled us before.

"Second, you know and I know we got two guys in the club who are on parole. You know who they are, I don't have to name names. One of the conditions of every parole is that they not hang around with disreputable people. If they knew that Lou had just been barred from all of the racetracks in the state, they would have to keep away from the club. They couldn't be here while Lou is here. It's not fair to them that Lou should stay and they have to keep away.

"Third, and maybe worst of all. The investigator from the Securities Department knows that the fraud they're investigating took place *in this club*." Sal jabbed the table for emphasis. "It happened right at our bar downstairs. And Tommy Benelli was part of it, he was looking up shit on his telephone while Lou was talkin'. As much as it might be to my advantage to want witnesses to come forward, the club doesn't need this. We don't want investigators coming in here to serve subpoenas and shit. We have enough trouble without that. I can tell the state people Lou isn't even a member anymore, and that I don't think there are any witnesses they need to talk to."

"So, OK, suppose all that is true," Enzo interjected. "It sucks, but what is the Executive Committee supposed to do about any of this?"

"That's simple," Sal replied. "Under the bylaws, the Executive Committee can temporarily suspend any member for 'conduct unbecoming.' Putting some distance between the club and Lou will solve all of these problems. Just vote to suspend his membership."

"Whoa," said Mario Beneventi. "This stinks. It smells to high heaven. All I've heard in the last few minutes is that Lou Incaviglia is somehow 'under investigation.' But the only reason we have to believe that shit is this: you filed a complaint in court, and then all of a sudden Lou is under investigation. But your complaint don't mean nothin' – nobody decided the case. No judge has said that Lou committed fraud. You're the one sayin' that. And it looks like you pulled strings and got the Racing Commission and the securities people and who the fuck else to supposedly investigate Lou for fraud. But the only one likely to benefit from kicking Lou out of the club is you. Because it hurts Lou and makes you feel better."

"Look," Sal replied, glaring at Mario. "I coulda played this a lot different. If I was just tryn'a look out for myself, I coulda called the Liquor Control Board myself. I coulda called parole officers myself. But I didn't do that. I love this club, and I came in here like a gentleman and told you guys about a problem we all have. And I didn't say, 'hey, we need to kick Lou out for good.' All I'm suggesting is that his membership should be suspended until all of these investigations are finished. If he clears his name – I mean, I obviously don't think he will, but just assume for a minute – if he clears his name, he can come back. No harm, no foul. The club has a right to protect itself till that happens."

"How long is the lawsuit supposed to last?" asked Eddie Esposito.

"Well, we could settle it tomorrow," Sal replied. "You never know. But my lawyer says we're probably looking at another year before it goes to trial."

All three Executive Committee members were quiet, staring at the tabletop.

"Look, I get it, we all want what's best for the club," Sal said, finally. "Remember two or three years ago I offered to make an interest-free loan to the club to renovate the kitchen? We sorta postponed the whole thing till we decided whether to expand the building out toward the back parking lot. But it doesn't look like there's much support for expanding, and we don't really need to wait on the kitchen. How 'bout if I pledge thirty grand for the kitchen, no strings attached? A gift, not a loan."

"No strings," said Eddie. "Meaning – you'll donate for the kitchen no matter how we vote on Lou's suspension?"

"This is bullshit," said Mario. "I can't believe what I'm hearing." He leaned back and crossed his arms.

"To answer Eddie's question: No strings. But I'm asking you to consider how much I've given in time and money to this club over the years. I think I've earned the benefit of the doubt. What I'm telling you about what's going on with Lou is all true. So will I be disappointed if you don't vote my way? Hell yeah. But, you know." Sal fell silent.

"Sal, can you give us a few minutes to talk about this?" asked Enzo.

"Sure," Sal replied. "I'll be downstairs."

Sal went down to the bar and found a stool. Lou Incaviglia was at the other end of the bar, talking to Carmine. Sal and Lou ignored each other. After about ten minutes, Enzo Primera appeared at Sal's shoulder.

"The vote was 2-1. I'll give the letter to Lou tomorrow," said Enzo to Sal. "I gotta find somebody to type it. And I'll announce your gift by email to all of the members."

"Easier still," said Sal. "I'll bring you a check for the 30k tomorrow, and I'll write 'Kitchen Renovation' on it. Put it in the bank, and then wait a few weeks till Lou's suspension is old news. Best for everybody."

CHAPTER 51

Lou was sitting on his usual stool at the club, eating lunch and talking with Tommy Benelli. Enzo Primera sat down to his immediate right.

"Yo, *El Presidente*, how you doin'?" said Lou.

"I'm good Lou, I'm OK," Enzo replied. "How are things going with you?"

"Can't complain," said Lou. "Tommy, can I get a beer for Enzo?"

Enzo held up his hand. "Tommy, no thanks." He turned to Lou. "Lou, uh, I need to talk to you." Just at that moment he couldn't come up with any words, so he handed Lou a letter he had been holding by his side. Lou was beginning to think that everybody in the world wanted to hand him something these days. He read Enzo's letter.

"*Marrone d',*" said Lou. "I gotta figure Sal Paglia put you up to this. Do you wanna tell me what 'conduct unbecoming' is supposed to mean?"

"Lou, we have to look out for our liquor license. When we heard you got suspended at the track, we knew that somebody's looking at what you're doing, whatever it is. And they might start looking here. You sit here and work out the bets you're gonna place for Carmine when you get to the track. We know — hell, everybody knows 'cause it's no secret — you and Carmine talk about betting in here every day."

"So does everybody else," said Lou.

"Yeah, but they're not under investigation for anything," Enzo replied. "You see our problem."

"I've been a member of this club for forty years," said Lou. It was a statement of fact, not a plea. "How much did he pay you to make this decision?"

"Lou, don't go there," Enzo replied. "Look, this is a temporary suspension, till you get all this shit straightened out. We gotta do this." He stood. "Lou, finish your sandwich. Then get this shit straightened out, will ya?"

Lou had never lost his appetite just because of something somebody said, at least that he could recall. Before now. "Tommy, be good." He stood, walked to the door, and stepped out onto the street.

CHAPTER 52

Lou was smoking a cigar on his stoop. Anna called him on his cell phone, which meant that she'd already tried his landline, and he hadn't heard it.

"Do you want to watch TV tonight?" she asked.

"I'm not in the mood, Doll. Maybe Thursday?"

"Something's wrong," Anna said. "You sound upset. What's going on?"

"The Italian Club suspended my membership today," Lou replied. "I'm still kinda digesting it."

"Are you serious? Did Sal Paglia have something to do with it?"

"Probably, but the letter didn't say nothin' like that. They said it was 'cause I got suspended at the racetrack, and they're worried about their liquor license if I hang around the club."

"Wait, what? You were suspended at the racetrack?"

Lou hadn't realized he hadn't told Anna about it. Talk about avoiding something subconsciously — jeez. He didn't want her to be upset about something she couldn't fix, and now there were two things she couldn't fix.

"Yeah, the manager at the track told me I was suspected of fraud. He gave me a letter and walked me out to my car. Last Wednesday."

"Lou, I'm so sorry. You don't deserve this."

"You know, it is what it is."

"Look, one thing I love about you is that you take life as it comes. You don't complain, you don't whine, you don't blame. Right now you need to remember you have Olivia, you have your friends, and you have your home. Nobody is going to shoot you, and nobody is going to put you in jail."

"Be thankful for small blessings," said Lou, without much enthusiasm.

"You always say, the secret to life is to play the hand you're dealt. More than ever, do that now. And you can drink. That's why they invented VO and Pabst Blue Ribbon. That's probably bad advice, but at a time like this, you'd be crazy not to drink a little, if you can. Hell, I'll drink with you. You're going to get through this."

"Thanks Doll," Lou replied. "My plan for tonight is to watch TV and go to bed early. How do you look for Thursday?"

"I'm good. I'll buy a bottle of wine for Thursday. Call if you need to talk?"

"Will do. Don't worry, I'll be fine."

"OK, bye-bye," said Anna.

"Bye."

Lou noticed that his ash had fallen on his pants. It was that kind of day.

CHAPTER 53

Olivia drove home from work tired. Hell, she did everything tired. She didn't want to admit it, but she felt the fatigue more when she was stressed, and the lawsuit against her dad was creating more stress than she would ever have expected.

Greg met her at the door coming in from the garage with a spoonful of Béarnaise sauce. "What do you think?" he asked, as he extended the spoon to her lips.

She tasted it and liked it. "The sauce is great. What are you making with it?"

"Salmon."

"Super! I'm in the mood for salmon."

"How was work?" he asked as they poured a glass of wine and sat at the island in the kitchen.

"Frustrating. One of the partners came to me with a leveraged buyout, straight out of 1983. I looked at the numbers. The client wants to borrow the money from his bank at SOFR-plus-two, variable. So I asked the partner, 'What happens if interest rates double?' And he says, 'That would be a problem.' And I said, 'Problem isn't the right word. More like disaster. They'd be bankrupt within a month.' So he asks me, 'Are interest rates going to double?' I say – as you'd expect — 'I have no idea.' Then he looks at me with this triumphant look and says, 'See? This deal will work!'"

Greg laughed. "As he sees it, his personality is what's paying the bills at Biddle & Co., and your brains are just overhead."

"I got the last laugh, sort of," said Olivia. "Two hours later, the client calls the partner and asks him, 'What happens if interest rates double?' The partner told him he'd just been thinking about that issue. Yeah, right. So they're going to go back to the bank to see if they can cap the variable rate, or tweak the deal somehow. They'll get it done – they almost always do."

Greg looked at Olivia for a long moment. "You a look a little stressed," he said. "Is there anything else going on?"

"My dad's lawsuit is making me miserable," she said simply.

"I know. Me too. We just got a document demand today from Sal's lawyers."

"Greg, I know we've talked about it, and I know we need to stay out of the case. But standing by is a lot harder than I thought it would be. I came to a kind of a conclusion today, and I need to tell you about it."

"OK." Greg waited.

"Nigel Branca is doing a better job than I would have expected, but in a very passive way. All he seems to be doing is reacting to whatever Sal Paglia's lawyers throw at him."

"Uh huh. Yeah, I think you're right."

"What I think I'm going to do is get together with Nigel and my dad and kind of vet the litigation strategy. I won't write anything down, and it would be a private meeting. There won't be any way for Sal and his lawyers to hear about it."

"Well, unless they ask the right question in a deposition or something."

"Maybe. But I think I would take that risk. My dad already gave his deposition. I think the benefits will outweigh the risks."

"OK, but what are you going to say? How are you going to help?"

"I'm going to tell them, 'fight harder, hit back.' They should put Sal under oath and ask him some hard questions, like, 'Why are you relying on a retired bricklayer to decide what companies you're going to invest in?' As I understand it, Nigel hasn't even decided whether he wants to take Sal's deposition. I think that's passive. Just plain passive."

Greg tapped the countertop where they were sitting, thinking about what he wanted to say. "Here's the thing. I don't know why, but I'm worried it's going to be really difficult for you to get pregnant while you're involved in litigation, even if you stay in the background. We're trying to have a baby. Who knows what effect all that stress might have?"

Olivia sighed. "I know. But doing nothing is stressful too. The bottom line is, we've been trying to have a baby for going on four years, and we'll keep trying for as long as it takes. Right now my dad's at the mercy of the lawyers on both sides. I don't think getting involved on an advice-only level is going to be any more stressful than what I'm going through now. It may even be a little less stressful, because maybe I'll be exercising some measure of control. Not much, but some."

"Can you take off work?"

Olivia considered the question. "That's a good idea, I think. I haven't taken even one vacation day yet this year. Maybe I'll just take as many days as I need to help with the case. That might mean we won't be able to go to St. Bart's in October. Would you be OK with that?"

Greg leaned toward her and gave her a hug. "Sure. I want you to do what you need to do. I love you."

CHAPTER 54

David Stein was 3Device's chief cook and bottle washer. Greg Morris thought great thoughts, fielded questions from the FDA, and plotted strategy, but David was the guy who made sure the FedEx's went out at the end of the day and the bills were paid on time. So maybe David's idea, when it came, was more applied common sense than genius. But it sure seemed like a stroke of genius.

"What about this," David said to Greg and Dr. Ableson. "We know we're never going to modify the geometry, shape or functionality of the hinge, during surgery or at any other point – we're just going to make different sizes, to different scales. We ourselves understood that the risks involved with letting doctors modify the hinge would be prohibitive. So why don't we go back to the FDA and say, 'Our device – our knee – is the hinge, 3D-printed. Period. That will always stay the same, in exactly the form you approve it. And as a bonus feature, we're going to make it fit better at point of care by allowing surgeons to modify contact surfaces. Framing it that way might get them off the dime, and we won't have to wait for the damn regulations."

There was quiet for a moment. "That is an excellent idea," responded Dr. Ableson, finally. "I think we've already told them we weren't going to vary the hinge, but it's kind of buried in the investigative phase material we submitted. We certainly haven't emphasized it at any point."

"We can call it an amended application," added Greg. "We can provide them some other examples of approved devices that are routinely modified to fit during surgery. Maybe we can persuade them their existing policies are adequate, and they can approve our application before they're finished creating their new rules. Anyway, it's worth a shot."

"Do you remember when the Chief Review Officer told us – in some phone meeting or other – that they want good devices to be approved?" asked David. "They want the public to have access to them. We can quote that back to her and see if we can change their perspective on this. We'll change the narrative."

"A knee is a hinge," said Greg. "Our trials have shown that our hinge works. Let's get Blue Tech on the phone and see what their reaction is. They're the ones who are going to have to sell the idea."

CHAPTER 55

Lou and Olivia and Nigel were sitting in Lou's kitchen in Norristown at noon on a Tuesday. Olivia had called Nigel and persuaded him that they needed to take Sal's deposition. Nigel sent Sal's lawyers a Notice of Deposition for October 19. After Sal's lawyer gave him the run-around for a few days, they finally agreed on the date – which was now a little more than three weeks away. There was some tiramisu on the table. Nigel had a whiskey tumbler; Lou was supplying the Jack Daniel's.

Lou's landline rang from the living room. Lou didn't like talking on the phone, but paradoxically, he loved his telephone. His phone was a red Western Electric table model from the early 1980's with a nice touch-tone grid. It had a heavy handset, and Lou paid for landline service through copper wires. Any time he had a choice of making a call from his landline or his cell phone, he made the call on his landline. Olivia usually tried calling him on the landline first – she understood his preferences – so that was good.

Lou walked out to his living room from the kitchen. "Hello?"

"Lou, it's Anna. Coffee's ready. Can I bring it over?" Anna had a ten-cup pot, which was a lot bigger than the pot in Lou's coffeemaker.

"Yeah, everybody's here. Thanks, Hon. See you in a bit." Lou walked back to the kitchen and sat back down at the table. Olivia turned to him to make a point.

"I'm listening carefully to what Nigel's been saying," said Olivia, "The best thing we have going for us is that a lot of people at the club heard Sal talking about how much money he was going to make. And they recall that he was talking a lot more than you were, Daddy. All of that is consistent with your testimony that he was the one pushing the deal. But nobody at the club can say for sure that you didn't say what he says you said. So we don't have corroboration for your side of the story."

"Honey, I don't care," Lou responded. "I don't own nothin' that he can go after when he wins. And he knows it too. He's trying to go after Greg and you, and not making any progress. Suing me is just a big joke."

"Which is exactly why I've wanted to pay for your defense," replied Olivia. "We can figure out a way to launder the payment, so Sal can never figure out it came from Greg and me. You shouldn't have to bear this alone, and neither should Nigel. We should hire a big law firm and fight back." She turned to Nigel. "No offense, Nigel. We would still want you involved."

"No offense taken," said Nigel.

Lou looked across the table at Olivia. "Honey, until a month ago, I never said anything like this to you in 35 years. But I'll say it again. If I find out you or Greg paid one penny toward my legal fees, or paid any other expenses, I will walk straight down to the judge and tell her that Sal wins, and I give up." Nigel didn't look happy about Lou's pronouncement, but Lou continued. "I caused this problem. I'm the one that listened to Sal even though I shouldn'a, and I'm the one that brought this mess to your door. The only way to keep this from hurting you is for you to stay clear. I'm not gonna let you pay money for this case, and I'm not sure anything you could do financially would help anyway. It's gonna be what it's gonna be. I'll deal with whatever happens."

All three were quiet. Olivia had figured she would fail, but she thought she owed it to her dad to try.

Anna knocked at the front door and let herself in. She brought the coffee back to the kitchen, placed the pot on the stove, and said hello to everybody. She poured a cup for Lou and Olivia; Nigel was happy with his flask. Anna smiled, patted Lou on the shoulder, gave Olivia a hug, and left quietly.

"All right, we can still talk about strategy," said Olivia, finally. "Nobody's quitting. But what our problem has boiled down to so far is that we don't have any leverage. Nigel, what can we do to gain some advantage?"

"Well, we have two possibilities that I can think of, although they haven't worked yet," Nigel began. "The first possibility is to push for a trial. Lou says he won't mind sitting in the courtroom for a few days. I hate trials, but I'm willing to do it. Trials are public. If we go to trial, Sal has to get up on the witness stand and claim that he lost a half a million bucks because a retired bricklayer didn't tell him enough about the company he was investing in. It'll make him look like an idiot. Lou, no offense. I can't imagine that's good for his business.

"The second possibility is we somehow persuade him to wait. Maybe do what's called a 'consensual stay.' His damages are all very uncertain right now, because 3Device is still in business, and still trying to get FDA approval for the knee. If the company turns itself around, he benefits financially, because he owns fifteen percent of the outstanding shares. There's a chance – hard to say how much of a chance – that the court is going to restrict him to his 'rescission' remedy if he wins, which would mean that he'd get his money back, but he'd have to give up his shares in exchange. So waiting would let him avoid a public trial for a while, and maybe he's still curious what would happen if the FDA let 3Device go to market with its knee. If he waits, maybe he can find out, and benefit."

"The problem we got is he's not worried about none of that," Lou responded. "He loves anything public. He's one of these pricks, you say his name out loud, he's happy. It don't bother him if you say somethin' bad about him, as long as you're sayin' somethin' about him. And I don't see him waitin', 'cause he's been pushin' me hard, and I don't see him lettin' up any time soon. Makes him feel important."

Lou paused and looked at his daughter. "I hate to admit this, but I never said one possible motive out loud. Remember when he called Greg and threatened him, right after the case was filed? Maybe that's what this is about for him. He loves the competition. He thinks Greg and you wear suits and drive fancy cars, and are too young to be where you are, and he just wants to hurt you. He's still a poor Italian kid from Norristown, and you represent every rich person who ever disrespected him in his life. Never mind you never did anything to hurt him. He don't care."

Olivia nodded slowly. She trusted her father's instincts about people. And what he said made sense. But she thought of strangling Sal Paglia and throwing his body off a porch somewhere so the crows could eat it. Maybe he was blind in one eye and wouldn't see her coming with a hatchet. Maybe he had some other weakness. Maybe he left all of his trucks unguarded overnight, and she could sneak in and puncture all their tires. Maybe she could put sugar in their gas tanks. Maybe he hadn't paid his taxes in ten years and she could report him. Maybe . . .

Olivia sat up straight and looked quickly from Lou to Nigel and back. "It's been staring me in the face for weeks, and it just didn't register. I know what we need to do, and it's not that complicated. You're going to go into that deposition ready for war. Asymmetrical war. He thinks he has you where he wants you, but he has no idea. I think you have him exactly where you want him. He walked out on a limb by filing this ridiculous lawsuit, and now you can saw it off."

"Not following," said Nigel.

"I need to do some research," Olivia responded. "Before I have you chasing after rainbows, I need to be confident we're going to find something. Give me two or three days, and I may not need even that long. But let me call you in a day or two."

Lou turned to Nigel. "I've seen her with this look on her face before. Let's just let her go with it. She's never wrong."

Olivia smiled, but her stomach was doing flips. "Let's just say that I'm hoping to justify your confidence."

CHAPTER 56

When Olivia got home, she turned on her computer and began to formulate search requests. Knowing that Sal Paglia, Inc., was a road contractor, she figured that the company was likely to have dealings with a lot of different cities and townships. To her surprise, she discovered that townships make extraordinary amounts of information about their operations and contracts available online. That made sense, sort of, because townships are governmental entities whose records are supposed to be available to the general public. And when she added "Sal Paglia" to her searches within township websites, she began to retrieve more hits than she had time to follow.

The website for Sal Paglia, Inc., was a treasure trove. It was full of information about the company's management, assets and operations. Olivia took notes furiously. When she finished with the company's website, it was also a simple matter to search for "Sal Paglia, Inc.," more generally. She turned up some information about its dealings with private developers – developers like to do press releases — as well as its contributions to various charities and non-profits.

As information accumulated, she began to realize that they would be greatly dependent upon Nigel's ability to use what she was finding at Sal Paglia's deposition. Sal Paglia, Inc., wasn't a party to the lawsuit. She had no idea whether Nigel would be permitted to bring up facts about the company during the deposition of its owner and president. She made a mental note to ask Nigel how, precisely, the information she was finding could be used during his questioning. She also needed to ask Nigel whether he would be prepared to meet with her daily to plan their investigation.

And perhaps the biggest question: Could they keep Sal Paglia in his chair during the deposition? What if he didn't want to listen to what Nigel was saying? What if he lost his temper and stormed out? Sal's leaving probably wouldn't be the end of the world, because they didn't require his cooperation just to inform him of what they found. They could always write him a letter, if it came to that. But Olivia understood that having Sal Paglia under oath would be a rare opportunity to confront him while he couldn't slither away.

In Olivia's mind, they would have one last, best chance to win the case – and Sal's deposition would be it. This was a guy who was prepared to file a federal lawsuit based on an elaborate series of lies. He was a talented liar, and it might be tough for them to prove to a jury that he was lying. But that wasn't where she was going with this. She wasn't interested in what a jury might conclude.

Olivia pulled out her calendar and began to create a project timeline. Three weeks. And she'd have talk to Nigel about whether her plan was remotely feasible in the time they had left.

CHAPTER 57

"Yeah."

For thirty-some years – since the verdict in the Scarfo trial – Tony Abruzzi answered his phone with one word. Whoever was calling knew who he was, and if they didn't, Tony didn't want to talk to them anyway. And the less information he gave to any Feds who might be listening in, the better. This particular Tuesday morning, he was sitting at his desk with his son, Joey, and his senior Capo, Angelo Cremonesi. Pete Fraterrigo was sitting in his usual chair in the corner, reading the sports page of *The Philadelphia Inquirer*. He still liked to read it on paper.

"Uncle Tony, it's me." Tony smiled. Hearing from Olivia was always a pleasure.

"Hi Honey, how you doin'?" said Tony. He mouthed "Olivia" to Joey and Angelo and popped a mint into his mouth.

Joey and Angelo listened to Tony's side of the conversation, and watched Tony's face go from happy, to contemplative, to serious.

"That prick," said Tony. "How's your dad doin'?" Tony nodded. And nodded again. Then Olivia talked for quite a while.

When Olivia stopped, Tony tugged on his ear and patted his hair down on the back of his head. "All right, that's good, that's a good plan. Sal Paglia is a twisted guinzo prick – always has been. He's overdue for some humility. Let me think about it and talk to the boys. Can I call you back in a day or two?"

Tony listened to Olivia, and nodded some more. "OK, I promise. I'll be back to you by close of business on Thursday." He smiled. "Love you too, Honey. Bye."

Tony placed the handset back in the cradle and summarized for Joey and Angelo. "Sal Paglia is a cocksucker. I hate the motherfucker." He turned to Angelo. "I tol' you he sued my brother-in-law, Lou Incaviglia? Lou did the brick work for the Knights of Columbus Hall over on Eleventh Street, remember? I introduced you while he was working there. Anyway, even if Sal Paglia wins, he knows he's not gonna get a dime. He just hates people. Well, Lou is family."

Tony looked at Joey, at Angelo, and back at Joey. Then at the ceiling. "Olivia had two or three really good ideas how to turn the case around," he began, as he lowered his gaze back to his two closest advisors. "And I have a couple ideas that might work. Joey, do me a favor and take a few notes, I'm gonna forget stuff. Angelo, why don't you push off tomorrow's meetings till Friday, and just work on this for a couple of days."

"OK, Tony," Angelo responded, and took out a notebook of his own.

"I don't pick fights with nobody," said Tony, "and I don't like to mix family business with, you know, family business. But this cocksucker started this fight, and we need to answer back. We don't need to do it all by ourselves, but we need to be heard from." Tony shook his head again. "Cocksucker."

CHAPTER 58

Lou, Nigel and Olivia were sitting at the kitchen table in Lou's kitchen. They had taken to calling the kitchen their "Command Center," and for all practical purposes it was. There were papers everywhere, Styrofoam coffee cups, half-eaten bagels, and dishes in the sink. They were four days into their preparation for Sal Paglia's deposition, and there were only two and a half weeks left before it would start.

"Try to think about everything you've ever known about Sal Paglia," said Olivia, "and then Nigel can think about whether any of it is going to be of any use. I'll give you an example – we talked about how his first wife, Consuela, is living in Doylestown. Maybe she'll talk to Nigel. Or maybe you know something about her, or can remember something about her, that would be helpful. The more facts we know about this guy, the more effective Nigel is going to be at the deposition. I have a pencil and paper, and I'm starting the recorder on my phone." She held them up. "Just relax and start talking."

"I think I get why we're doing this," Lou began, "but most of what I knew I prolly forgot, and I don't know whether half of what I know is true."

"Just about everything is potentially important — rumors, comments, vague recollections," Nigel responded. "Things you heard that aren't true aren't going to help, but we won't know whether something is true until we've investigated it. So don't worry about whether something is true or not, at this stage."

"OK, got it. I'm goin' with the program. I'll do my best." Lou thought for a long moment. Where to begin?

"I've known Sal for about 30, 35 years. I met him at the Italian Club, and ninety-five percent of what I've ever known or heard about him, I picked up at the club. He's got a lot of money – prolly more than anybody else at the club – and he likes to think he's a big shot. He hands out twenty dollar cigars. He buys a round of drinks for everybody pretty often. He thinks he's important, and he enjoys the attention.

"If I'm bein' honest, he fits in pretty good at the club. He's mostly just one of the guys. So when he reminds you he's rich, it's kind of like subtle. I don't know how to explain it.

"The other thing is, he's sort of a celebrity, so people talk about him time to time when he's not there. Give you an example. There's a story – true story – about how he was in the club one day at lunchtime, and one of the guys at the bar got a call from his wife saying that their dog had just been hit by a car, but was still alive. She didn't have no car. Sal was sitting next to the guy at the bar and knew where the guy and his wife lived. He called one of his drivers who was in the area, and the driver loaded the dog and the wife into the cab of the truck and took them to the vet hospital. I forget how the dog made out, but everybody had this image of that big dump truck being used as an ambulance. That story still gets told around the club.

"There was the story about how Sal had a hole-in-one over at Norristown Country Club and didn't know it. He's nearsighted, but he wasn't wearing his contacts, and the guys he was playing with knew it, so they told him his ball went over the green. He's looking for his ball, they made him take a stroke for a lost ball, he's all like 'I thought I hit that ball good.' It must a been funny as shit. So they let him play the second ball, and then finally pretended to be confused when the first guy finished putting and there was an extra ball in the cup. They straightened it all out and busted Sal's balls. Sal took it pretty well, apparently, and bought drinks afterwards like you're supposed to.

"And you know me, I hear things. I heard other stuff. One afternoon, Lenny Delgado was sittin' at the bar. I know him good, 'cause he's a bricklayer, and we've done a couple a jobs together. He's telling me that he did a job at Sal's house out in Blue Bell. He met Sal's second wife. 'Sallie's' her name, believe it or not. Sal and Sallie. She's not Italian. Younger than Connie, real pretty. She wanted hand-made bricks for the new patio and barbeque in the back yard, so they ordered Glen Gery's. That's a high-end brick, costs a fortune. Lenny did the job moonlighting, took vacation to do it. Most union guys – Lenny is union – will do a private job without getting the hiring hall involved, and will set their own rates. I never liked to do that, but I didn't think it was union-busting or nothin' when guys did it. But he told me Sal had one of his trucks out there, so it was almost like a company job. And Sal's company is non-union. Close to the line, you ask me, I wouldn'a took the work."

"That's interesting," interjected Olivia. "I wonder if the truck drivers were working on company time. There's probably not anything illegal about using company assets for personal projects – he owns the company – but maybe it crosses some line, somewhere. Nigel?"

"Mostly tax issues," Nigel replied. "I'll give it some thought. I'm thinking about state taxes, especially." Nigel took a sip of Jack Daniel's from his little flask. "Go ahead, Lou."

"So, I'm tryn'a think a other stuff. Sal has season tickets to the Eagles, and every once in a while one of the tickets is gonna go unused, and he'll offer a seat to the game to guys at the club. That happens maybe once a year, I don't know. Carmine DeLuca said 'yes' once – this was just a couple a years ago — and Sal told him to get in touch with a nephew, Sal's sister's kid. Carmine called the kid, and the kid asked him to come pick up the ticket. Carmine had to drive pretty far to get it, I remember. He said he had a good time at the game. By coincidence, he was sitting next to the Township Manager from Penn Manor Township, which is where Carmine lives, just outside of Norristown. Carmine says to him, 'tell you what, you can buy me one beer for every pothole I don't complain about.' I always remembered that line. The guy laughed, and Carmine said they had a good time."

"Do you think Carmine would remember the nephew's name?" asked Olivia.

"Yeah, Carmine don't forget nothin'," said Lou. "I can ask him if you want."

"Yeah, please, do that," said Nigel.

Lou continued to search his memory. "What else? Sal's favorite expression is 'God forbid I ever have to go back to sealing driveways.' That's how he started his business, spreading hot tar on people's driveways. He would charge a hundred bucks for a top coat that would last you a couple a years. He's proud of where he came from.

"I don't know nothin' about his family or what he was like growing up. I know he grew up in Norristown, but he was over in St. Francis Parish, so I didn't go to grade school with him. He was at Bishop Kenrick High School for one of the years I was there, but I never knew him. He never went to college, and he was proud a that.

"He smokes Macanudo cigars. He drives a Land Rover. What self-respecting guinea from the neighborhood drives a Land Rover? What's the matter with a Chevy Tahoe? Or even a Cadillac Escalade, shit. Don't make no sense, unless he's tryn'a impress somebody who's not Italian. Or maybe Sallie picked the car, who knows?

"He has a mean streak. We know that, but I think he keeps it hidden from a lot of people. He tortures Tommy Benelli about the fact that Tommy's eyes don't look in the same direction at the same time. I don't like when Sal does that, and I used to say somethin' to him when he did it. Then he'd say he was just kidding, and I should lighten up. I'd like to lighten up his face.

"What else? He drinks V.O., like me. He usually comes into the club in work clothes, directly from work. He's a hands-on boss and likes to visit his jobs, so he wears jeans and boots. Every coat or jacket or sweater he has says 'Sal Paglia, Inc.,' with like a little logo thing. I mean, every one. That's probably smart – if you're gonna own a company you might as well advertise it every chance you get.

"I don't think he has no hobbies. He doesn't collect coins or stamps or cars or nothin'. The only sport he likes is baseball. I woulda thought he was a football fan, with the Eagles tickets and all, but he don't follow the game.

"I know he hates unions. He only ever said something once, maybe 15 or 20 years ago. His company is mostly non-union, but his asphalt plants are unionized, and the guys in the asphalt plants did a one-day walkout. Over not havin' enough safety equipment or somethin', I forget what. Sal was pissed, and started bitchin' to Gino Tonelli about it at the club. He said some terrible things about unions. Bad idea. There's a lot of union guys in the club – including Gino — and people were actually getting out of chairs to come over to where he was. I don't think we've ever had a fight in the club, at least not when I was there, but this was close. And he's clever at dealing with people – he looked around and said, 'OK, I've said my piece. Just lettin' off some steam.' What were we gonna do at that point, break a chair on his head? So people went back to their seats, and everybody moved on. But Gino has never really stopped being pissed at him.

"I'm tryn'a think if I've heard anything else about his business. Danny Garibaldi is a member down the club, and he drives for Sal. Big dump truck. I haven't talked with Danny about the lawsuit, I don't wanna get him in the middle. Anyway, the company used to put Santa Claus on the roof of Danny's cab at Christmas, and fill the bed up with presents. They would drive around neighborhoods in Montgomery County, with Santa waving to kids and Danny honkin' the big air horn. They took the presents to poor neighborhoods in the city and gave them out. Danny loves that truck. But he almost blew it up once. He was drinking in the club and told us about how he left the fueling hose unattended at the fueling station in the company yard – he was taking a piss, I think — and that little trip lever thing didn't work to stop the pump when his tank was full. He dumped a hundred gallons of diesel on the ground. He was still rattled about it when he told the story."

"When was that?" asked Nigel.

"Mmmm, I'm tryn'a think," said Lou. "Wait, I remember Danny had one of those blue paper masks hanging off one ear when he tol' me the story. He must a been getting ready to leave the club, or maybe he just came in. So that means it hadda be 2020, 2021 or maybe even 2022. During the whole COVID thing."

"Good, that's good," said Nigel. "Keep going."

"What else? Sal's first wife, Connie – Consuela – was from Brazil. She was a nice lady, came into the club for the Christmas party most years. I would say they got divorced about ten years ago, maybe more. I don't think the divorce was nasty. They just fell out of love, maybe. They are both close to their sons. Like you said, I think Connie lives in Doylestown, last I heard."

Lou continued to talk for another hour. Some of it was going over things twice or three times, with Olivia and Nigel asking a lot of questions. At the end of the process, Olivia wasn't sure how much progress they'd made, but she trusted her instincts. She had a good feeling about their ability to accumulate a great deal of additional information about Mr. Salvatore Paglia. And about his company. She and Nigel set up a time to get together for the next phase of their effort.

CHAPTER 59

Olivia's home was orderly. And she carefully monitored things that ran out. In a house that large, it was a simple matter to store copious reserves of paper towels, toilet paper, AA batteries, bath soap, light bulbs, dish liquid, laundry detergent, coffee, toothpaste, and beer without Greg's noticing. The fact that she had a 24-month supply of dinner candles wasn't hurting anyone. And when Nigel asked if she had any AA batteries on hand – he needed one for his mouse – she was equipped and happy to help.

Olivia and Nigel had agreed to work at her house for the day. When she made the plan she had forgotten that Nigel didn't own a car. When she realized he was going to have to take the Red Arrow Line to Villanova and then walk a mile and a half to their place, she volunteered to pick him up and drive him home.

They were sitting in Olivia's home office, staring at the screens on Olivia's desktop and Nigel's laptop. The two of them had been involved in mostly unproductive online searches for about an hour. It was their assumption that Sal Paglia, Inc., had probably been involved in a lot of litigation over the years, either as a plaintiff or defendant, and that they would be able to identify some adverse parties who might be able to provide information about the company. And who would be happy to share it.

They turned up a few cases, but nothing that looked like nasty, contentious litigation. Most of the cases they found were auto accidents. Big trucks hitting smaller cars. But those kinds of cases are handled by insurance companies, and they don't generate a lot of motions and court opinions. Sal's divorce, in Montgomery County, was on the docket. But the divorce had been consensual, and the docket showed only three documents, all mostly uninformative.

Olivia walked down to the kitchen, poured some coffee and brought it back to the office. This time, Nigel accepted a cup. They let the screen savers take over for a while.

"He's such an ornery human being that I expected to find a bunch of lawsuits, either by him or against him," said Nigel. "We're missing something."

"Is it possible he just settles them all?" asked Olivia.

"Sure, but for there not to be anything on the dockets, he would have to settle his disputes before complaints are filed. Even if it were just a complaint and then a prompt settlement, the case would be searchable on a court docket," Nigel replied.

"How about arbitration?"

"Well, that's a good point. If virtually all of his contracts include arbitration clauses – and he's a road contractor so they probably would – a breach of contract case wouldn't show up on a public docket.

"Just for the hell of it, let's search for cases involving one of his competitors," suggested Olivia. "Let's try Heritage Paving."

They went back into the same dockets they had just reviewed, and turned up more than 20 cases by or against Heritage Paving during the prior 15 years. The company was involved in the ordinary run of public disputes – like truck accidents, employment discrimination claims, a tax claim by Bucks County, and two or three disputes with vendors.

"I wouldn't read too much into it," Nigel volunteered, "but I suspect Sal Paglia picks his battles. You'll notice that he hasn't been sued by employees or ex-employees, which suggests that he settles those cases before they go to court. Which might be a smart business strategy. Those are the people who know his secrets, who know where the bodies are buried. He doesn't want to be fighting with employees in court. Maybe he avoids cases that could open cans of worms."

"Are there any more court records we could check?" asked Olivia.

"I don't think so," Nigel replied. "We've looked at all of the federal districts and all of the civil dockets in Pennsylvania." Nigel thought for a second. "I guess we can try the criminal dockets."

Nigel navigated through Pennsylvania's online judicial portal, looking for the name "Salvatore Paglia" as a defendant in any criminal case. To his astonishment, a case popped up in Berks County.

"Holy shit. A Salvatore Paglia was a defendant in a case that came out of Shillington in 1995. The charge was simple assault, which is a misdemeanor. He was found not guilty. Can you search for a 'Sal Paglia' and 'Salvatore Paglia' in Berks County, to see if it could be somebody with the same name?"

Olivia searched while Nigel thought. "The people-finder databases don't suggest anyone other than the Sal Paglia we know and love," she said, finally.

"The fact that the case was in Berks County probably explains why nobody at the club heard about it. Sal was obviously keeping it quiet." Nigel paused. "Let me try something," he said. After a minute of searching, he turned his laptop screen half way toward Olivia. "I was searching the Reading Eagle archives. The paper had an article about the case." Both of them read the brief story.

"So some guy drives onto Sal's new asphalt by accident, and he and Sal get into a tussle," said Olivia. "And Sal gets found not guilty. Why do you think they weren't able to convict him?"

"Well, I handle these cases for a living, so I can give you some informed speculation. 'Not guilty' probably means that there was solid evidence that the other guy started it. Maybe Sal yelled at him for driving on the asphalt, and maybe the guy got insulted and popped Sal on the chin. Or maybe he just shoved him. In either case, Sal had the right to use equivalent force to defend himself, assuming he didn't initiate the altercation."

"What is 'simple assault'?" asked Olivia.

"Simple assault is when you intentionally hit or shove somebody, with an intent to cause 'substantial pain.' Sal was charged with a second-degree misdemeanor, which means the DA had some evidence that he started it. If the DA thought it was mutual combat, they would have charged it as a third degree misdemeanor. So the complaining witness must have been claiming that Sal clocked him without physical provocation. And the judge or the jury probably rejected that story and concluded that it was self-defense. I don't know, I'm just speculating."

"Is there anything we can do with this information?" Olivia asked.

"Not really. He was found not guilty. If he had been found guilty he could have faced a lot of collateral consequences, like loss of the ability to bid on government contracts. That's probably why he took the case to trial. He needed that verdict. And his decision paid off, because 'not guilty' means 'not guilty.' As far as the law is concerned, it's as if the criminal case was never brought."

"Can we re-investigate the criminal case – maybe talk to the witnesses – and use the evidence somehow?"

Nigel smiled. "You're thinking like a lawyer. But no. The fact that he got in a physical dispute decades ago isn't going to be relevant to our case, and I can't think of any other use we can make of it."

"In any event, you had a grown man, who owns his own business, acting like a kid on a playground," said Olivia. "What kind of company president gets in fights?"

"I think that's just the way Sal is," Nigel replied. "He's got a temper."

Olivia shook her head slowly. "OK, back to our case," she said, finally. "It looks like Sal Paglia avoids certain types of litigation. Then why would he sue my dad? I know you can't read his mind, but what do you think is going on?"

"Most litigators claim to know what the other side is thinking, but that's all bullshit. When I was doing civil litigation, I never had much of an idea why the other side did anything. Your opponent is not going to tell you why he's doing X instead of Y. But often, you find out what he *wants*, because he'll tell you. And in this case, Sal Paglia has told us that he wants to own and control 3Device, Inc. That's what he's demanding to settle the case, and that's probably why he brought it. So our job is to frustrate that desire."

"Why would he want to own 3Device?" asked Olivia. "He already owns a company with a hundred and fifty mil in annual revenues, and 3Device barely owns its own office furniture. It doesn't make sense."

"There are only two possibilities," replied Nigel. "Either he believes 3Device is going to be very successful, or he wants to harm Lou – and you and your husband. And it doesn't have to be either/or. It could be both."

Olivia nodded slowly. "I agree with you," she said. "So we need to make it sufficiently painful for him that he'll re-think what he's willing to do to get what he wants. We can remind him why most businesses, including his own apparently, do their best to avoid litigation."

"Yup. All right, let's go to the next item on our list," said Nigel. He signed on, again, to the business search portal of the Pennsylvania Department of State. "It says here that Sal Paglia, Inc., is a Pennsylvania corporation formed in 1986. The company is in good standing with the state – which means its taxes have been paid – and its registered office is at 7740 Ridge Pike in Collegeville, Pennsylvania. Every corporation has to have a 'registered office' so that parties can know where to serve a lawsuit against it. It looks like Sal has used his business address as his registered address."

Nigel clicked a few more keys as Olivia watched. "Well, this is interesting," said Nigel. "I searched whether there are any other companies present at that address. It turns out that there's a company called 'Autumn Events,

LLC,' that has the same registered office address in Collegeville. We should probably try to figure out what they do."

Nigel went back to the Department of State portal and determined that Autumn Events, LLC, was formed in 2011 as a Pennsylvania limited liability company. No additional information was available from the state. Nigel searched for domain names and websites that contained "Autumn Events" as part of the name, and didn't turn up any hits. Google only turned up the basic information from Pennsylvania's business search portal. So whatever Autumn Events did, it apparently didn't advertise its products or services to the world. "How can a company not sell anything?" asked Nigel.

Olivia's eyebrows shot up. "Maybe they buy things. I have a girlfriend who buys pottery, and has for years. She has a little company. Lots of people are like that. Let me check in Craigslist, ebay, Etsy and some classifieds. I'll search 'Autumn Events' and '7740 Ridge Pike,' and see if I can find a trader – somebody who buys and sells gold, or art, or guitars, or fine china. Whatever. It shouldn't take too long."

Olivia went to work running searches on the big trading websites. Autumn Events wasn't running any ads currently. She cross-checked some things with Internet Archive, and used Google's search cache function that lets you search other people's searches and find the results that they got. After 25 minutes, she struck gold. "Nigel, check this out. There was a 'Wanted to Buy' ad on Craigslist for three months at a time in 2013, 2014 and 2015. The buyer was looking for Eagles season tickets. 'Will pay substantially above face value.' It says 'email us through Craigslist, or call Autumn Events at 610-772-9911.' And the little circle map centers on the Collegeville area."

Nigel smiled. "This is great stuff," he said. "But it almost raises more questions than it answers. We know from Lou that Sal has some Eagles season tickets, and when he lets people use them, he sends people to his nephew to get them."

Olivia nodded. "Yeah."

"It appears that Autumn Events, LLC, wants to own Eagles tickets, but doesn't really sell anything," Nigel continued. "But why wouldn't Sal just have Sal Paglia, Inc., buy the tickets? Entertainment expenses aren't deductible, but the paving business is where the cash is. It seems like a lot of wasted motion to have the tickets owned by a separate company. What's the point?"

"We'll figure it out," Olivia replied. "Let's keep moving. You said we could look up information on the company's pension plans?"

Nigel opened up another tab on his browser. "Yeah, it's an easy process. A company is required to submit an annual form to the federal government providing details about its pension plans and other kinds of employee benefit plans. It's called a Form 5500, and each company's submission is a public record. Amazing, really. There's a lot of information in those forms. So I'm bringing up last year's Form 5500 for Sal Paglia, Inc."

Nigel worked his keyboard while Olivia headed to the kitchen to find more coffee and some cookies. They'd been at it for almost three hours, and it felt like 10 minutes. Too much to do, and too little time.

Nigel turned his laptop toward Olivia as she walked back in with coffee and some shortbreads. "Here's the company's Form 5500 for its 401(k) plan last year. It says there are 30 participants in the plan. That's odd. The company's website says it employs more than 900 workers." Nigel made a note. "I'll check to see what the story is on that."

"Were you able to dig up any records from any of the local townships?" asked Olivia.

"I'm making some progress," Nigel replied, "but it's slow going. The company's contracts with townships are all public records, but copies of the contracts themselves are not online. You have to make a public records request, and the township thinks about it for two months, and then they make you pay a dollar a page for copying. So we can't get contracts in time for them to help. And we might not find much anyway. I talked to a lawyer here in Norristown who does township work, represents a lot of township boards. I went to law school with him. I asked him if there were a lot of reported instances of townships getting in trouble over contracting. Apparently not, although he says it happens."

"Maybe it just doesn't get reported," said Olivia.

"Possible," said Nigel. "But there may be a more important reason. The guy I talked to says sealed bidding and fixed-price contracts are required for almost everything major that a township buys, and sealed bidding is very hard to rig. When they unseal the bids, they read them out loud in public. And the big bidders tend to police each other. They can file bid protests if they think something wasn't kosher.

"There is one thing though. I noticed that Sal Paglia, Inc., has been approved for a bunch of change orders on its contracts with townships. Mostly for 'unforeseen conditions.' Township boards have to approve major change orders, and so some of those were searchable. But a lot of townships have published policies that say the Township Manager can approve a change order up to $25,000. I'll keep going on that, see what we can find."

Olivia sighed. "Nigel, I'm starting to think that we have too much to do, and too little time. Can we get the deposition postponed? I'm not sure the two weeks we have left are enough time to get ready."

"I wish I could be more encouraging, but I think it would be a mistake to postpone the dep. The court set a discovery deadline of December 1, and if we postpone the deposition, Sal is going to resist setting a new date for it. He's going to say we had our chance but didn't take it. He could make us file a motion to compel the deposition, and there's no guarantee that the motion would be decided before December 1. And the court might say we had our chance and gave it up. In short, it'd be risky to postpone. That's all I can say."

Olivia nodded and fidgeted with her coffee cup. "Yeah, but litigation is all about risk."

Nigel stood and stretched, drummed his fingers lightly on the back of his chair, and considered Olivia's comment. "When you called me a couple of weeks ago to insist that we take his deposition, I was a little hesitant. I think I know what he's going to say about the stock transaction, and I wasn't necessarily keen on giving him an opportunity before trial to practice what he's going to say during trial. But you convinced me. Having him sitting at the deposition table, under oath, is the best opportunity we're going to have to beat the bastard. He can't get up and leave – or at least he's not supposed to – and we can make him sit there and listen to every question we have. All the while, the court reporter is taking it all down, and anything Sal says can be used against him. We desperately need to sit him down in that chair, and October 19 may be the only chance we'll have. Two more weeks is going to have to be enough to get ready."

Olivia nodded again. "I get it." She stood and clasped Nigel on the shoulder. "Nigel, let's call it a day. I'll drop you off at home on the way over to my dad's. How are you doing? Is it causing problems for you not to be doing any criminal work right now?"

"Naw, the money your dad gave me has been more than enough to pay my bills," said Nigel. "I can go back to accepting court appointments any time I want. I'm going to see this case through Sal Paglia's deposition, and then we'll see where we are. Your idea was brilliant, that's all I can say. I think this is going to work."

CHAPTER 60

Lou arrived at Empire Brick Supply at 3:00 in the afternoon, an hour before closing. He figured, any supply house, the counter man is busy in the morning. Guys are picking up materials for their jobs that day. It's hard to get a minute to talk to him. The time to go is later in the afternoon.

Empire Brick Supply was owned by Arturo Angeloni. Nigel had talked about serving him a subpoena, and Olivia and Lou had brainstormed some other strategies for obtaining information from the business. They agreed, finally, that there was no harm in trying Lou's idea first. Lou knew – because he heard things – that Nico Salamone, the counter man for Empire Brick Supply, drank too much, liked to bet on sports, and was behind on his child support. They would try the direct approach first.

"Nico, how you been?" said Lou, as he entered the store and approached the counter.

Nico looked up, registered who it was, and smiled. "Louie, how are you my friend? It's been a while." Lou had often come into the store to pick up bricks for jobs.

"I'm doin' good, can't complain," Lou replied. "I wanted to stop by to see if you could help me with somethin'. You know I been retired for a little while. But I'm trying to price out a backyard patio and barbeque that my daughter and her husband are thinkin'a building. Anyways, I remember a conversation I had with Lenny Delgado at the Italian club about five, six years ago where he was sayin' he built a brick patio and fireplace for Sal

Paglia, and they used Glen Gery handmades for the job. Since your yard is only a mile from Sal's place, I figured he probably bought the brick from you, and you might be able to help me budget it."

"Yeah, I remember that job," replied Nico. "I've special ordered Glen Gery's a few times, and that was one of them. I can ask them for a quote. I can probably get back to you in two or three days."

"I don't want to tie you up with all that if we can avoid it," Lou replied. "Here's my business proposition for you. If you can let me look at your invoice to Sal Paglia for the job, I'll give you a thousand bucks, cash. I don't even need to make a copy, and nobody will ever know I was here."

Nico was not born last week. "Lou, this is too weird, man. I have no idea why you want to look at that invoice, but whatever you're cooking up, I don't wanna be involved."

"I get it, Nico, I'd say the same thing. But there's no law against you showing me one of your invoices. It belongs to Empire Brick Supply, not to the customer. You can just pull it up on your computer, turn the screen out a little bit, and go check your stock room for a minute. I promise no one will ever hear about this conversation." Lou placed the ten 100's flat on the counter.

Nico looked at Lou, looked at his computer, and then silently moved his mouse and clicked a few keys. He moved his mouse again, and fingered the wheel a little bit. "Lou, I need to check something in back, I'll be with you in a couple of minutes." He took the ten bills with him.

Lou looked back through the front door to make sure that the parking lot was still empty. He turned back to the counter, bent his torso across most of it, and tipped the computer screen further in his direction. The result was as good as, or better than, they had hoped. Lou took out a pen and a small pad, noted the names, date and amounts, and wrote down the most important fact they were after. He smiled to himself, turned the computer screen back to where it was, and texted Nigel: "Success." He was standing at the counter for another two minutes, at least, when Nico came back.

"Lou, we're always happy to help," offered Nico. "Let me know if I can make a call about those Glen Gery's."

"I will, Nico. I'll be back with you, let you know how the project is going." Lou turned toward the door, and gave a little half wave to Nico. "Bye Buddy."

"Bye Lou. Take care of yourself. And thanks for coming in."

CHAPTER 61

Lou and Anna were having lunch at the Cracker Barrel with Carmine and his girlfriend Martina. The restaurant displayed rocking chairs out front, all of which were for sale. That made sense to Lou – once you eat their biscuits and gravy, the first thing you think of is falling into a rocking chair, taking a nap, and hoping that you'll be hungry again by dinner.

"I was doing her hair at Trans World Hairways," said Martina. "She probably came to me for two years, before I left."

"How did you get her talking?" asked Lou.

Martina gave him a "What planet are you from?" look. "The only problem we ever had in that shop was shutting these ladies up."

"Did you like her?" asked Anna.

"Yeah, I did," Martina replied. "Sallie was a trophy bride. She didn't brag, or whine, or complain, or celebrate it. She just owned it. Like, 'I may have won the marriage lottery, but I have to deal with his temper, and I still have to get under the sink and crank the garbage dispose-all when it clogs.' That kind of thing."

"She talked about his temper?" asked Lou.

"Yeah, she told me about a picnic they had in their back yard. One of Sal's adult sons was there – Sallie's stepson, not her child – and the kid said something to his father. I don't remember what it was, but I do remember thinking it wasn't that horrible. So Sal jumps up from his chair, slaps his son hard across the face, picks him up by the collar of his shirt, and tosses him over the patio wall."

Lou, Carmine and Anna digested that information. "Did it seem like she was afraid of him?" asked Anna, finally.

"No. I got the sense, or she may even have said, that he never hit her. She was just upset that he was like that with his son. Like I said, she talked a lot about his temper."

Lou asked Martina, "Did you ever meet Sal?"

"I did once, at the Christmas party down the club. Sallie was with him, and she introduced us. I remember thinking he's a big man. And he was complaining about the meatballs. He looked to me like an angry human being."

Lou wasn't afraid of Sal Paglia. But he wondered how they were going to manage his temper during the deposition. In the meantime, they had a lunch to finish. "Carmine, you gettin' dessert?" Lou asked.

"A course I'm gettin' dessert. Key lime pie. And a Bud."

"I'll make that two," Lou replied. He didn't always drink Pabst. "Ladies?"

The girls exchanged looks, like, "Unbelievable." But they also knew that a piece of pie and a beer after biscuits and gravy would make Lou and Carmine happy. Never hurts to be happy. The girls ordered raspberry sherbet and coffee.

CHAPTER 62

L ou, Olivia and Nigel were in the Command Center for their daily meeting. They were working on a Saturday. "We need a young guy to go talk to Sal's nephew at the Valley Forge Cucina in King of Prussia," said Olivia. "Anybody have any candidates?"

"The problem is, I heard he hangs out there," replied Lou, "but I don't know for sure. I don't wanna send nobody on a wild-goose chase."

"At this point, we need to start taking some chances," Nigel responded. "Our working theory is that the nephew – his name is Wayne Locatelli, he isn't a Paglia — is going to have information that will help, a lot. We need to go get it."

"Dad, I was being a little coy; I apologize," said Olivia. "What I wanted to say was, 'Do you think Ziggy Gallo would be willing to help?'"

Lou looked up, surprised. "Aw, Honey, I couldn't ask Ziggy to get involved in this shit show. That wouldn't be fair to him."

"Daddy, I knew that was what you would say, but hear me out. You taught Ziggy everything you know about bricklaying and horse racing. You literally changed his life. Ziggy would walk through walls for you. You've helped him in a million ways, and he would want to help if we asked. What I need to tell you – and I asked Nigel about this, he can confirm it – is that Ziggy can't get in any trouble from this. We're not asking him to do anything illegal. He won't get pulled into the litigation, because the information he'll be looking for isn't anything you could use at trial. And if it were, Nigel says we can prove it some other way, we won't need Ziggy to testify. This will be fun for him – a little private investigator action, maybe he'll tell his kids about it some day."

Lou sat quietly for a half a minute. Neither Olivia nor Nigel interrupted his thoughts. "OK, we can do it. But if I get uncomfortable, or if I think Ziggy is getting himself into a tight spot, I'm gonna pull the plug on his involvement. End of story."

"Deal," said Olivia, quietly. "Thank you, Daddy. Now, we talked about sending Carmine around to scope out the asphalt plants. Were either of you able to talk to Carmine about that?"

"I called him yesterday," said Lou. "He's happy to do it. He don't get much chance to drive anymore."

"I went online to find these places," said Nigel. "And I cross-checked on Google Earth. I think six of the eight asphalt plants could be visible from the road. He'll have to leave early in the morning if he wants to do it all tomorrow."

"He won't be happy about gettin' up early, but he won't complain," said Lou. "He wants to help."

"OK," said Olivia, "would it be possible to print the addresses and maybe some Mapquest directions? Nigel, can we do that?"

"Sure, but it'll take an hour or two, at least. We're at the point where everything takes time, and we don't have much." He sighed, and took a sip from his flask. "Let me get started." In the meantime, Olivia called Greg to fill him in, while Lou read an old copy of People Magazine. Lou wasn't much help with a computer.

CHAPTER 63

L ou's sister Rita and her partner Karen were coming around Mario's and Paulette's side yard to the picnic in back. Lou saw them from the lawn chairs and made a beeline.

"Hi Hon. Hi Karen. Good to see youse." He gave each of them a hug. Olivia and Greg were trailing after Lou, and stepped up beside him. "Hi Aunt Rita," said Olivia. "Hi Aunt Karen. Where's the puppy?" Greg and Olivia hugged their aunts, who were both in their late fifties but looked younger. "That little bastard, he ate a cushion on the couch while we were out walking our three miles," Rita replied. "I kept whispering to him, 'SPCA, SPCA' while we were getting ready to come over. I plan to crate and ship his shaggy ass back to where he came from first thing tomorrow morning."

Lou gave her a skeptical look. "What, a girl can't dream?" she said. She had been making similar threats against Bigsby for eight years. Karen and Rita had rescued Bigsby from the SPCA and had joked about giving him back every week he'd been with them. They loved him like a son, but he was – difficult. "So, he's not here because he's literally being punished. We penned him in the back yard with some water and the remains of the cushion, as a reminder. Let him reflect on his sins."

Mario and Paulette guided everyone onto the back patio. They hosted a fall family picnic every year. As it happened, this year was a little different – both of their kids, Marty and Stacey, and all of the grandchildren were with in-laws, so Olivia wouldn't get to see her cousins and their kids. But she and Greg had been looking forward to catching up with Mario and Paulette and Rita and Karen, and the mood was good. Greg was with Mario at the grill, observing his technique. The Phillies were on, so Mario, Greg and Lou stole a glance every few minutes at Mario's patio TV. Playoff baseball.

Rita sat down next to her brother while they were having beers and waiting for the chicken-tender appetizers to finish cooking. "You look like shit, Lou. What's up with the lawsuit?"

Lou shook his head. "It's hard to tell. We have a deposition coming up. Maybe we'll know more, after."

"Have you been sleeping?"

"Yeah, I never have no problem sleepin'."

"I haven't seen you look this bad since Gabby died. We're worried about you."

"You don't need a be worried. I'm doin' fine, and I'm almost able to laugh about all a this. It's more like . . . Do you remember when me and Mario used to go with friends down to the trees between the river and the railroad tracks?"

"Yeah."

"One time, we found one of them portable electric speed limit signs that somebody parked next to the tracks, where the access road crosses. And somebody thought it would be fun to break it all up, because everybody hates speed limits, right? And then a detective from the Norristown Police Department starts knockin' on doors in the neighborhood, askin' if any of the parents know anything. So for two or three weeks me and Mario were worried that we were gonna get caught, and Mom and Dad would find out."

Rita nodded as if she were following, but she wasn't, really.

"That's what defending a lawsuit is like," Lou continued. "You know somethin' bad might happen. Even if it won't be the end of the world if it does happen, some part of your brain is worried about it. And so it feels like you're worrying all the time, even though you're not. It's makin' me tired."

"You should get some antidepressants, Big Brother. They really do work."

"Olivia said somethin' like that. There's two problems. One, I don't like takin' mental meds. Two, they supposably take about six weeks before they start workin'. By that time, this case will hopefully be over."

"All right then, promise me you'll drink a lot," said Rita.

Lou laughed. "My friend Anna said the same thing. Liquor is quicker, I guess."

CHAPTER 64

Nigel and Lou were meeting with Carmine DeLuca at the Swede Street Diner. It was 3:30 p.m. They could have met at Lou's place, but Lou hadn't eaten since morning, and he was hungry. Lou had picked Carmine up at his home in Penn Manor Township and brought him over. Nigel had done the research and was leading the discussion.

"The trouble with asphalt plants, for our purposes," said Nigel, "is that they're automated, and you're not going to see very much in the way of people. But what you might be able to see is the loading process."

Carmine nodded. Nigel explained what Carmine should be looking for if he was able to see asphalt being loaded.

"What do I do if somebody asks me why I'm sitting outside the plant entrance?"

"Tell them you're waiting for Triple-A," said Lou. "See if you can borrow or steal an orange cone somewhere. Or get a white T-shirt and hang it out a window."

"How much time goes by between loads?" asked Carmine. "What's the likelihood I'm gonna see a truck being loaded if I spend a half hour at one of these plants?"

"We have no idea," said Nigel.

"How likely is it that I'm gonna have a clean line of sight to the loading area?" Carmine's skepticism was showing.

"We don't know that, either," said Nigel. "Best we can tell you is what we know from Google Earth – these plants seem to be sitting out in the open. They're probably designed that way. And the driveways seem more straight than twisty and curvy, probably because they don't want the trucks to have to maneuver all over the place."

"Will I have binoculars?" asked Carmine.

Nigel and Lou looked at each other. Ooops. "Walk with me to the ATM after we eat," said Lou. "I'll give you some money and you can head over to Target on the way home, pick up a pair."

"Seems to me you're grasping at straws," said Carmine.

Nigel and Lou nodded together. "Yup," said Lou.

"Well, OK then." Carmine had another thought. "If this works, will I be testifying against Sal at trial?"

"Maybe. It depends on whether I can get your testimony admitted into evidence," said Nigel. "If I can, are you OK with that?"

"Sure," Carmine responded. "I'd be happy to bury the cocksucker for what he's doin' to Lou."

Lou paid the bill and all three left the diner together. Nigel headed home to continue his online searches. Lou and Carmine went to the deli across the street to use their ATM. That ATM was out of money, so they drove over to try the ATM at the Wawa. Lou took out $200 and gave it to Carmine. As they left the Wawa, Lou flipped his keys to Carmine. "Good luck at Target. Take your time tomorrow C," he said. "And don't worry about bringing it back tomorrow night. You can go straight home if you want."

For Carmine, having a car, even for a day, was a nice change of pace. He had forgotten that he didn't have a driver's license anymore. When that thought occurred to him, he decided not to mention it to Lou. He didn't think Lou would care, but Lou had enough worries, and there was no reason to add any stress to his life, however minimal. Lou started the short walk home, and Carmine headed out of town in the Mercury.

CHAPTER 65

"I'll do my best, but there doesn't seem to be any guarantee this will work," said Ziggy Gallo to Lou, Olivia and Nigel. They were meeting in the Command Center on a Wednesday evening. Sal's deposition would begin in eight days. They had been talking and planning for over an hour.

"You may be right," Nigel responded, taking a sip of whiskey from his flask. "We're not sure. But the thing to remember is, he has no reason to be defensive. There's no reason he won't talk to you if you can get him talking."

"I'll see what I can do," said Ziggy. "But jeez, a lot of things have to go right."

"Zig, you don't need to worry about whether it goes right or not," Lou replied. "Anything you find out will be gravy. And if you don't find out nothin', that's OK too."

"All right," said Ziggy. "Tell me again what you want me to do with this list." He held up a printed chart in his right hand.

"It's going to be a challenge," replied Nigel. "A bunch of information was available to us online, and we've summarized it for you on that chart. You need to memorize the whole list. You can't play the game if you don't know the players and where they're from. There's a lot there, but it's doable, I promise."

"Lou, if this thing is possible, I will make it happen," said Ziggy, turning to Lou. "Thanks for asking me."

CHAPTER 66

Carmine's apartment complex in Penn Manor Township was smack in the middle of Sal Paglia's business territory. Carmine decided, arbitrarily, to drive out to Chester County first, and then work his way from west to east through four counties to see each of the six plants that they thought might be visible. He'd go to Chester, Delaware, and Montgomery, and then he figured he would end his day at the plant in lower Bucks County – coincidentally, not far from Pennsylvania Park Racetrack. Racing would be almost done for the day, but maybe he could catch a race or two at the end. And he could stop at the Hooters across the street.

Nigel had explained to Carmine that his principal task was to observe human beings, and not to worry so much about the plants themselves – although if he saw something about any of the plants that didn't look right, he could certainly note it. Pictures would be nice, but not strictly necessary. Nigel just needed information, and Carmine's description of what he saw would be enough, if it came to that. "Make sure you have a notebook," was their only request along those lines. "We don't want you to forget anything." But as far as Lou could tell Carmine never forgot anything, so what they were really doing was building in some redundancy.

Carmine spread the Mapquest printouts on the big front seat, took a swig from the Thermos of coffee that his girlfriend Martina had made him, and put the car in "Drive." As he headed out to Chester County he turned the radio up and thought about – well, nothing, really. The job was not that complicated.

Four of the plants were busts. In three of them he saw no trucks go in or out, and in a fourth, he could see trucks stopping to load but couldn't see any people. The two plants in Bucks County, however, were gold mines. He even got a few pictures.

He got to the racetrack in time for the last two races. He sat down in the bar across from the betting windows. A woman holding a Groucho Marx ventriloquist dummy was imitating Groucho and using the puppet to pinch other women on their breasts. Most of the victims laughed, because the woman was really funny. It gave Carmine an idea for a bet in the tenth race – a filly named Marxist Theory was starting on the rail. Carmine didn't think much of her chances, but he liked her name. What the hell, the binoculars had only cost sixty bucks. Carmine would put the rest of the money to good use, and if he lost, he'd pay Lou back somehow.

Marxist Theory led from wire to wire, and Carmine collected a thousand bucks, which he planned to split with Lou. He thanked the lady with the puppet on his way out. She smiled and gave him a kiss on the cheek.

CHAPTER 67

"All right Ziggy, we have you on speaker phone," said Olivia as she placed her iPhone on the table. "How'd it go?"

"Hard to say," said Ziggy. "I was thinking it was gonna be hard to find him, but that turned out to be the easy part. I got into the restaurant – the Valley Forge Cucina's a nice place, by the way – and there was only one person at the bar. The guy was eating, and looked about the right age. I sat two seats away, ordered a beer and some tapas, and looked sideways at this guy to say 'hi.' He had a golf jacket draped over the back of his bar-stool – Cutter & Buck or some brand like that – and it said 'Wayne,' sort of on the upper left side of the front of it. I thought, 'damn, that was easy.' Pretty good start. The local sports report was on the TV above the bar, and they were talking about the Phillies. So I made a couple of comments and started a conversation. Then, 'Hey, I'm Ziggy,' and 'hey, good to meet you, I'm Wayne,' that kind of thing, and we shook hands. So I didn't have to do the thing with the barmaid that we practiced, and finding him turned out to be easy."

"How'd the rest of the conversation go?" asked Olivia.

"Well, we talked about the Phillies 'cause the sports reporter had just talked about the playoffs. We talked about the weather a little bit. And about the Chicken Parmigian' they were serving. But then he had to go. He had just finished his meal, and he must've gotten there at 5:30. He said, 'gotta run, good to talk to you,' and that was it. So we couldn't have talked for more than about five minutes."

"All right," Nigel replied, "that's a good start. Seriously. Finding him and starting a conversation was going to be a challenge. You got that done, Ziggy, and that's important. Can you keep memorizing your list and head back there for the next couple of evenings? Maybe get there at 5:30, if you can, and nurse a beer or two? Wait for him to show up?"

"No problem," said Ziggy. "I get off work at 3:30 the rest of this week, and can change in the car in the parking lot. He seems like a nice guy. I don't think it's gonna be hard to get him talking."

"Thanks Zig," said Lou. "Think about where you wanna eat the big dinner we're gonna buy you."

CHAPTER 68

"You're depressed," said Anna. She and Lou were having breakfast at McDonald's. Lou was getting ready for another day planning Sal Paglia's deposition.

"I'm not depressed," Lou replied. "I'm just not happy. There's a difference."

Anna thought about it and realized Lou had a point. There was a difference. But she hated to see him like this. "Do you want to go to Cracker Barrel tomorrow?"

"I don't think it would cheer me up. The only two things I really want to do right now are the two things I can't – go to the track, or go to the club."

"That's the thing about life," Anna replied, "you almost never get what you want. The trick to being happy is appreciating what you have."

"I know."

"You have Olivia. You have your house and your car and your Daily Racing Form. You don't have to give up on horseracing. You can adapt. Go to OTB or go to Delaware Park instead of Pennsylvania Park. And the Italian Club isn't the be-all and end-all. Go to D'Angelo's – it's right up the street, it's a nice bar, and we're always bumping into people we know."

Lou thought she had a point. And he liked that she wasn't babying him. Life sucks, she was saying. Deal with it. "And we can always go to Cracker Barrel," he said.

Anna smiled. "Yeah. The other thing to consider is that this lawsuit isn't going to go on forever. When it ends, that'll bring more change. When you win, you get everything about your old life back."

"We're gonna try to win," Lou replied. "We'll have to see."

CHAPTER 69

A preview of the Eagles' game against the Saints was on the TV over the bar. The Valley Forge Cucina was more crowded than it had been the night before. Wayne Locatelli settled into an empty seat next to Ziggy Gallo. "Hey man. Ziggy, right?"

"Hey Wayne. They just picked up a cornerback off of waivers," said Ziggy, pointing at the screen. "Somebody from Jacksonville."

"Yeah I saw that," Wayne replied. "Maybe it'll help. How're you?"

"I'm good. I can't wait for Sunday. Even with the Phillies in the playoffs and all, baseball just doesn't do it for me."

"Yeah, me neither," Wayne replied. "I have a ticket for the Saints game."

"Aw, man, I'm jealous," Ziggy replied. "Do you get to go down to the Linc pretty often?"

"Season tickets at the 45-yard line. Inherited. And before you say anything, yeah, I was born lucky."

Ziggy laughed. "I'd give my left nut to have season tickets. But that's why God invented the flat screen television and 1080p."

They started talking about newly-signed free agents, the Quarterback Controversy, the state of the offensive line, and the price of beer at Lincoln Financial Field. Wayne fielded a quick call, probably from his wife or girlfriend, hung up, and took a sip of his beer. "What kind of work do you do?" he asked Ziggy.

"I'm in sales," replied Ziggy. "How 'bout you?"

"I'm the assistant golf pro at Norristown Country Club," said Wayne. "I teach little old ladies to slow down their backswing. But I like my night job better. I'm just starting to get into DJ work. You know anybody who needs a DJ?"

Ziggy laughed. "We all do, man. Alexa don't cut it. Why don't you work in here?"

"Nah, a quiet bar doesn't need turntables. You need to work parties and dance places to make it as a DJ. How about you, what do you sell?"

"I sell street signs to local governments," Ziggy replied. "Stop. Yield. Maple Ave. Speed Limit 35. It's a living."

The bartender came over with bar menus, and both men placed their orders. Talk continued on about fifteen different subjects – only one of which was the reason for Ziggy's presence there that evening — and the bartender refilled glasses periodically.

It turned out that they knew some people in common. Ziggy did not disclose, of course, that his familiarity with those people was based on Olivia's and Nigel's research and his own memorization. Wayne, in turn, was happy to explain how he knew them. After an hour or so, Ziggy asked for his check, and paid it in cash. He turned to his left. "Wayne, buddy, my girlfriend's getting off work in 20 minutes. She's a nurse over at Children's Hospital across the street. I gotta go pick her up. See you back here, I'm sure. I'll buy the first round next time." He clasped Wayne on the shoulder as he got up to leave. "Go Birds!" he said.

"Amen, Brother," Wayne replied.

When he reached the parking lot, Ziggy pulled his cell phone from his pocket and called Lou. "Yo, Lou, you have a pencil? I gotta tell you this while I still remember it."

"Yeah, I'm right here at the kitchen table. I'm waitin' for Olivia and Nigel. Whaddaya got?"

"Ellis Gardner. Frank Wilson. Matt Henderson." Lou noted the names. Then they talked about horseracing.

CHAPTER 70

"Yeah."

"Tony, this is Tyrese Miller from Local 882. Catch you at a good time?"

"Absolutely," said Tony Abruzzi. "I was hopin' to hear from you. Thanks for getting back."

"No problem. I ain't see no reason we can't help, but my committee wants some things. This ain't any kind of thing like we do, ordinarily."

"Like I said when we first asked, we don't expect you to do this out of the goodness of your hearts. What's your committee sayin'?"

"A lot of our guys are gonna hafta call in sick to do this. They don't have no sick time left, half of 'em, 'cuz of the picket line we put up in Jersey back in March. And we gotta arrange transportation. We know we got no chance of organizing truckers out in the counties. So we're thinkin' the easy way to do this is cash. Know'm say'n? Simple. That way we don't have to change none of our other deals wit' you. Just a cash deposit to our Christmas Party Fund, and we'll make sure each of the guys on the line gets a share from that."

"How much are you looking for?" asked Tony.

"We think we need $15,000 a day."

"How many guys will that put on the picket line?"

"We can do at least twenty guys. Twenty large black men on a suburban picket line is gonna be somethin' to see, and none of these truckers is gonna wanna fuck with 'em without backup. We'll close it down good."

"Done," said Tony. "Thanks for the quick work."

"Just curious, man," said Tyrese Miller, perplexed. "Why aren't you talkin' to the Teamsters about this? They'd likely do it for free for y'all, 'cuz they might have a real shot at organizing these drivers."

"Truth is, they're still mad at us about Hoffa. They won't work with us. Maybe some day." Tony realized he'd said too much to somebody who didn't need to hear it. You're gettin' old, Tony, he reminded himself for the tenth time that week.

"Tyrese, thanks again for gettin' back to me so quick. I'll have Joey give you a call to work out the details. Don't hesitate to call me back if you need to talk to me."

CHAPTER 71

A heavy, late afternoon rain was pelting the knee-to-ceiling windows in Major Boardman's offices. The large ceiling lights, suddenly visible, made all of the space in the office look different, like an elementary school classroom at night. Neither Palmer Eastman, nor his client, Sal Paglia, wanted to be preparing for the next day's deposition. Each would have preferred to have been home with a dog and a glass of scotch. But there was always a chance – stopped clocks, and all that – that defendant's counsel, Nigel Branca, would come up with a challenging question or two for the named plaintiff in *Paglia v. Incaviglia*. Preparation, therefore, was the order of the afternoon. That's what lawyers do.

"We have to watch out for overconfidence," said Palmer Eastman, "especially given that Lou Incaviglia's deposition was such a disaster for them. They essentially admitted every element of our case. He never informed you of negative information about the company that was material to the risk, and never offered you a scrap of paper. What little he did tell you was a bunch of lies intended to induce you to buy his shares."

"The man knows how to lie, I'll give him that," said Sal.

"They have to grasp at whatever straws they can," Eastman continued. "I've probably mentioned to you a couple of times that a plaintiff in a securities fraud case has to prove that he 'reasonably relied' on the misrepresentations of the defendant. I'll give you an example. Suppose Mr. Black, a professor in a business school, studies up on a tech company for a year, talks to management, reads the financial press, and talks to his own financial advisors. He decides to buy shares in the company being offered to him by an eighty-five year-old nursing home resident and retired mailman – Mr. White. Before they agree on a price, Mr. White says, 'this company is going to report billions in profits for this year.' And that's all he says. Well, that's a statement of fact, and the fact would be material to Mr. Black's decision if it's true, but compared to everything else Mr. Black knows, that single comment is just not that important. He's not going to rely on it to make his decision about whether to purchase the shares. So Mr. Black almost certainly loses that case if he sues Mr. White, because his reliance on that single statement would not have been 'reasonable.'"

"Yeah, I noticed that in the complaint," Sal responded. "We said it about six times — that I 'reasonably relied' on what he told me."

"Because lack of reliance is all they've got, you're going to hear about it a lot," said Eastman. "Questions like, 'You're the CEO of a large company, aren't you?' And then, 'You knew that Mr. Incaviglia is a retired bricklayer, didn't you?' And so on. He'll probably ask you about your familiarity with financial statements, that kind of thing. Those kinds of questions are not going to get them anywhere, so just admit that you're a CEO, he's a brick-layer, you know how to read a balance sheet. Admit that kind of stuff, and wait for the next question."

"Tell me again why that doesn't help them," Sal responded.

"I wouldn't say it doesn't help them," Eastman replied, "because it's all they've got. But they're not going to win with that."

"Again: Tell me why not," Sal insisted.

"Because he had access to information that you couldn't get," responded Eastman. "3Device is a private company. Nothing about its financial circumstances or its communications with the FDA was public knowledge. Mr. Incaviglia knew those facts because his son-in-law runs the company, and he had access to their Private Placement Memorandum. But you didn't know those facts, and he didn't tell you."

"Why didn't I ask him for more information?" asked Sal. Neither lawyer nor client acknowledged that Sal was asking his lawyer to tell him something that only Sal would have known.

"It's in the complaint, Sal," Eastman responded, with a trace of impatience. "We talked about this before your complaint was filed. You asked him for some documentation, and he told you that he couldn't give you any, because 3Device is a private company, and its technology is closely guarded. He told you that you would need to trust him, that he wouldn't mislead an old friend, and that he would get you answers to your questions. That's why the second conversation in the club was so important – he brought you back answers to your questions. And everything he told you was a lie."

"Well, yeah," said Sal.

"I can't emphasize enough how important it is that you re-read the first fifteen pages of the complaint a few times tonight. That's where all the facts are. Really lock those facts in. In almost every case, when the plaintiff sits down for his or her deposition, the defendant's lawyer picks up a copy of the complaint and asks the plaintiff questions about it. A lot of plaintiffs get tripped up, because they didn't write the complaint — their lawyer did. So Nigel Branca is going to try to trip you up. Don't let him."

"I should be OK," Sal responded, "because I told you everything that's in the complaint. You just wrote it down." Actually, Palmer Eastman instructed a young associate to draft the complaint, and that associate interviewed Sal over the phone before he started writing.

"Yes, and that's the way I want you to be thinking about it," Eastman responded. "I'm not going to have any problem with your repeating the language in the complaint. All of his statements that you could remember are written down in that one document. It also describes everything you asked him. There are no points for originality during a deposition. Stick to the script, and the script is in the complaint. Again, please: Read it 10 times tonight, and memorize the conversations that are described to the extent you can."

Sal was not pleased by what he heard. He and his wife were going out to dinner with a township manager, and he knew perfectly well he wasn't going to be reading shit tonight. "I'll do that," said Sal. And I promise to floss regularly between now and my next appointment.

Sal's nonchalance was not going to be a problem. Not because he knew how to handle the questions Palmer Eastman was expecting – but because Mr. Eastman had guessed wrong. Nigel Branca would not be asking Sal Paglia about the complaint.

CHAPTER 72

Nigel, Lou and Olivia were in the Command Center, going over Nigel's questions and each of the exhibits for the tenth time. The number of Styrofoam coffee cups scattered around had doubled over the past few days, and the copier they rented was blinking a toner warning. Sal Paglia's deposition was the next day, and if Olivia's plan were going to work, tomorrow was it.

"I want to be there," announced Olivia.

"Out of the question, we've talked about this," Lou replied.

"We're renting a bunch of meeting rooms. I can stay out of the way in one of them. Sal won't even know I'm there. But if you need research help I can go online, and I can fetch anything you need."

"I don't see how it can hurt," said Nigel, turning to Lou. "The door will be closed. Olivia has been the one making most of this happen. We may need her input on stuff."

Lou hesitated. "All right. Stay out of sight, please." Olivia smiled.

Shifting gears, Nigel asked, "All right, what haven't we thought of?"

"I hope that's a rhetorical question," Olivia replied, smiling wanly.

Nigel paused. "Actually, it is," he said. "Or let me put it this way. Everything we've thought of is somewhere in these questions, or in this stack of paper. We can't do much more."

"What's the worst that could happen tomorrow?" asked Lou.

Nigel paused again, and thought hard. "The worst thing that could happen is if he walks out before he hears us out," he said, finally.

"I don't think he will," Lou replied. "He's gonna get really pissed, I mean really, really pissed. But Sal isn't afraid of nothin'. I don't think he avoids shit. He couldn'a built his business if he was puttin' his tail between his legs every time he heard somethin' he didn't like. He won't leave, 'cause every time you ask him somethin' that surprises him, he's gonna want to know whether you got anything else."

"Can his lawyer tell him to leave?" asked Olivia.

"A lawyer is not supposed to do that," Nigel replied. "He'd really be risking sanctions. The court can impose a fine if they walk out of a duly scheduled deposition. But yeah, they could walk out. Nothing's stopping them."

"Sal's not gonna leave," said Lou. "In his mind, only pussies run away. He's there to beat us, not run away from us."

"Nigel, when will you bring up settlement?" asked Olivia.

"I won't," Nigel responded. "Your dad and I talked about it before you got here this afternoon. Lou's going to bring it up when the time is right, if he brings it up at all. We'll be ready to write up a settlement agreement, but it doesn't have to happen tomorrow." Nigel thought for a second. "I'd be surprised if it didn't," he said.

"Why?" asked Lou.

"Because of the transcript," Nigel replied. "The way it works is the court reporter records everything, and the voice recognition software creates a first draft of the transcript. But there's a lot of work that the reporter has to do to clean it up and make it accurate. And she has to mark and organize the exhibits and get them attached to the transcript. So the transcript doesn't get distributed to the parties for at least a week after the deposition, and sometimes it's a month or more. When she sends it out, the court reporter certifies the transcript as accurate, as an officer of the court. That allows the parties to file an official transcript with the court in support of motions, or they can use it at trial to question witnesses. If we're right about how this is going to go down, Sal won't want that transcript ever to be created. So he knows that if he doesn't settle, unpredictable things can happen a week or a month from now when the transcript is ready."

"Can I get one of those the next time my dad promises me he's going to stop eating chicken wings?" asked Olivia.

CHAPTER 73

Greg Morris burst into David Stein's office first thing in the morning with a letter in his hand. "This was a pdf attached to an email," he began. "I printed it out. Does this mean what I think it means?" Grinning like a parrot, he handed the letter to his business partner. David read it slowly.

"I don't think there's anything ambiguous about it," said David, finally. "The FDA says they're going to consider our application on the basis of existing regulations. They say they're still going to issue revised regulations, but we don't need to wait for them. We can disregard the advice we received in their previous letter." David began to grin too.

"They copied Blue Tech on this, so we'll probably hear from them shortly," said Greg. "They're an hour behind. Or we can try to call them. Boris may be in the office by now."

"Shouldn't you call Olivia?" asked David. "They've got the deposition this morning."

"Yeah, you're right," Greg replied. And then, "No, come to think of it."

"Why not?"

"They'll do better if they think they're hitting with two out in the bottom of the ninth. We can always tell them about this tomorrow. Let's see how it goes."

PART III

CHAPTER 74

Lou, Olivia and Nigel had settled into a small meeting room at the Plymouth Meeting Suites Hotel and Conference Center. It was Thursday, October 19, a date that had been circled in red on their calendar in the Command Center for the previous three weeks. There was coffee on the table, and some pastries. The mood was a little tense, mostly because Nigel and Olivia were jittery. Lou seemed fairly relaxed.

Olivia's phone dinged, and she checked a new text. "OK, this is good. The Warehousemen's picket line went up at the Ambler yard at 6:30, and there were a lot of picketers there. Sal's trucks were not crossing the line, or even trying to. So most of his business is likely shut down for today. One of the trucks stopped right at the picket line, and one of Tony's guys was able to confirm the measurement we talked about. They could see some other trucks in the yard, and got pretty good information. On some of them, the stencil is missing altogether."

"That's great," said Nigel, making a note on his yellow pad.

"Did the temp agency come through for us?" asked Olivia.

"Yeah, I just heard from her," Nigel replied. "She's ten minutes out. We'll put her in Meeting Room 4 down the hall."

"I talked to my Uncle Tony this morning," said Olivia. "Pete Fraterrigo is on his way."

"Good," Nigel replied. "Hopefully, that's one more precaution than we'll actually need."

"Livvie, why don't you head home," said Lou. "There's no reason for you to sit in this little room all day. We can tell you about it tonight."

"Dad, we've talked about this. You may need somebody to find some information you don't have," Olivia replied. "Or maybe we'll need a document from the Command Center. Or maybe you'll just want to talk about what's going on in there. I wouldn't consider leaving."

"I love you, Honey. But stay in here. I'd be sick if Sal saw you here and tried to make something out of it. We've kept you out of this thing – let's not change that now."

CHAPTER 75

Nigel and Lou walked into the bigger meeting room where Sal's deposition was to be held. Sal and Palmer Eastman were already there, as was Sandy Wells, the court reporter. The court reporter was always hired by the party taking the deposition, and Nigel hired Sandy Wells because he'd been told she was widely respected in Montgomery County. Nigel nodded hello to Sandy and ignored Sal and Eastman. He opened his loose-leaf binder. "Swear the witness please."

Sandy turned to Sal. "Raise your right hand, please." Sal did as he was told. "Do you swear that the testimony you will give today will be the truth, the whole truth, and nothing but the truth, so help you God?"

"Yes," replied Sal.

Nigel had decided to dispense with the preliminaries. Why would he spend 15 minutes letting the witness get comfortable? Better to go right at him.

"Mr. Paglia, did you have some issues with a union early this morning at your Ambler yard?"

Sal looked up in surprise and alarm. "Word travels fast."

"What makes you think we had to wait for word to get to us?" Nigel responded, looking at Sal directly.

"Objection to the question and the answer," interjected Palmer Eastman, belatedly. He had been digging in his briefcase, and hadn't expected the deposition to start at full speed.

"The question has been answered, Mr. Eastman," Nigel replied. "If you want to move to strike it, you can, of course, file an appropriate motion with the court after the conclusion of the deposition."

"Thank you for the tutorial on federal procedure, Mr. Branca," said Eastman. "I suggest the deposition will be more productive for you if, henceforth, you confine your questioning to matters at issue in this litigation."

Nigel ignored Eastman, and continued to stare at Sal. For his part, Sal looked at Nigel with something close to reptilian attention, and waited for the next question.

"Mr. Paglia," Nigel began, "does Sal Paglia, Inc., maintain what's known as a '401(k)' plan for its workers?"

"I instruct the witness not to answer that question," interjected Eastman, "on the grounds that it seeks information that is neither relevant to this litigation, nor likely to lead to the discovery of admissible evidence."

Sal sat silently.

"Mr. Paglia, are you a designer, administrator or trustee of any '401(k)' plan for employees of Sal Paglia, Inc.?" continued Nigel.

"Same instruction, same grounds," said Eastman.

Nigel smiled. "Just for the record, Mr. Eastman, one of your burdens in this case is to prove that Mr. Paglia reasonably relied on Mr. Incaviglia – a retired bricklayer – to provide certain information in connection with Mr. Paglia's purchase of securities. You have just instructed Mr. Paglia not to answer a question directed to discovering information about his past experience and familiarity with investment securities. I look forward to your attempt to defend that instruction when we are before Judge Lester seeking sanctions from you and your client."

Eastman said something in response, but Nigel wasn't much interested in whatever it was he was saying. Nigel lifted the top document from a short pile of documents sitting at his right elbow, and turned his attention back to the witness.

"Mr. Paglia, I am showing you a document that has been marked 'Paglia Deposition Exhibit 1.' I will represent to you that this document is a Form 5500 report filed last year by Sal Paglia, Inc., with the United States Department of Labor." Nigel handed an additional copy to Eastman, and kept a copy for himself. "The document is a matter of public record, and we obtained our copy online, directly from the Department of Labor. Do you recognize this document?"

"I instruct the witness not to answer that question," said Eastman.

"Mr. Paglia, do you see that on the – fourth; fifth, I guess sixth" – Nigel was counting down from the top – "let's call it the sixth line of this document, Sal Paglia, Inc., reported that there are 30 employees participating in the "Sal Paglia, Inc., Section 401(k) Investment Plan?"

"I instruct the witness not to answer that question," said Eastman.

"Approximately how many employees did Sal Paglia, Inc., have two years ago?"

"I instruct the witness not to answer that question," said Eastman. Eastman was puzzled by Nigel's demeanor. Nigel didn't seem bothered by instructions not to answer that were, if not categorically improper, at least highly questionable. Eastman knew he would have been on thin ice if he were opposing a litigator from another big firm in town. But he was damned if he was going to hesitate to frustrate this gin-soaked refugee from the Montgomery County criminal appointments list. Trouble was, Nigel didn't act frustrated or unsure of what he was doing. On the contrary, he seemed — to Eastman at least — disturbingly calm.

" Mr. Paglia, I am showing you a document that has been marked 'Paglia Deposition Exhibit 2.' I will represent to you that this document is a screen grab from the very first page of the website of Sal Paglia, Inc." Nigel handed copies to the witness and to Eastman. "Do you recognize that document?"

"I instruct the witness not to answer that question," said Eastman.

"Mr. Paglia," Nigel continued, "do you see where it says, 'with more than 900 dedicated employees, we provide exceptional service to our municipal clients and private developers'?"

"I instruct the witness not to answer that question," said Eastman.

"Mr. Paglia, going forward, I'll sometimes refer to Sal Paglia, Inc. as 'your company' or 'the company.' Did you have an accounting firm perform an analysis to determine whether the company's 401(k) plan was 'top-heavy,' that is, whether it provides an improper share of benefits to highly-compensated employees?"

"I instruct the witness not to answer that question," said Eastman. Sal looked a little nervous.

"Were you aware that you might have to pay money to lower-paid employees, or give back some of the tax benefits that accrued to higher-paid employees, if your plan is top-heavy?"

"I instruct the witness not to answer that question," said Eastman.

Nigel continued to pose questions about the 401(k) plan, its funding, its participants, and the total funds involved. In response to every question, Eastman instructed his client not to answer.

Nigel turned to Exhibit 3. "Mr. Paglia, I am showing you a document that has been marked 'Paglia Deposition Exhibit 3.' I will represent to you that this document is an IRS Form 3949A. Form 3949A permits anyone – an employee, a union rep, a stranger, or even, say, an adverse party in litigation – to, quote 'report suspected tax law violations by a person or a business,' close quote. Do you know if anyone has filed a Form 3949A in connection with your 401(k) plan, or has anyone advised you that they're thinking of filing one?"

Sal literally gulped. His Adam's Apple rose and fell, and, as he had for the prior 20 questions, he sat silently.

"I instruct the witness not to answer that question," said Eastman.

"OK," said Nigel, looking at his opponents. "I'll just leave the Form 3949A on the table, and if you, Mr. Eastman, or you, Mr. Paglia, want to take a closer look at it at any point, I'll be happy to give you time to do that."

CHAPTER 76

Nigel turned back to his notes. "Mr. Paglia, is your company obliged to comply with U.S. Department of Transportation regulations governing the use of your heavy trucks?"

"I instruct the witness not to answer that question," said Eastman. "That's it, that's enough of this nonsense! We are going to call Magistrate Judge Martinez and put a stop to this."

In the United States District Court for the Eastern District of Pennsylvania, each District Judge has a Magistrate Judge "assigned" to him or her. The principal job of a Magistrate Judge is to handle arraignments, bail determinations, and other preliminary phases of federal criminal cases. As a somewhat secondary role, a Magistrate Judge handles various motions and other preliminary matters in civil cases for his or her assigned judge. One of the long-established powers of each Magistrate Judge is to act as a "referee" when disputes arise during depositions in civil cases.

The case of *Paglia vs. Incaviglia* was assigned to United States District Judge Marcia Lester; Juan Martinez was her assigned United States Magistrate Judge. Palmer Eastman was invoking the authority of Magistrate Judge Martinez to consider his objections to the questioning, and stopped the deposition to do that.

The Plymouth Meeting Suites Hotel and Conference Center had an old-fashioned star-shaped, landline speakerphone installed on the big table in the meeting room. Eastman pressed "9" for an outside line and dialed a number he found in the contacts list on his cell phone. The ringing sound came through the speaker, followed by, "Magistrate Judge Martinez's chambers."

Palmer Eastman recognized Gloria Peterson's voice, because she used to work at Major Boardman, and he had helped her get her job with Magistrate Judge Martinez. "Gloria, hi, this is Palmer Eastman. Is he available to act as a deposition referee for a few minutes?"

"Mr. Eastman, hello. He's on the bench at the moment handling a bail application, but I can have him call you when he's free."

"That will work, we'll wait. Let me give you the number over here." He read from the little white cardboard insert in the phone. And then, "The case, in case he needs to look at the complaint, is *Paglia vs. Incaviglia*."

"OK, I'll give him the message, and I expect he'll be able to call you. Who is your opposing counsel?"

"This is Nigel Branca," said Nigel. "I represent the defendant."

"Thank you gentlemen," Susan responded. "We'll be back to you. Bye-bye."

"Bye Gloria," said Palmer Eastman. "All right, this deposition is suspended until we have a chance to get a ruling from the court."

Nigel didn't say a word. He picked up his yellow pad and his briefcase and motioned to Lou to follow him. They walked down the hall to the smaller meeting room where Olivia was waiting.

"We're taking a break until we can get a ruling from the court on Eastman's objections," Nigel said to Olivia, as he came through the door. "Shouldn't be long."

"Why is the court getting involved?" asked Olivia.

Nigel explained the role of the Magistrate Judge as deposition referee, and explained what Eastman's objection was. He added, "I think we win this one. We'll see."

"Do you have time for a cup of coffee?" asked Olivia. She didn't mention whiskey.

"No, we just wanted to check in with you," Nigel responded. "The magistrate could call at any minute; we need to be there."

"How are you holding up, Daddy?" Olivia asked.

"Aw, honey, I'm fine. Nigel's doing all the work. I'm just watchin' the fireworks." Lou turned and began to follow Nigel back out the door.

"All right, see you in a bit," said Olivia.

Nigel and Lou walked back into the deposition room and sat down. Sal Paglia, Palmer Eastman, and the court reporter were still there. No one said a word for fifteen minutes. Finally, the phone rang.

"Palmer Eastman," said Eastman, as he pressed the call pick-up button.

"Mr. Eastman, this is Juan Martinez. Is Mr. Branca there?"

"I'm here, Your Honor," Nigel replied.

"OK, I have the complaint on my screen. Do you want this call to be on the record or off the record?"

"I suggest we stay off the record until we need to memorialize a ruling," replied Eastman.

"I'm fine with that, Your Honor," said Nigel.

"OK," continued the Magistrate Judge, "who is being deposed, who is seeking a ruling, and what's the issue?"

"Your Honor, this is the plaintiff's application," Eastman began. "I represent the plaintiff, Salvatore Paglia, who is being deposed by the defendant. So far this morning – and we're now almost an hour into the deposition – the defendant hasn't asked a single question having to do with the issues in this case, which is a claim for securities fraud. The plaintiff is being harassed. We ask for a ruling to the effect that any questions posed must bear some relationship to the issues in this case. The pending question is a good example . . ."

"I'm not sure I follow," interrupted the judge. "Relevance isn't normally a proper objection at a deposition. And if the questions and answers are irrelevant, Mr. Branca won't be able to use them at trial. Why do we need to make a ruling on something like this?"

"Respectfully, Your Honor, relevance is not the basis for my objection. Harassment and burdensomeness are. Under Rule 26(b)(2)(C), a party may not engage in discovery that's burdensome or outside the scope of the matters at issue in the case. Here, we've got a situation where Mr. Paglia has taken a day off from running a large corporation. Mr. Branca's questions are all directed, so far, to matters related to the operation of that corporation, which is not a party to this case. We are concerned that the questions are intended to suggest technical violations of law by a non-party. Because the questions don't relate to this lawsuit, the only reason to pose them, it seems to us, is to suggest that a non-party has done something wrong. So the mere posing of these questions might cause substantial damage to the corporation and its reputation if the transcript of this deposition were to be made public. It would be one thing if the corporation were a party to this case – but this is a dispute about a purchase and sale of stock in a completely different company, operated by the defendant's son-in-law. So we ask that defendant's counsel's questions be confined to matters bearing some plausible relation to this case, and that questions about the plaintiff's corporation be barred altogether. And defendant's counsel should be subject to sanctions if such improper questions continue to be posed."

The Magistrate Judge thought for a moment. Finally, "Mr. Branca, what's your response?"

"Your Honor, I have to admit that this is the first time I have ever heard a party to a deposition object to the posing of questions, as opposed to making an objection about having to answer them."

"I'll grant you that," interjected the judge, "this is kind of a first for me, too."

"So to be clear where we are procedurally, I can tell you that Mr. Eastman has instructed his client not to answer virtually every one of my questions. I'm sure you're familiar with Judge Gawthrop's famous opinion that made clear that an instruction not to answer, if not accompanied by a claim of privilege, is absolutely indefensible. I should be the one applying for sanctions. But that's why I mentioned the procedural context. The present application is not by a party objecting to having to provide answers; this is a party objecting to having to listen to questions.

"In all my years of practice – other than, perhaps, in a jury trial where certain subjects have been ruled out of bounds by the court beforehand – I have never heard an objection to the posing of questions. If I can't put the question on the record, how can we ever have a discussion with the court later about whether an answer should be required during continued discovery? This is just ridiculous. And while I shouldn't have to say more, I will address Mr. Eastman's argument that the questions are improper. They aren't. The corporation to which Mr. Eastman refers is Sal Paglia, Inc. On information and belief, the plaintiff, Sal Paglia, is the sole owner of that company, and directs its affairs. My questions so far this morning relate to two matters: first, Mr. Paglia's familiarity with his 401(k) plan; and, second, regulatory compliance on the part of Sal Paglia, Inc. The defendant will show at trial that plaintiff Sal Paglia, as CEO of his company, failed to report a bunch of regulatory issues to appropriate authorities. We are confident he will ultimately testify, when asked, that the violations were no big deal, or words to that effect. Well, if regulatory matters are not material enough to report to responsible authorities, then similar issues are not material enough to have to be disclosed in connection with a private stock transaction.

"I also want to show, in this securities fraud case, that Mr. Paglia could not reasonably have relied on my client for information about an investment in a privately owned company, when Mr. Paglia was ten times more familiar with how companies operate, and the regulatory challenges they face, than Mr. Incaviglia – a bricklayer by trade – will ever be.

"Additionally, many regulatory schemes require reporting by responsible management, and provide for criminal penalties if management has covered up violations of regulatory requirements."

Sal and his lawyer, both of whom had been more or less staring at the speakerphone while Nigel spoke, looked at Nigel quickly. Criminal penalties?

"If Mr. Paglia has covered up criminal conduct, then that cover up is *crimen falsi*, and I can use the evidence to impeach his credibility at trial. So we need to see where that goes.

"And finally – the court can very easily deal with Mr. Eastman's real objection, which is his fear that the questions themselves might become public. We have no interest, at this point, in making the deposition questions public. The defendant, Mr. Incaviglia, has no objection to the transcript of today's deposition being sealed by the court, until a party moves to unseal it and the court grants that motion. And we might make that motion at some point. But for now, public disclosure is not at issue, and I respectfully request that the plaintiff's application be denied."

"Your Honor, may I respond?" said Eastman, immediately. "Mr. Branca has completely misstated the real issues in this case . . ."

"I think each side has had a fair opportunity to make its argument," the judge interrupted. "To the extent that Mr. Branca has characterized the record, and to the extent you want to dispute any of those characterizations, I can tell you that I'm not relying upon Mr. Branca's descriptions of the evidence or the issues in the case in making my ruling. Right now, I'm looking exclusively at your application, and frankly, I don't see much there."

Magistrate Judge Martinez cleared his throat. "Let's go on the record. We'll use your court reporter, if that's OK."

"Yes, Your Honor, I'm ready," replied Sandy Wells from the deposition room.

"OK, thanks," said the judge. "I think one of the reasons we don't get very many requests to serve as deposition referees is that litigators in this court are generally competent, they know the rules, and they understand that if they bring an issue to the court, it has to be well-defined, and it has to be the kind of thing where, if you can get a ruling, it will make an important difference in the record that's going to be created at a deposition. We don't have that here. Mr. Branca's questions, themselves, are not evidence, and nothing he asks is going to affect the record in this case until an answer is offered. Only answers count. Obviously, I can't come into this case cold and jump into an analysis of how plausible the defendant's lack-of-reliance argument might be when the case gets to trial. We're not going to hold a three-hour hearing, lay out half of the evidence in the case, and decide whether the defendant's theory makes sense. But you're both experienced litigators, you know the drill during a deposition. Objections to relevance are reserved for trial, period. I don't see any indication that Mr. Branca's questions, at least as they've been described to me, are so far out in left field that they constitute harassment.

"I also want to make clear, Mr. Branca, that under no circumstances will you be permitted improperly to smear a non-party to this case. I've seen that non-party's big black trucks all over the Philadelphia suburbs. They are obviously a substantial, well-known company. And I certainly haven't seen any suggestion in the press or online that the company is anything but responsible and reputable. So I'll accept your offer to seal the transcript – which I think is a good indication that your questions are not asked for the sole purpose of making them public. Mr. Eastman, please submit a form of order to seal, so that I can look at it and make a recommendation to Judge Lester.

"And while I'm lecturing Mr. Branca, I ought to direct a comment to Mr. Eastman as well. Instructions to a witness not to answer a deposition question are a very risky tactic in this court. I know it's done, but Mr. Branca is right about Judge Gawthrop's opinion – it carries a lot of weight down here. I suggest, Mr. Eastman, that if you're going to instruct a witness not to answer a question, you had better have a very good argument prepared for why the question was obviously and manifestly improper. But Mr. Branca has not moved to compel those answers, and I don't need to address the issue now. I will stand by, however, and I expect both counsel to conduct the deposition professionally.

"Is there any other matter to address?"

"No, Your Honor," said Nigel.

"No, Your Honor," said Palmer Eastman. "Thank you for taking our call."

"OK, folks, have a good day," said Magistrate Judge Martinez. The speakerphone went dead.

CHAPTER 77

Nigel went back to his notes. "Mr. Paglia, is your company obliged to comply with U.S. Department of Transportation regulations governing the use of your heavy trucks?"

Sal had become used to his lawyer telling him not to answer. When no objection came from Eastman, Sal put his brain back in gear. "Repeat the question, please."

"Is your company obliged to comply with U.S. Department of Transportation regulations governing the use of your heavy trucks?"

"Yes, I believe we are."

"Do your company's trucks display U.S. Department of Transportation registration numbers on the doors of their cabs?"

"Of course they do," replied Sal. "That's the law."

"Agreed," said Nigel. "Do some of those trucks have fresh paint jobs?"

"Sure. We like to keep 'em looking nice, and we repaint the cabs when we do engine overhauls, and other heavy maintenance."

"Is it possible that someone forgot to include the DOT number on some of those trucks when they came out of heavy maintenance?"

"I suppose so. But if they did, we'll just add the numbers. No big deal."

"OK, but maybe it's not that simple," continued Nigel. "Were you aware that DOT regulations require your DOT number to be visible at fifty feet, and that the normal standard applied is that they be at least two inches in height?"

"No."

"We believe, Mr. Paglia, that if you take a look at your trucks, you'll find that your DOT numbers are only about an inch high, on all of your trucks, except the ones that are missing DOT numbers altogether. And here's my question. Do you find, when U.S. Department of Transportation inspectors are dealing with America's truckers, including Sal Paglia, Inc., they are models of good humor and a spirit of compromise?"

Sal smiled grimly. "No, I do not."

"Do you find that they are usually inclined to treat violations of DOT regulations as 'no big deal,' as you put it?"

"I don't know."

"Does Sal Paglia, Inc., own about 100 large dump trucks?"

Finally, another question Sal knew how to answer. "Yes, 102, last count."

"Would you agree with me that repainting 102 front cab doors, in that very high quality paint scheme you use, could cost you $50,000? Assuming, hypothetically, that a DOT inspector instructed you to do it?"

"I don't know. If so, it's a cost of doing business."

"Those seem to be adding up this morning," observed Nigel.

"Objection. That's not a question. We will move to strike that comment," Eastman interjected.

CHAPTER 78

Nigel turned a page in his notes. "Mr. Paglia, your website suggests that your company has eight different asphalt plants. Is that the correct number?"

"I don't know." Sal was sullen.

"Do you have a lot of asphalt plants because your hot asphalt needs to be close to a road where it's going to be applied?"

"Yes, obviously."

"At the end of the liquefaction process, do you pump the asphalt into tanker trucks?"

"Yes."

"Is that liquid asphalt hot?"

"Yeah, 300 degrees."

"Do the truckers who refill their rigs in your asphalt plants wear face shields, hard hats, tunics and insulated rubber gloves when they're loading hot asphalt?"

"Well, we do whatever the law requires."

"If I told you that OSHA and industry standards require a full face shield, a long thick tunic, and insulated rubber gloves for loaders and drivers, would you see any reason to disagree with me?"

"I've disagreed with a lot you've said so far."

"Hot asphalt is petroleum-based, is it not, and the fumes are bad for your health?"

"You wouldn't want to breathe asphalt fumes for too long, but I don't think they'll kill you."

"Well, aren't there regulations that define maximum exposure to asphalt fumes?"

"I don't know."

"If I told you that our investigator recently drove past a couple of your plants and observed workers loading asphalt who were not wearing hard hats and face shields, would you say that he was mistaken?."

"If he said that he's a liar, so yeah, he's mistaken."

Nigel pulled out Paglia Deposition Exhibits 4 and 5, and distributed copies. "Mr. Paglia, I'm showing you pictures of tanker trucks, which I will represent to you are loading at two of your plants in Bucks County." Carmine's pictures were many times blown up and grainy, but the bare-headed and bare-handed truckers were visible standing under the loading derricks that led to their rigs. "Do you see any personal protective equipment, or PPE, on the men seen in these photos?"

"You tell me, counsel." Sal was becoming surly.

"OK, Mr. Paglia, I'm happy to do that," replied Nigel. "The pictures show two men under asphalt loading equipment who are not wearing PPE."

Nigel checked his notes. "Were you aware that OSHA regulations – that is, regulations issued by the United States Occupational Safety and Health Administration – permit any person who is aware of serious health or safety violations in a workplace to file a complaint?"

"I'm sure you're going to tell me about it."

"Well, I just did. And wouldn't you think that 'any person' who could make that kind of complaint to OSHA might include, say, an adverse party in litigation, you know, somebody you might have recently sued?"

"You're the lawyer, counselor."

"Yes, I am," Nigel replied. Nigel was surprised by his own statement. He put down his notes and took a sip of water. "All right, Mr. Paglia, Mr. Eastman, I would propose to take a ten-minute break at this point. Any objection?"

"No," Eastman replied. He looked relieved. "Do you have much more?"

"Oh, we're just getting started," replied Nigel. "We're adjourned for ten minutes." Nigel and Lou left the deposition room to Sal Paglia and his lawyer, and walked down the hall to rejoin Olivia.

CHAPTER 79

"You should see Nigel," said Lou. "He's killin' 'em."

Olivia smiled in response. "I believe it. Nigel came loaded for bear."

"I don't want you to get too excited about this early stuff," said Nigel. "Some of these violations are easily fixable if they got cited for it. So part of what I'm doing is getting him to think his business is vulnerable to anyone who wants to dig hard enough. But I also want him, maybe, to think 'if that's the best they have, we're doing fine.' Hopefully it's going to be deflating for him when we pull out the heavier ammunition."

"What have you covered so far?" asked Olivia.

"I would say, four of our seven subjects," Nigel began. "He knows we knew about the union organizing campaign before he did. We talked about his 401(k) and the Form 5500. We covered the DOT lettering. And we talked about the asphalt plants. So, yeah, four down, three to go."

"Have we heard from Pete?" asked Lou.

"Yeah, he got here a few minutes ago," Olivia replied. "He stuck his head in to say hello. He's in the meeting room around the corner."

Nigel and Lou both went to the bathroom – Nigel took a few sips from his flask – and returned to the deposition room.

CHAPTER 80

"Did you build a backyard patio and barbeque at your home in Blue Bell, Pennsylvania, three years ago?"

Sal hesitated. "I don't know. Three years?"

"Let me restate the question. Did you ever build a backyard patio and barbeque at your home in Blue Bell, Pennsylvania?"

"Yes."

"Just for the record, your home and the patio and the barbeque are not the property of Sal Paglia, Inc., are they?"

"No. My wife and I own our home."

"Was that patio and barbeque at your home in Blue Bell constructed largely out of bricks?"

"Yes."

"Was that patio and barbeque constructed with Glen Gery bricks?"

"Is that a type of brick? I don't know what kind of bricks they were."

"Are you familiar with Empire Brick Supply?"

"Yeah. They have a brick yard a mile or so from my house."

"Did you buy the bricks for your patio and barbeque from Empire Brick Supply?"

"Yeah. And I borrowed a truck from my company to pick them up and deliver 'em to my home. Do you have a point that you're trying to make with all of this, counsel?"

Nigel ignored the question. "How much did you pay for those bricks?"

"I don't recall."

"Does the figure sixteen thousand nine hundred dollars refresh your recollection?"

"No."

"Mr. Paglia, are you aware that the Commonwealth of Pennsylvania has created and published a form of sales tax exemption certificate for businesses who purchase goods for resale in the ordinary course of their business?"

"Yeah, I think I know what that is," Sal replied.

"Does Sal Paglia, Inc., issue sales tax exemption certificates to its vendors when it buys materials that it plans to resell to its customers?"

Sal connected the dots. He seemed to take a couple of slow breaths before he answered.

"I believe we do."

"Mr. Paglia, we have examined Empire Brick Supply's invoice for Glen Gery bricks that were delivered to an address in Blue Bell. You will not be surprised to learn that the invoice in question, which was paid, included a notation that a sales tax exemption certificate was presented by the buyer. So no sales tax was charged on the transaction, despite the fact that the bricks were used in a consumer's back yard. We will subpoena that invoice, if necessary, so that you and your lawyer can examine it too. Although, come to think of it, you probably have a copy somewhere in your files at home, so perhaps you wouldn't really need or want us to subpoena it. In all events: Were you aware that fraudulent use of a sales tax exemption certificate is a crime in Pennsylvania, punishable by up to a year in jail?"

"Don't answer that question," said Palmer Eastman.

"Mr. Eastman, I'm happy to give you a citation which will get you started. You might take a look at 62 Pa. Code 32.2(c)." said Nigel.

Turning back to the witness, Nigel said, "Mr. Paglia, sales tax in Pennsylvania is six percent. By our calculation, you saved $1,014 dollars on sales tax, assuming for purposes of argument, that sales tax was due on that purchase. Do you agree with our math?"

"Don't answer that question," said Eastman. Turning to Nigel, he said, "The math is what it is. And yours is probably wrong. This witness doesn't need to perform calculations for you."

CHAPTER 81

Nigel looked at Sal Paglia and continued his questioning. "Mr. Paglia, did your company report a petroleum spill to the Pennsylvania Department of Environmental Protection during any of the years 2020, 2021 or 2022?"

Sal hesitated. He expected an instruction not to answer. Eastman, however, was being much less aggressive about instructions not to answer since he spoke with Magistrate Judge Martinez. "You can answer," said Eastman, finally. "Note my objection to any question having to do with any petroleum spill."

"I don't recall us reporting any spills during that period," Sal replied. "But we might have."

"Were you aware that one of your dump truck drivers accidentally poured about a hundred gallons of diesel fuel on the ground at your refueling station in the Ambler yard?"

Sal's face flushed with anger. "No I was not. And if that happened – and I don't think it did – that driver is gonna be fired tomorrow."

"Well," replied Nigel, "I was going to tell you how we knew about the spill that I mentioned, but now that you've threatened the employee involved, I think we're going to make you and Mr. Eastman make a request in discovery if you want more particularized information." He turned to Eastman. "Of course, we will move for a protective order when you ask for it – to protect the whistleblower's identity – and in the process, your demand for information about the spill will become public record. Or maybe, I don't know, you can just take our word for it for now."

Nigel turned back to the witness. "Mr. Paglia, were you aware that any spill of diesel fuel larger than 25 gallons must be reported to the Pennsylvania Department of Environmental Protection?"

Sal hesitated again. "I can't say I'm familiar with the exact regulation."

Nigel knew that he could have delved in excruciating detail into exactly what Sal Paglia knew about spill regulations. But that wasn't where he was going with this. "Your Ambler Yard is right next to the Wissahickon Creek, is it not?"

"Yes," Sal replied. For once, an easy question to answer.

"And the Wissahickon Creek flows into the Schuylkill River down in Manayunk, does it not?"

"Yes, I believe so."

"And the Schuylkill flows into the Delaware River down near the old navy yard, does it not?"

"Yes."

"Were you aware that any spill that could significantly affect navigable waters of the United States has to be reported to the federal Environmental Protection Agency?" Nigel knew that the spill was reportable to the state; he wasn't as sure about the federal rule. It sounded plausible.

"Again, I'm not familiar with that regulation," Sal replied.

"If a spill goes into the ground, it can affect groundwater for a long time, correct?"

"I don't know," said Sal.

"Were you aware that failure to report a spill can be a crime under federal law? And Mr. Eastman, for your benefit, I'm referring to 18 U.S.C., Section 3571."

"I don't know anything about that," replied Sal.

"Were you aware that failure to report a spill can be a crime under state law? And Mr. Eastman, that's 35 P.S., Section 691.611."

"I don't know nothin' about that, either," Sal responded.

"Mr. Paglia, were you aware that when a road contractor is found to have violated an environmental law, that violation can result in debarment – in other words, exclusion – from participating in any further governmental contracts in Pennsylvania?"

Sal's face had lost almost all of its color. "No."

"Were you aware that both the Pennsylvania Department of Environmental Protection and the federal Environmental Protection Agency maintain tip lines that would permit any person – let's say a former employee, a union rep, or even an adverse party in litigation – to report a spill of a pollutant into the environment?"

Sal looked sick. But a very angry sick. "No," he replied.

"And, thus, if that tipster reported something that, hypothetically, resulted in your being found to have violated the environmental laws of Pennsylvania or of the United States, you could possibly lose most of your government business for a while?" Nigel waited a beat, as Sal considered his answer. "That's OK, Mr. Paglia, I withdraw that question. We know what the answer is, and you don't have to respond."

CHAPTER 82

"Mr. Paglia, does Sal Paglia, Inc., do road work for townships in Southeastern Pennsylvania?"

"You know the answer to that question. We do paving, repaving, road construction, road repair, road drainage systems, you name it."

"How long has your company been doing road work for townships?"

"I don't know. At least thirty years. Maybe more."

"Do you also do road work for counties, like Bucks, Montgomery and Chester?"

"Yes."

"And occasional special projects for the state, through PennDOT bids?"

"Yes."

"What percentage of your annual revenue is derived from government work?"

"I'm not telling you that. That's highly confidential information."

"Maybe, but it says on your website that Sal Paglia, Inc., is the leading contractor for public right-of-way repairs and improvements in Pennsylvania, correct?"

"If that's what it says, that's what it says."

"How did you come up with that claim about being the leading road contractor in Pennsylvania?"

"I don't know. We have people for that. But I'm sure it's true."

"I think it's probably true as well," Nigel responded. "'Nice business you got there,' as the saying goes. Have you ever been debarred from public contracting, that is, prohibited from submitting a bid or bids?"

"Never. In fact, the question's insulting. We follow the rules, counsel. We pay Mr. Eastman's law firm a lot of money to make sure we follow the rules. We provide the best work for the best prices, and that's why we do so well with fixed-price, sealed bidding."

"Fixed-price? What do you mean by 'fixed-price'?"

"Just like it sounds. The request for bids from the township describes the work they want done, and we submit a bid telling them we'll do the work for a fixed price." Sal wasn't done. "In other businesses, like defense contracting or whatever, you can have cost-plus contracts where the government will pay you what it costs to do the work, plus a profit that's set in advance. Or you can have requests for proposals, where it don't matter who the low bidder is, because the government can pick the bidder it likes best, even if their price isn't the lowest. Almost all of our contracts come from sealed, fixed-price bidding. You can't cheat, you can't kiss the asses of contracting officers to get the work, and sometimes you lose money if you bid low and then run across problems on the job. It's the only honest way to do government contracting, in my opinion."

Nigel affected a perplexed look, and pretended to shuffle some papers. "Well, Mr. Paglia, maybe you can help me understand something better. We have been doing online searches trying to educate ourselves on the ins and outs of public contracting, and we have come across probably fifty examples in the past 20 years where one township or another has approved a contractual change order requested by Sal Paglia, Inc. And those are only the ones we found by means of online searches – there could have been a lot more. Can you tell us what a change order is?"

Sal sat a little straighter in his chair and took his time answering. "Sure. That's where the township and the contractor agree that the contractor will do some extra work for a specific amount of money. And then you amend the contract in that amount. It's done all the time. And sometimes a change order will take work out of the contract, and we get paid less."

"Well, when you say 'extra work,' that doesn't always mean an extra benefit to the township does it?" asked Nigel. "Isn't it true that a change order is often approved when the road contractor encounters 'unforeseen conditions'?"

Sal liked it when he could talk about road building. He was in his element. "Yes, absolutely."

"Could you give me an example, please, of when a change order might be approved for 'unforeseen conditions'?" asked Nigel.

"Sure," Sal replied. "Suppose we bid a three-foot road bed, which means we're gonna give them three feet of compacted fill underneath the new road surface. And the road needs to be level, not going up and down hill every hundred feet. And suppose we're going along and we discover a big underground scarp of granite just under the topsoil. For a bunch of engineering reasons – often because we have to level the road, and the underground condition is in the way — we might have to take some of that granite out of there. We have to bring in drills and blasting equipment and extra wheeled and tracked vehicles to carry all the granite out. So it wasn't our fault the granite was there, and there's no reason we should have to lose money on a contract when we're giving the township the new road they wanted. And the townships recognize that – they want good contractors to bid their contracts in the future – and they'll approve a change order to cover our extra costs for working around the unforeseen condition."

"If you do get a change order for extra work approved, that means you'll be paid more on the contract, correct?"

"Yes, of course."

"So when you call one of these sealed bid contracts 'fixed-price,' what you really mean is that they're fixed price as long as there are no change orders, correct?"

"I don't know what you mean," Sal replied.

Nigel ignored the answer. As far as Nigel was concerned, having Sal hear the questions was more important than whatever answer Sal might choose to give in return. "What if the subterranean condition wasn't really unforeseen?" Nigel continued. "Are you supposed to be able to get a change order approved if the condition was something that your engineers should have anticipated?"

Sal hesitated. "Well, no, of course not. It all depends."

"How many times, say, in the past ten years has your company had a change order request denied?" Nigel asked.

"Every so often," Sal replied.

"How often?" asked Nigel.

"Occasionally," said Sal.

The answer wasn't important. "Well, we can get that information by asking the townships involved," said Nigel.

Sal glanced at Eastman as if to ask, "Can he really do that?"

"Which township official typically approves a change order?" Nigel continued.

"I don't know what you mean. Which township?"

"In a typical Pennsylvania township, is a change order usually approved by the Board of Supervisors, the Township Manager, or the Township Engineer?"

Sal was getting tired, and his guard was down a little. And because he saw no harm in telling the truth in response to Nigel's question, he answered it. "Larger change orders have to be approved by the Board of Supervisors. Change orders below a certain amount can be approved by the Township Manager alone. And the Township Engineer makes recommendations to the Township Manager and to the Board about whether a change order should be approved, and if so, in what amount."

Nigel figured that it was about time to explain to Sal where he was going with all of this. "Mr. Paglia, let me ask you this. If 'unforeseen conditions' weren't really that unforeseen, and if they weren't really going to cost you extra money to fix, and if you had a change order with extra dollars approved by the Township Manager, and/or recommended by the Township Engineer, you could make a lot more money on your sealed bid contract, could you not?"

"Don't answer that question," Eastman interjected. "It's argumentative and completely hypothetical."

Nigel didn't care what Sal's answer would have been, but he was surprised that Eastman saw enough risk in the question that he cut off Sal's ability to answer it. If you're taking flack, it means you're over the target. Or maybe, if your enemy starts throwing up barricades, you're attacking at a weak point.

"Well, let me ask you a different question," said Nigel. "Does Sal Paglia, Inc., do its best to maintain cordial customer relationships with Township Managers and Township Engineers in the townships for which you do work?"

"No. Not particularly."

Nigel viewed it as a good sign that Sal chose to tell such an obvious lie.

"When you apply for a change order, isn't it a good thing to be on good terms with the Township Manager and Township Engineer who will need to review it?"

"You tell me, counsel," Sal replied, now sneering at Nigel.

Nigel ignored Sal's failure to answer the question. He shuffled a paper or two and collected his thoughts. He wanted to be careful and precise about the questions he was about to ask.

"Mr. Paglia, are you familiar with a company called 'Autumn Events, LLC'?" asked Nigel.

"No, it doesn't sound familiar." Nigel noticed that Sal had hesitated again before giving his answer.

"Well, that's odd," continued Nigel, "because according to the website of the Pennsylvania Department of State, Autumn Events, LLC, shares a registered office address with Sal Paglia, Inc., out in Collegeville." Nigel handed Sal and his counsel copies of Paglia Deposition Exhibit 6, which was a screenshot from the Department of State website. "Do you have any explanation as to why state officials believe that Sal Paglia, Inc., and Autumn Events, LLC, seem to be sharing space?"

Sal shook his head slightly. "No."

"We've driven past your Collegeville facility, and it doesn't look like an office park. Do you rent out space in that facility to any other businesses?"

"No."

"We have previously marked, as Paglia Deposition Exhibit 7, twelve screen grabs from Craigslist.org." Nigel handed copies to Sal and to Eastman. "I'll read you the language that I want to ask you questions about. Quote: 'Wanted to Buy: Eagles Season Tickets between the 40 yard lines. Will pay substantially above face value. Email us through Craigslist, or call Autumn Events at 610-772-9911,' close quote. And, for the record, you'll also notice, to the left of the ad, a little circle with a map in it that centers on the Collegeville, Pennsylvania, area. Do you see all that?"

Sal didn't respond. But Nigel knew he was looking right at it.

"OK, Mr. Paglia, these screen grabs are from Google and Internet Archives, and date back to 2013, 2014, and 2015. Do you see that?"

No reply.

"Do you recognize those Craigslist ads?"

"No."

"Do you recognize the phone number, 610-772-9911?"

"No."

"Do you know of anyone within your company who might be able to explain why a company that shares your address in Collegeville was advertising to purchase Eagles season tickets?"

"No."

"If we were to send a subpoena to the telephone company, would you expect that we might be able to obtain subscriber information for telephone number 610-772-9911?"

No response.

"Let's take a break," said Nigel.

CHAPTER 83

Lou, Nigel and Olivia were seated around the small table in Olivia's smaller meeting room. For the first time that day, there was a genuine disagreement about tactics.

"I don't think it's fair," said Lou. "The kid didn't do nothin' to us. Sal Paglia is a vindictive son of a bitch, and just because the kid is his sister's son doesn't mean Sal isn't gonna hurt him. The minute we say his name, the kid's life is changed. And for what?"

"Lou, you're not responsible for your opponent's misconduct, if it happens," responded Nigel. "You have a right to name names in litigation. What happens next is between Sal and his nephew. It's not your responsibility."

Olivia responded quietly. "Nigel, I agree with my dad on this one. Enough people are looking at serious disruption in their lives as a result of this lawsuit. Can't we leave the kid's name out of this?"

Nigel thought for a little while. "The problem is this. If we don't explain how we know what we know, Sal is going to assume we can't prove it. In that case, we get no leverage at all."

"All right, I got an idea," said Lou. "I'm not under oath today, am I?"

"No," replied Nigel. "But I get the feeling I'm not going to like what's coming next."

Lou chuckled, and then explained his idea. He concluded by saying, "Nobody's telling no lies today – except Sal, a course."

Nigel nodded agreement, and Nigel and Lou got up to walk back to the deposition room. "See you in a bit," said Nigel to Olivia.

CHAPTER 84

Nigel signaled to the court reporter that they were going back on the record. Sal Paglia and Palmer Eastman waited for the next question. Neither looked happy to be where they were. Nigel made a show of placing his chart of townships, Township Managers and Township Engineers on the table. It was the same chart that Ziggy had consulted and memorized, and, as they worked in the Command Center, they had filled it full of red circles, underlines, handwritten notes, question marks and exclamation points. Nigel knew and intended that Sal would be reading it upside down.

"Mr. Paglia, do you know Matthew Henderson, the current Township Manager in Brittany Township, Pennsylvania?"

Sal's reptilian look returned. He answered slowly and carefully. "Of course I know Matt Henderson. Brittany Township is a good customer of ours."

"Has Matthew Henderson at any time attended a Philadelphia Eagles game sitting in a seat controlled by Autumn Events, LLC?"

"I have no idea. I told you I never heard of this 'Autumn Events.'"

"Do you know Frank Wilson, the Township Manager in Guilfoyle Township, Pennsylvania?"

"Yes. Guilfoyle Township is a customer of ours."

"Has Frank Wilson at any time attended a Philadelphia Eagles game sitting in a seat controlled by Autumn Events, LLC?"

"Same answer, counsel. I have no idea."

"Do you know Ellis Gardner, the Township Engineer in North Cornwall Township, Pennsylvania?"

"Yes. Same reason. North Cornwall is a customer."

"Has Ellis Gardner at any time attended a Philadelphia Eagles game sitting in a seat controlled by Autumn Events, LLC?"

"I don't know."

Nigel paused for a few seconds and shifted his approach slightly. "Mr. Paglia, do you know Carmine DeLuca?" asked Nigel.

Sal looked surprised. "Sure. He's a member of the Italian American Citizens Club of Norristown. Like me."

"Did you ever arrange for Mr. DeLuca to use an Eagles ticket that was otherwise going to go unused?"

Sal hesitated. "No."

"Did you tell Mr. DeLuca to call a relative of yours to obtain that Eagles ticket?"

"No."

"Did you know that Mr. DeLuca accepted your offer, and wound up sitting next to the Township Manager of Penn Manor Township during an Eagles game?"

"I instruct the witness not to answer that question. It assumes facts not in evidence." The basis for Palmer Eastman's instruction to his witness was specious, but he didn't care. The point was to keep Sal from saying anything that would dig the hole deeper.

"And did you know that Peter Cooper has been the Township Manager for Penn Manor Township for at least the past 10 years?"

No response.

"Well, I'll move on," said Nigel. "Mr. DeLuca can tell the story himself at trial."

Sal's jaw opened slightly and then closed again. The room was quiet for a moment.

"Do you have any reason to believe that Mr. Henderson, Mr. Wilson, Mr. Gardner, and Mr. Cooper did *not* attend Eagles games sitting in seats controlled by Autumn Events, LLC?"

"You're making this stuff up," Sal replied. "You know you can't prove any of this, and you're just trying to slander public officials and public contractors. This is bullshit."

Lou literally tugged at Nigel's sleeve. "Nigel, dammit, tell him about the video," he said, loud enough for the court reporter and everyone else in the room to hear. "Tell him about the video."

Nigel turned to Lou. "It's your case – I'll do what you want. But they haven't asked for it, and I don't want to produce something we haven't been asked for."

"Tell him about the video," said Lou, again, firmly.

Nigel let out an exaggerated sigh, and turned back to Sal. "Mr. Paglia, have you ever watched a football game, and sometimes the TV feed will include shots of spectators in the stands?"

Sal was interested now. "Yes."

"Were you aware that football coverage is archived, and for a fee, you can review all of the material that's telecast during an NFL game?" Nigel had no idea whether this was true. It seemed plausible.

"I have no idea," Sal replied. Fair enough, thought Nigel, neither do I.

"Do you have any idea why three men who are officials in three different Pennsylvania townships – Messrs. Henderson, Wilson and Gardner – have been seen sitting in the same seat or seats, but during different games, on approximately the 45 yard line a few rows behind the Eagles' bench?"

"No." Sal looked sick again.

"Just as a person who has contracts with a lot of different townships, wouldn't you find it extraordinarily coincidental that officials from different townships wound up in the same seats at different times?"

"I don't have any idea," Sal responded.

"Would you find it coincidental that a company you seem to share space with was looking to purchase Eagles tickets, and then different persons you do business with seemed to sit in the same pricey Eagles seats at different times? And what's more, each of those customers has approved change orders for the benefit of Sal Paglia, Inc. in the past ten years. Do you see some extraordinary coincidence there?"

"I instruct the witness not to answer that question," said Eastman. "This is absurd."

CHAPTER 85

Nigel turned to the court reporter again. "Please label these ten letters that I'm handing you, collectively, as 'Paglia Deposition Exhibit 8.' And please label these additional ten letters I'm handing you, collectively, as Paglia Deposition Exhibit 9.'

I am providing copies of the exhibits to plaintiff and his counsel." He handed the copies across the table.

"Mr. Paglia," continued Nigel, "I will represent to you that these letters, signed by defendant Louis Incaviglia, will be sent to the townships indicated in the address blocs at the conclusion of this deposition. A version of Exhibit 8 is addressed to, and is being sent to, Porter, North Cornwall, Penn Manor, Morris, Hancock, Brittany, Tacony, Neshaminy Springs, Quaker Heights and Guilfoyle Townships, which are all townships in Bucks, Montgomery, Delaware or Chester Counties in Pennsylvania. A version of Exhibit 9 is addressed to, and is being sent to, each of the same townships. I'm going to be asking you questions about your company's dealings with those townships, and, with respect to Exhibit 9, some of the persons named in those letters. I will first read into the record the text of the first letter in Exhibit 8, addressed to Porter Township, quote:

"Ladies and Gentlemen, Pursuant to Pennsylvania's Right to Know Law, Pennsylvania Act 3 of 2008, the undersigned requests that you identify and produce copies of all contractual change orders approved by your Township with respect to any contract between your Township and Sal Paglia, Inc. The undersigned will assume copying costs. Sincerely, Louis C. Incaviglia. And copy recipient: Office of the Attorney General of Pennsylvania.

"The text of Exhibit 9, page 1, addressed to Porter Township, reads as follows, quote:

"Ladies and Gentlemen, Pursuant to Pennsylvania's Right to Know Law, Pennsylvania Act 3 of 2008, the undersigned requests that you identify and produce copies of all documents, including electronic documents, by which Township Manager Edward Ross or Township Engineer Robert Meyers has reported to your Township the receipt of complementary Philadelphia Eagles game tickets from any person, whether or not such person does business with your Township. The undersigned will assume copying costs. Sincerely, Louis C. Incaviglia. And copy recipient: Office of the Attorney General of Pennsylvania.

"I will further represent to you that the final nine letters in Exhibit 9 contain the same text as I just read you, and vary only by township, and by the individuals named as Township Manager and Township Engineer, respectively. Those nine letters are addressed to North Cornwall Township, naming Albert Stone and Ellis Gardner; Penn Manor Township, naming Peter Cooper and Charles Parker; Morris Township, naming Elizabeth Dixon and Bruce Adams; Hancock Township, naming Richard Williams and Paul Brooks; Brittany Township, naming Matthew Henderson and James King; Tacony Township, naming Melinda Hill and John a/k/a Jack Collins; Neshaminy Springs Township, naming Barry Jones and George Reynolds; Quaker Heights Township, naming Thomas Kennedy and Samuel Gibson; and Guilfoyle Township, naming Francis Wilson and Donald Smith.

"Mr. Paglia, does your company do business with the ten townships that were named in Exhibit 9?"

Sal Paglia sat still as death. He didn't look at Nigel, and he didn't look at his lawyer. He wasn't looking at anyone.

"I instruct the witness not to answer," said Palmer Eastman, although it was clear that the witness wasn't going to answer anyway.

"Mr. Paglia, if, hypothetically, any of the officials in the townships identified in these letters were to believe, for whatever reason, that your company had some connection with Eagles tickets that township officials might, hypothetically, have used, do you think they might get in touch with you about these letters?"

Sal was silent. "Don't answer that question," said Eastman.

"If, hypothetically, any of the township officials identified in these letters were to sense some – shall we say – increased public scrutiny concerning their possible use of Eagles tickets, might those officials call you to ask what's going on?"

"Same instruction," said Eastman.

"Well, let me get to more of a technical, lawyer's kind of point," said Nigel. "If, hypothetically, criminal investigators from the Pennsylvania Attorney General's Office were to interview some of these township officials, do you think some of them might name some names to save their own skins?"

Eastman was enraged; worse, he was enraged and powerless. "Do not answer that question."

CHAPTER 86

"**M**r. Eastman," said Nigel, "I would propose to give the court reporter a break, let's say for an hour or so, while the parties and their counsel discuss the case. Is that OK with the plaintiff?"

"Sure," replied Eastman. His heart was not in his job at that point, and he didn't check with his client before agreeing to go off the record.

Nigel turned quietly to the reporter. "Sandy, please give us an hour. We'll come find you in an hour or so to let you know whether we're going to keep going with this."

The court reporter turned off her recorder and quietly left the room.

"Before we talk, I'm going to find the men's room," said Nigel, as he stood and turned for the door. Lou fixed his gaze across the table at Sal.

Sal let Nigel leave, and then exploded at Lou. "You little cocksucker. I'm gonna fucking kill you. You've had your little fun today. But you have no idea of the shit that's gonna fall down around your head, startin' tonight."

Eastman put his hand on Sal's forearm in a gesture that said "stay calm, we've got this." Sal responded by slapping his hand away. "Don't touch me, you fuckin' weasel." He turned back to Lou and described the parts of Lou's anatomy that wouldn't leave the hotel with the rest of him. He was still ranting when Nigel came back in with Heidi and Pete.

Per the plan they'd worked out beforehand, Lou took the lead. "OK, gentlemen, let me introduce the rest of our team," he said. "Heidi, here, is a legal temp, and she's really good at typing up documents in a hurry. She has been in one of the other meeting rooms all day. I think we rented every meeting room they had."

Lou turned to Heidi with a smile. "Thanks for standing by, Doll. They have a little 'business center,' I think they call it, right down the hall on your right. It's got computers and printers and all the stuff you'll need. Could you wait down there for a little while longer?" Heidi had been briefed on how the day might go, and nodded her agreement. She left to assume her new post.

"And I also want to introduce this large man with the large coat." Lou continued. "This is Pete. You can probably guess who Pete's current employer is." Lou reached beneath his chair and located a small cigarette-pack-sized device and placed it on the table. "This is a baby monitor. Pete has the receiver down the hall, and if Pete hears this thing turn on, that will mean I pushed the button because somebody in this room isn't controlling his temper very well."

Sal knew exactly who Lou's brother-in-law was – it was common knowledge at the Italian Club – and he was able to guess who Pete's employer was. Lou nodded to Pete, and they all watched Pete leave the room, slowly and calmly.

As Pete left, Olivia came in the door. Lou saw her, and a lump of alarm rose in his throat. Nigel was standing behind Lou and put a hand on his shoulder. "It's OK," he said, "we weren't going to be able to keep her away."

Lou nodded. He turned back to Sal and Eastman. "Gentlemen, on my left here is my daughter Olivia. I suppose she'll talk whenever she has somethin' she needs to say." He turned to Olivia: "Have a seat, Honey." And then to Sal and Eastman again: "Olivia isn't offended by bad language, 'cause she lived with me for so long. I just wanted to let you know, Sal – well, you already know – I'm a peaceful guy. You can raise your voice at me – we're all Italian here – but if you raise your voice to my daughter, or direct any foul language toward her, I will call Pete, and he will hurt you." No one responded to Lou's statement.

"Now, down to business," said Lou. "Sal, why don't we ask the lawyers to leave the room?"

"Why would we do that?" Sal replied.

"Because if we don't, I'm going to leave here and drop those letters to those townships in the nearest mailbox." Lou stared across the table while Sal thought about his options.

"OK, no lawyers," said Sal. "I'm surprised you have the balls to talk to me without Nigel here to hold your hand."

Lou turned to Eastman. "Mr. Eastman, there are plenty of nice seats in the lobby, and even a little bar. I started a tab, and you're welcome to order somethin'. Nigel, in the meantime, will be in Olivia's little room, with Pete, who you just met."

"I will be calling the police," said Eastman, as he stood up. "You have threatened physical harm to my client, and that will not stand. This has all gone too far."

"Mr. Eastman, would you please leave your telephone with Sal?" Lou replied immediately. "Pete is not going to have to hurt anyone, so there's no need for you to call anybody. We have business to finish. The police showing up would just speed up a lot of bad things happening to your client's business, and you don't wanna see that. You can call the police later if you want. Come on, phone on the table please."

Sal turned to Eastman and nodded. Eastman placed his phone on the table next to Sal. As he and Nigel reached the door, Lou said to them, "Counsel, thanks for your patience. We're probably gonna need your services, so please stay around a while."

The lawyers left. Lou and Sal and Olivia looked at each other.

"Sal, you've known Nigel for a while from down the club," Lou began. "I'm like you, and everybody else I guess. I thought he probably drinks too much to be a good lawyer. But you know what? He's a great lawyer. Amazing, really, what you don't know about people sometimes. And Nigel says – and I believe him – that the penalty in Pennsylvania for bribing a public official to give you a government contract is up to 7 years in prison and a $15,000 fine. And that's for each time you do it. You done it, what, at least ten times, prolly? You're lookin' at seventy years, altogether. A hundred and fifty grand."

"Good luck with that," Sal replied. "I don't have nothin' to do with Autumn Events, or whatever the fuck you're calling it. And my company didn't buy no tickets."

"Well, Nigel tells me, he says that because Sal Paglia, Inc., wasn't directly involved in this whole thing with the Eagles tickets, the DA will be looking for a real living, breathing person to charge. The highest up person involved in all of this – the one people are gonna be pointing at when they're lookin' to save their skins – is you. And Nigel showed me some newspaper articles – district attorneys in these counties really don't like it when public officials get bribed. I were you, I'd plan on goin' to jail for a long time."

Sal began to interrupt, but Lou held up his hand and cut him off. "Let me just talk for a little while longer. You need to hear this, and I promise I'll listen to you, I'll hear you out. This isn't no one-way street. We're negotiating here." Most of the time, Sal would never have tolerated somebody telling him not to talk. But the truth was, he wanted to hear the rest of what Lou had to say.

Lou cleared his throat and looked across the table. "I'm not gonna lie to you. If you'd a told me all this shit about your company a year ago, I'd a said, 'Wow, good for him. Sounds like a pretty good business strategy, you ask me. A course he bends the rules. I don't know a rich cocksucker who don't.'

"But then you went after my family. You hadda know I'd fight back. So that's where we are now. I gotta be honest here, I been really confused about what we did to make you so mad. I like to think I know people. I like to think I knew *you* pretty well. But I didn't. You got anger issues, as

Carmine DeLuca likes to say. You're really mad. We been tryn'a figure out why you're so mad, and today I think I finally did.

"You think you've been done wrong. You do. Somehow my son-in-law really embarrassed you in that shareholders' meeting. And you're really pissed that he wouldn't agree to give you control of his company, because you figure you deserve it. You got a case a what Father Lamonica back at Kenrick used to call 'righteous anger.' You think, because you're so mad, we must a really wanted to hurt you. But you know what, Sal? We didn't want that. And there's no such thing as righteous anger. It's just anger. Don't do you no good, don't do anybody no good, but when you leave here tonight, you're still gonna be mad the same way. You think you got a right to be mad, you think we're wrong, and we're not gonna change your mind.

"So all I can do is take you down with me. You and your company. And I'll do that. But me, I'm retired and I live in a rowhouse. You got a lot farther to fall.

"So I'm hopin' you can think a yourself like a badger – the meanest animal in the forest – who just jumped on a porcupine. You're mad, and you don't wanna let him go, but things are gonna turn out really bad for you if you don't.

"What we're lookin' for is just to make all this go away. That's all. Make it like this never happened, like you never heard of 3Device. We're not gonna try to get your money back from this Paul Smythe guy – that one's on you – but you'll still have your business, and everything will be like it was before you sat down beside me at the club. We won't even ask for the 15 grand I hadda pay Nigel. That one's on me. I shouldn'a listened to you. And if you agree to make this all go away, nobody ever hears nothin' about all the stuff we dug up on you. Or about the other stuff we would dig up if we kept digging.

"Nigel and your lawyer can agree on how to do this, and somebody can draw up the papers. This needs to end."

Lou was quiet.

"Thanks for the speech, you asshole," Sal began. "Guys like you get killed in the movies 'cause you're too fuckin' stupid to realize you pissed off the wrong person. Well, I'm the wrong person, you little prick.

"You're wrong about somethin' major here. You may not have far to fall, but your son-in-law and your daughter have a lot to lose. I've seen pictures of that big house in Villanova. We've done investigations too, you cocksucker. It'd be a shame if they couldn't live there anymore, and if their neighbors heard stories about what kind of people they really are." Sal was looking at Lou, and not at Olivia. Apparently, he wasn't interested in seeing Pete come back.

"Look at my face and tell me whether you think I'm serious. I don't need Sal Paglia, Inc. I can go back to spreadin' sealcoat on driveways. I got a lot of money put away in stocks, real estate, gold. I can use that money for the next few years, figuring out ways to fuck up your son-in-law's life, and your daughter's life. I'm glad she's here today so she can hear that. Your family knows what's coming. Your little dog and pony show today gave me a good lesson on what to do.

"I don't have to say much more," said Sal. "Look at my face. You know I mean what I say, and you know what to expect. So maybe that's where we'll leave it today."

To Lou's ears, Sal's words didn't add up. He didn't seem to believe what he was saying. Lou started to reply, and Olivia put a hand on his arm. "Daddy, let me talk." She looked at Sal and gathered her thoughts.

"My husband Greg and I expected you to say what you just said," she began, "so we were able to talk about it before I came over here today. I have a few responses, and I think you should consider them carefully.

"To begin with, you're old. Greg and I are not. People in their thirties get ruined all the time. It's no fun, I imagine, but it doesn't kill you. If your fantasies about ruining us came true – and they won't – we would still have a lot of time to recover. Maybe we can start a little sealcoating company to support ourselves, and see where it takes us. In the meantime, you'll get even older, and senile or dead. If you think family doesn't mean enough to us to risk those consequences, then you couldn't be Italian. And don't sell Greg short. He agrees with me. He's Italian by marriage.

"Your next problem is, what you're talking about doing probably won't work. Go online and read about the collapse of Commercial Bank of New York. I was working there when it happened. The bank failed because they didn't follow a bunch of laws and rules. The same reason that Sal Paglia, Inc., is going to fail if you don't dismiss this case today.

"But Greg has followed the law. The lesson of our 'dog and pony show,' as you call it, is that you have to follow the law or you get in trouble. Simple as that. You can't take Greg down that way because he follows the law. And me? I'm generally law-abiding, but I don't like being pushed around. You'll find that out if you take us on."

Olivia interrupted herself. "I want you to know, by the way, that what hit you today was *my* idea. I only thought of it three weeks ago. Consider what I could've done today if I'd had more than three weeks to plan this." She gestured toward the exhibits on the table.

"And then your next obstacle, of course, is that you'd probably be making your efforts to ruin us from inside a jail cell. You certainly have more money than Greg and I do, but we have more than enough resources to investigate your contracting practices and turn the information over to at least four county district attorneys, as well as the state Attorney General. The Eagles are always big news in this town, and district attorneys are elected officials looking for headlines. You *will* go to jail.

"Lastly, you mentioned family. Let's talk about family. You have hypothesized – I guess that's the right word – that Sal Paglia, Inc., will be gone, and you and your wife will be living off your savings, spending most of them trying to destroy us. But we will have my Uncle Tony Abruzzi and his people on our side. He is my favorite uncle, and I am his favorite niece. He's very upset right now. More particularly, he's not very happy with one Sal Paglia. If that doesn't scare you, it should. If you hurt my dad, or if you try to harm my husband, I will call in reinforcements. They will come running." She paused. "Look at my face."

Olivia hadn't raised her voice. Her eyes were hard and focused, but that was the only emotion she showed. Lou was proud of her. The room was quiet.

At that moment, and for the first time in twenty-five years or so, Sal Paglia was viscerally aware that there were organizations in the world — governmental and private organizations – who were a lot more powerful than he was. And he had a lot to fear from them. He hadn't expected to discover anything like that when he put his shoes on that morning. But he had underestimated Lou Incaviglia. He shouldn't have. Sal knew that when Lou bet, he preferred to win.

"Let me hear it," said Sal, finally breaking the silence. "Bring the lawyers back in."

CHAPTER 87

"Mr. Eastman," said Nigel, "we want four documents sitting on this table within two hours. Please take some notes while I'm speaking. First, we want a signed, voluntary withdrawal of this litigation, with prejudice, in form suitable for filing with the court. We will be happy to file the signed document with the Clerk of Court.

"Second, we want stock certificates endorsed by Mr. Paglia for transfer to Mr. Incaviglia representing all of the shares of 3Device, Inc., that were purchased from Mr. Incaviglia and Mr. Smythe. Or, in the alternative, a signed stock power transferring the attached share certificates to Mr. Incaviglia, with right of registration with the company. In either case, Mr. Paglia's ownership stake in 3Device, Inc., ends today. Mr. Incaviglia will sign a receipt for those shares.

"Third, we want a signed unconditional release of all claims that Mr. Paglia or Sal Paglia, Inc., has or may have against Louis Incaviglia, Olivia Incaviglia, and Gregory C. Morris, Jr., 'from the beginning of the world to the date of these presents,' etc., etc.'

"Fourth, we want a letter signed by Mr. Paglia permanently resigning his membership in the Italian American Citizens Club of Norristown, Pennsylvania, effective immediately.

"In return, Mr. Incaviglia will agree never to order a transcript of this deposition from the court reporter – we sent Sandy home, but I'll let her know — and no transcript will ever become part of the public record in this case. Mr. Incaviglia will agree not to send the letters to municipal governments included within Paglia Deposition Exhibits 8 and 9, or, indeed, communicate with those municipal governments, or any other governments, concerning any of the matters raised during this deposition.

"Stated even more clearly, Mr. Incaviglia will agree – and he'll be speaking for his daughter and his son-in-law as well – that Mr. Paglia can go about his business as if this litigation had never happened, without interference from Mr. Incaviglia or anyone connected with him. Mr. Incaviglia will not sign any documents memorializing that commitment, because he is not about to be complicit in Mr. Paglia's future decisions about his business practices, whatever those decisions may be. But Mr. Incaviglia will shake hands with Mr. Eastman confirming what I just told you. As Mr. Paglia knows – and has known all along — Mr. Incaviglia can be trusted to keep his word.

"We believe, although we can't promise, that the efforts of Local 882 of the Warehousemen's and Produce Workers International Union to organize Sal Paglia, Inc., will not be resumed tomorrow, and pickets lines will not be reestablished. We will make a call or two. But under the National Labor Relations Act, the decision whether to continue those organizing efforts is up to the workers and their union.

"Gentlemen, you can prepare documents in the business center down the hall. Heidi, whom you've met, will assist you. I talked to the hotel, and they're happy to bring sandwiches to the business center if you need to eat while you're working. The documents we're looking for don't have to be neat and flawless, or in any fancy format. However, if those documents are not on this table in two hours, we will be leaving. Two hours is plenty of time for you to make a call and get the share certificates here. This is a one-time offer. After two hours, consequences will flow with no further notice to you. We're not going to debate all of this any further."

Nigel had run out of things to say, so he just set his chin and stared.

CHAPTER 88

One hour and fifty-eight minutes later, Nigel reviewed the four documents sitting on the table, signed in the appropriate places by Sal Paglia and his counsel. Nigel showed Lou where to sign and date the receipt for shares of stock.

"What's the date today?" Lou asked.

"October 19th," Nigel replied.

Lou automatically scribbled "Lou 1019" on the signature line of the receipt before he realized what he was writing. He looked up quickly at Nigel.

"Leave it," said Nigel. "It's your mark. And it happens to be the date. So just leave it."

Then Nigel looked across the table at Eastman, who looked at Sal. Sal nodded. Eastman extended his hand to Lou, and they shook hands. Eastman didn't look like he wanted to.

With that, Nigel gathered up the signed documents and led Lou and Olivia out of the deposition room, leaving Sal and his lawyer slumped in their chairs. Sal was shaking his head slowly and fingering the key to his Land Rover.

Nigel took a sip from his flask as they walked down the hallway. Olivia gathered up her things from the small meeting room, and they thanked Pete for coming. Lou asked him to tell Tony they'd be calling later. They thanked Heidi, gave her a $100 tip, and offered to call her a cab. She said she'd take Uber, because it was simpler. Nice person, Lou thought. Why did nice people get involved in other people's lawsuits? Strange way to make a living.

Olivia, Lou and Nigel had all arrived in Olivia's car, and their first stop on the way back was to drop Nigel off at his apartment. Lou stepped out onto the sidewalk as Nigel got out, and extended his hand. "Nigel, thanks. I need to get you those 15 shares of stock in 3Device. Who knows, maybe they'll be worth somethin' some day." They shook hands, and Nigel shuffled over to the front door of his apartment building. He felt good, which didn't happen very often.

Lou got back into Olivia's car and closed the door with a tired sigh. "Drop me at home, Sweetheart. I'm gonna order pizza and go to bed early."

"Nope, that's not the plan," replied Olivia. "We're going over to our house for a celebration. Greg will have dinner ready, and we have a cake, and even the cat is wearing a bow."

"Aw Honey, we don't have nothin' to celebrate, really. I mean, what you did today was really great, and I'll always appreciate it. I can't thank you enough. But it would be like celebrating 'cause your tooth stops hurtin'."

"What in the world makes you think we're celebrating the case being over?" asked Olivia, with a big smile. "You're right, *that's* no reason to celebrate."

Lou looked at her, puzzled. She glanced over at him and saw his look.

"We're having a baby, you idiot."

EPILOGUE

A little less than three years after Sal Paglia dismissed his federal lawsuit against Lou Incaviglia, the Wall Street Journal reported that a growing Philadelphia-area company, 3Device, Inc., had captured 45% of the American market for artificial knees. The Journal noted that, following approval of its knee by the FDA, 3Device began to train young doctors in every major city in the use of its software and 3D printers, and 14 of the 15 largest orthopedic practices in the country were using 3Device's technology for at least some of their surgeries. Some observers quoted by the Journal attributed the company's success to the persistence and strategic savvy of its management, and to the vision that Gregory Morris had shown in directing 3D printing technology toward the market for joint replacements. The article also noted that 3Device had obtained a patent on its new hip, and the company was hopeful that any competitors would be obliged to seek a license from 3Device before attempting sales of 3D printed hips. The company's earnings had risen quickly, to about 14 million dollars per year.

Following publication of the article, there were many requests by individuals and hedge funds to purchase shares in the company, but neither the company nor any of its shareholders were inclined to sell. Lou Incaviglia's ownership share in the company – including the shares he received from Sal Paglia – totaled about 15% of the equity outstanding, and was worth about 22 million dollars. His allocable earnings exceeded two million dollars per year.

Nigel Branca found that his one half of one percent interest in the company was returning more than $70,000 in annual dividends, which allowed him to retire from the practice of law. Before he stopped practicing law, he handled Lou Incaviglia's appeal of his exclusion from Pennsylvania Park Racetrack in Bensalem. That appeal was successful, and to everyone's great relief, Lou was able to return to the track. Nigel also persuaded the Pennsylvania Department of Banking and Securities to close its file on the *Incaviglia* matter. After his retirement, Nigel continued to spend time in the Montgomery County Law Library reading cases.

Lou, Olivia and Greg attended Tony Abruzzi's retirement party in South Philadelphia, at which Tony received a gold watch and some nice luggage. Tony relocated to Boca Raton, Florida, promptly thereafter, with his lovely wife Angela. His older son Joey took over leadership of the family business, and, despite some rough patches, was said to be doing well.

Sal Paglia continued to do what he had always done – run his business. Autumn Events, LLC, relinquished all of its interests in Eagles season tickets, and the company was quietly liquidated. At about the same time, the revenues of Sal Paglia, Inc., derived from municipal contracting dropped off measurably, but not disastrously. The 401(k) plan sponsored by Sal Paglia, Inc., was expanded to include all regular full time employees of the company. Sal Paglia no longer frequented the Italian American Citizens Club of Norristown, of course, but, truthfully, he wasn't missed all that much by the other members. Lou Incaviglia kept his promises to Mr. Paglia – a deal is a deal – and never had cause to communicate with him again.

Lou's daughter Olivia managed her father's stake in 3Device as his agent, and invested his quarterly dividends. In contravention of every known rule of fiduciary duty, she did not inform her father that he was now a multi- multi-millionaire. Olivia never had been much of a stickler for rules. Lou may have suspected that his investment was doing well – Olivia did, after all, arrange to renovate his house in Norristown, and she sent him on a package tour of Sicily and Italy for his sixty-fifth birthday. He did not know that she had bought a small, upscale nursing home not far from her home in Villanova and placed title to the business in his name, reasoning that no one could ever kick the owner out if he ever needed to live there.

Lou Incaviglia continued to pass a substantial part of his time on his front stoop on Walnut Street – he loved a good cigar – and at the Italian American Citizens Club of Norristown. He was spending time at the track, of course, but less — he was too busy babysitting his granddaughter, Gabriella. And he was looking forward to a grandson, due before the end of the year.

Lou did not know, but would probably learn at some birthday celebration or another, that Olivia had traveled to the yearling sale at Saratoga, New York, and bid successfully on two racehorses to be registered in Lou's name, a colt and a filly. The colt was to be called "Lou," and the filly was to be called "Gabby."

THE END

ABOUT THE AUTHOR

Richard G. Tuttle lives and writes in Philadelphia, Pennsylvania. *Lou 1019* is his second novel. His first novel, *Wyoming*, is available at BookBaby.com, Amazon.com and other online outlets.